A Promise of Stone and Shadow

Meadow Spurr

A Promise of Stone and Shadow

Meadow Spurr

First published in 2021

ISBN 978-1-7779262-0-5 (paperback)

This paperback edition first published in 2021 by Meadow Spurr, meadowspurrbooks@gmail.com

Cover artwork by Michal Kvac
Map illustrations by Adam Boardwell

To Willow the dog, because even though you eat my socks, I love you and you smell nice.

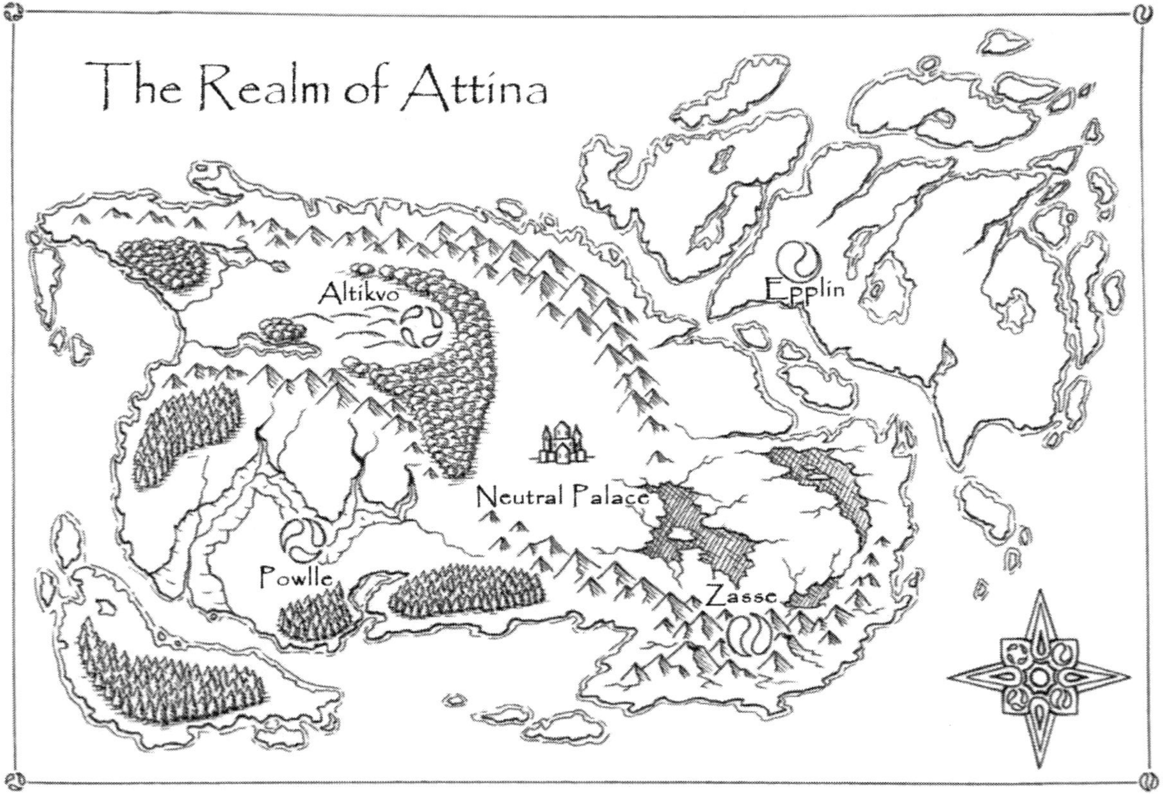
The Realm of Attina
Altikvo
Epplin
Neutral Palace
Powlle
Zasse

Chapter 1

Attina was a realm in which times of peace were known only through legend and prophecy. It was a land spun with great magic, but that magic only served as a catalyst for battle and bloodshed.

Across the land, four dominant clans vied against each other throughout the ages, and had done so since the beginning of memory. Each of these groups had been blessed with elemental control in the early years of the world, and had since segregated themselves based upon those gifts; Fire, Air, Water, and Earth. Each member of the respective clans could exert some measure of control—in varying degrees of power—over the element of their bloodlines. Any individual could practice and strengthen the single gift they had been blessed with, but there were limitations.

One such limitation was that no person in the spoken or written history of Attina had ever been able to control multiple factions of the same element. If one person could freeze the rain, for example, they would have no control over the tides of the sea. If another person could direct the wind, then they would not be able to fly.

Each clan was identical in the way that power was manifested and controlled, but that was where the likenesses between the groups stopped; in fact, they had been separated from each other for so long, that each clan had developed unique appearances over time.

The Water clan folk had hair and eyes coloured anywhere from blue or green to black, and they were often tall, with long limbs and slim fingers. They were mostly land dwellers, of course, but they were adept at swimming, and some had even been blessed with the ability to breathe underwater. On the rare occasion, one might see a Water clansman with vibrant blue or green skin, but typically, their tones were more subdued, often ranging from pale olive colouring, to deep brown.

The Fire clan were some of those whose bodies actually reflected their gifts; for example, it wouldn't be strange to see someone from the Fire bloodline with bright red skin, since their tones tended to range from coal black to infernal red. Most of them had some resistance to fire, as well. Fire folk's hair and eyes also followed the same pattern as their skin, typically ranging from black or brown to red. The largest of the clans in physical stature, those from the Fire bloodline were usually tall and powerfully built.

People from the Earth clan were typically the slightest people on any given battlefield, but one would be foolish to assume that meant they lacked power. The bloodline's preference for small physiques was often the most easily identifiable feature in Earth folk, because they tended to exhibit the broadest range of other physical attributes. They had hair and eyes that could vary in colour from green to brown, or from black to grey. Their skin, as well, typically spanned the entire neutral range between pale creams and deep browns.

Finally, the Air clan. The heights of people in the clan ranged all over, but rarely did the bloodline produce broad or heavy-set people. Air folks had hair that was typically white—but occasionally bled into stormy grey—and their eyes were always some form of white, grey, or blue, as a rule. Those from the Air bloodline also had the palest skin in Attina, and were similar to the Fire clan in that this tone was directly in relation to their elemental gifts.

The four Attinian clans boasted values and ideals that seemed to be largely preferential to each respective group, which made intermingling even more troublesome. They were too dissimilar to properly coexist together, yet too tied in their likenesses to ever truly dominate the others.

The realm had been unofficially split into four "kingdoms" by the clans themselves, but without an actual sovereign rule, many things fell by the wayside. Trade between elemental groups suffered magnificently, and those within the four territories often found themselves having to go without certain properties until an arrangement, however tentative, was reached between the arguing parties. Trade agreements didn't last long.

As a result, food and other crops that could only thrive in the Fire territory, for example, rarely made their way to the Air population. On the other hand, the healing crystals and medicines from Earth were almost never traded within the Water zone. Each clan suffered, due to the stubbornness of the nation as a whole, and yet none of them were willing to make the first move towards reconciliation.

Decades' old social hierarchies pervaded the clans themselves, which resulted in high tension, even within each local society. These levels of importance were based on magical power alone, and as such, would have been all but impossible to disestablish from within—if anybody had bothered to try. For example, a person born with formidable control over their element would undoubtedly have more opportunities throughout their life than someone born with lesser power. Throughout the years, certain families had climbed these social ladders, and were producing more and more powerful offspring at every turn, through either luck or careful breeding. These families had become loud voices within their respective cultures, and could often too-easily sway local law in their favour.

This was the story of the clans throughout Attina, and because of that, the conflicts between each other were even more poisonous. With no clear overarching goal, yet without a happy society to return to should they fail, and with a bone deep desire to see victory over their brothers and sisters, the people of the country rarely backed down from a fight.

Sometimes these fights became so magically charged, that what might have started out as a simple trade disagreement between family groups, became full-fledged clan wars. And, with so many capable people holding so much hate for those from other bloodlines and with other magic, agreements were often ungraspable. The worst wars, those that had been named throughout history, had spanned decades; though typically, the time spent on the actual battlefield was far less.

These problems, among others, had gotten so pronounced over the course of time, that the elemental elders had eventually felt the need to step in. Each clan was minimally overseen by the eldest people within the society—those too old to fight or hold grudges any longer. They weren't actual rulers, by any means, but they demanded and received respect, for any group of people who had survived to their elder years in such a war-entrenched world clearly held some manner of wisdom and power.

And so, in a summit that had held the nation's attention, the clan elders met on a large expanse of neutral ground in the heart of the country, right at the corner of each of the four realms. It was decided, over the course of the meeting, that the clans of Attina and their precious bloodlines would truly not survive long-term if things continued as they had done throughout the previous generations. Already, in their lifetimes, the elders claimed they could see the toll that the wars were taking on their people. Discussions of solutions were long and arduous, however, and old prejudices between the bloodlines began rearing their heads, even during talks of peace.

Fearing the meeting would all be for naught if they were unsuccessful in finding an answer, the elders called upon the witch doctors of the four nations—a last-ditch attempt at coming to an understanding.

The elemental witch doctors were strange folk, even amongst the blessed, and each clan had only ever had one or two appointed witches at any given time. Granted with the ability to communicate with the higher powers which had blessed the Attinian people centuries in the past, true witch doctors were few and far between.

Five of them were sent to the summit. Two from Water, and one each from the other clans.

Witch doctors had never gotten involved in the petty bloodline conflicts throughout Attina's history, and these five were no different. They arrived to the neutral ground and heard the elders' pleas, then withdrew as one to a nearby cave to begin spinning their strange magic—as if they were all cut from the same cloth and had nothing to disagree about.

Days passed, and though food was brought and left at the mouth of the cave by order of the elders, all of it went rotten and uneaten. As time wore on in silence, rumors began spreading in the clans that no formal decision would ever be made, and even that the witches had killed each other and would remain in the cave forever.

But finally, the witch doctors re-emerged, looking no worse off after not having eaten anything in weeks; that is, not having eaten anything that had been brought to them, anyway. None of the five doctors spoke a word to anybody, not even amongst themselves, until they were seated in front of the elders once more. They explained that, indeed, if things continued as they were currently between the clans, Attina and all of the people in it were doomed.

However, they whispered to the elders of a promise. A promise of redemption they had woven and spun from the spirits of the elements themselves. With that promise, the witches claimed, had come a vision.

A vision of the future.

In an untold number of years, a great shadow would settle across the elemental lands. With the shadow would come a threat the likes of which the people of Attina had never seen in all of history—a threat which the spirits themselves dared not name. The only way to overcome the shadow truly, would be to wield all four gifts; Earth, Fire, Water, and Air.

The elders had balked at the bad news, for nobody had ever even wielded multiple facets of the *same* element, let alone all four. Before panic could settle in, however, the witch doctors had calmed their worries.

There was a way, they said.

The period of time directly after the witch doctors made their claim is where accounts become muddy between clan historians. Some claim the witch doctors led the elders on a trek into the dangerous northern mountains of the neutral territory, where magical beasts were rumored to roam, angry and unchecked. Others claim the doctors gave each elder a drink infused with Earth medicines to allow them to hallucinate visions of the spiritual world. Still others think it was merely a conversation.

In any case, all historical accounts agree on what happened after.

No matter how they came to it, the witch doctors revealed to the elders four glowing Stones of Promise, from the cave where they had convened; one blue, one white, one green, and one red. These Stones, the witches said, each contained a power that would provide the ability to control one of the four elements in its entirety; however, there were guidelines to follow, else all would be for naught and Attina would fall to its doom.

Each Stone would be protected above all else, staying hidden from public eye until a prophecy that the witch doctors foretold came to pass.

Four babies would eventually be born within the four clans, to parents with no other children, and all on the same day. That day would fall somewhere between the year's autumn harvest and Winter's first snow.

The births must be natural, the witches warned; there would be no forcing the labour.

And on the day when each clan had produced offspring who fit the criteria, the four babies would be taken from their families—a high honour—and brought to the cave where the Stones of Promise had first been gathered. There, each baby would given a Stone, and together, they would become the unopposed leaders of Attina.

The last baby to be born, the doctors amended, would also be the last to be gifted their Stone when the time came. Though the youngest by right, that baby would be the one who would truly fulfill the prophecy; for until they entered the world, the other three births, though falling on the same day, would be ordinary. Not until the fourth child took its first mewling breath would the preparations begin.

It was decreed that the babies would grow up as true brothers and sisters, and learn to wield their powers together. It would be only their familial bond that would have the strength and longevity to hold the clans united, and eventually, defeat the coming shadow.

The witch doctors' words were accepted as law, and when the summit came to a close, the elders began organizing the construction of the great palace that would one day house the Promised Four. It was to be built on neutral land, within a day's travel of the cave where the Stones had been gathered, and where the prophesied babies would one day begin their blessed elemental journey.

In the months and years following the summit, a tentative harmony was reached between the four bloodlines. Knowing and accepting that one day they were to be united against some great evil, the clans slowly began to bury age-old feuds. It was slow work, and would not truly be finished until there were ruling heads in place to ensure peace was maintained—but it was a beginning, as well as a good indicator that the witch doctors had indeed spoken truth.

A tax was put in place for all people in the realm. The money and riches would be saved in a vault hidden deep within the neutral palace, and kept until one day the Promised Four had need of it. Every year, each family would give a percentage of what they'd earned to their city elders, who would transfer the reserves to the neutral territory. The settlement could be anywhere from 1-10% (or higher), depending on what the families chose, but everybody had to give something. In this way, as the years went on, the palace began cultivating a great wealth for their would-be rulers. The giving of the tax became so engrained in society that it became second nature to tithe, and most citizens did it without a thought. It was understood that if they could give more, they would, and if for any reason they could not manage a high sum, meeting the minimum requirement was no reason to be scoffed at.

Births and pregnancies became highly documented across Attina after the famed summit.

Any births which could possibly fall in the timeframe were marked and thoroughly checked. There were laws set in place about informing clan elders of pregnancies and births, and procedures laid out about what would happen when potential prophecy babies were born. There was also a plan made for the parents—how they would be reimbursed and honoured after having their first-born children taken from them. It was decided that they would never want for money or social position afterwards, but would also not be permitted to view or refer to the would-be royals as their relations or children, ever again.

Should the law be broken, the utmost of punishments would be delivered. The Promised Four would be children of the realm, until they grew up to lead it.

And even with the potential threat of losing a child forever, during the first decade or so after the summit, the birth rate of Attina spiked right around the end of autumn and the beginning of Winter. It seemed almost every pair of first-time parents, no matter the cost, wanted to be a part of the prophecy that would save their world.

Understandable, perhaps, but largely useless; for though there were many close calls in the years following, never were there four babies born that fully fit the criteria.

—

Midnight had settled restlessly over the Water clan township of Epplin that evening. The moonlight, when it was not obscured by the unseasonable clouds, made the water along the coast sparkle in the darkness seconds before it cascaded high onto the well-kept beaches and water fields.

Epplin was situated off the coast of the large Water island, and out of season mists and rain were tolerable, but sudden changes in air pressure, especially overnight, often effected the tides before somebody could come and put things right. Ocean shallows and flat reefs pervaded most of the town's agriculture, and the population had long-since adapted their farming practices to make use of the salt water; however, when it was harvest time and the tides started changing unpredictably, the seaweed and kelp fields often became muddy and miserable to work.

And, just as the tides and those trying their best to calm them were feeling restless, so too was Neerna, as she tossed and turned in her bed. She'd lived in Epplin all her life, but even still, had never gotten comfortable with the way the air felt when the late summer and early autumn pressure systems rolled in.

Compiled with everything else going on for her right then, suffice it to say that Neerna didn't think she would be getting any sleep that night. She cursed to herself as she changed position yet again, rolling over and fixing her sleeping bedmate with an accusatory stare.

"How can you sleep at a time like this?" She squawked, causing her husband, Nakk, to crack open one sea-green eye. She wasn't referring entirely to the uncomfortable weather, but was rather referring to the news they'd received earlier in the evening.

It seemed that their surrogate, Flyyn, had *finally* gone into labour.

Neerna had, of course, insisted on staying at the healer's house while the poor girl went through it; after all, a mother should be there for the birth of her first child. It went well at first, and the healer had allowed her to stay. She'd even been allowed to braid shells and seaweed into Flyyn's long hair for good luck; however, when the contractions started getting worse, and Neerna's anxiety started bleeding over to Flyyn, she was asked (rather, *told*) to go back to her hut and get some sleep.

Like such a thing were even possible.

"Nakk!" She barked, as her husband let out a snore.

Neerna's initial goodwill about the pregnancy had faded into something a lot more sharpened as Flyyn's original due date faded into the past. Originally, when she had been inseminated, the healer had told the three of them that Flyyn would give birth in early autumn—well before the autumn harvest, and therefore, well out of the range of the prophecy. Flyyn's name had been removed from all of the birth checklists, and Neerna had been generally left alone to prepare for motherhood since then.

As it would happen, however, the baby was in no rush to come, and Flyyn's original due date was quickly lost behind them. Not only that, but Epplin's aquatic fields had gone into a forcedly early harvest due to the increase in the pressure systems and unpredictable tides. By then, the fields had already been getting worked over for a week. So, with such an early harvest, the prophecy birth windows were extended, and that meant Flyyn's name was dusted off and dragged back onto the lists.

"What do you want me to do?" Nakk grumbled, sinking a little deeper into the pool of their bed and drifting blissfully close to sleep once more.

"Go to the healers," Neerna pleaded, splashing him until he finally opened his eyes properly. "Let me know how it's going."

To Nakk's credit, he didn't argue, and instead swam out of bed and leapt out of the window. As soon as his feet touched the shallows bordering their hut, he vanished—off to the healer's house.

Nakk could reorganize his genetic makeup while in the water and reform in another body of water almost instantly; as long as they were connected to each other and he'd been there before. He was the only one with such a gift in the entire clan, supposedly, and when he and Neerna had first fallen in love, he'd often used it to get out of her way.

Nakk was back in the shallows and shouting into the hut after mere moments.

"The baby's coming!"

And like a tsunami, Neerna was off.

Their son was born quickly thereafter, perhaps as an apology for having refused to vacate Flyyn's body for so long before then.

Now, when an Attinian child was born between harvest and the first snow, in any of the four clans, an order of business had to be followed.

First, the elders of whatever townships had had births were to be notified and introduced to the child. From there, the elders would send word to the neutral palace, where a clan representative from each bloodline lived, waiting to document the date and time of any possible-prophecy births.

If things went according to plan, each clan could generally make contact with the neutral territory in one day's time. Records of the year's births were kept until the first snow, and when the prophecy was one day fulfilled, messengers would immediately be sent out from there to notify the townships and remove the respective children.

As the sun rose on Nakk and Neerna's son's first day of life, the Zasse township of the Fire clan was already in the midst of a busy harvest. It had been an unseasonably rainy autumn for the southern village, and the crops had just dried out a few days prior, and only then with the help of their most dedicated and powerful farmers. Usually, the mountains and volcanoes protected the valley from the worst of the precipitation, but that year, it seemed the winds and weather systems had other ideas.

Crops grown in the Fire region did best in dry, hot weather, and were in danger of rotting if things stayed too wet. Fortunately, almost anywhere could be an agricultural zone within the clan territory, as long as the temperature laborers kept a close eye on things; however, not even they could stop a monsoon. Not safely, anyway.

In the past, they had risked lifting the temperature of certain regions high enough so the rain simply couldn't fall—or evaporated before it hit the ground—but this had typically brought in a host of other issues, ranging from crops not getting *enough* water, to damaging the actual plants with the excess heat. Without crops, there would be no food, and trade in the region would take a serious hit; so sometimes, even for the most experienced, farming was a patchwork quilt of luck and guessing.

It was hard work being a farmer in the Fire region no matter the weather, but those that did so were typically proud of their work, and highly praised within their societies.

One such farmer was named Jenothii. He was well known within Zasse as one of the hardest workers in the fields. He and his partner always collected a good yield during harvest, and were often the first to arrive and the last to leave.

Jenothii's skin was naturally of dusky red colour, but a life full of long days spent under the sun had darkened it to more of a brick-like red. With black eyes that had no hint of a pupil, and standing well above the others in the fields, he struck quite an imposing figure; however, he also possessed one of the biggest hearts that could be found.

Jenothii was currently stationed in a field already drenched in morning light, doubled over in a patch of leafy plants. His large hands were half buried in the dirt, and his teeth were gritted in concentration. The moment he closed his eyes, the temperature of his body began to rise. Soon, he was so hot that the air around him began to shimmer, though not a bead of sweat fell from his brow.

"That's great Jenothii, hold it right there," Said a woman beside him; his partner Bara. She had a long, thin basket tied vertically across her back, and she began pulling the plants free from the dirt closest to Jenothii's red-hot fingers.

In that particular field, the crop yielded long, edible root growths which fetched a high price on the interclan market; however, extracting them was a tricky science. If plucked from unheated, wet, or too-hot ground, the delicate tubers would split and spoil in the oxygen. The dirt had to reach and maintain the right temperature before they could be harvested.

This was what made Bara and Jenothii such good partners.

While Jenothii could manipulate his own basal body temperature to the point of affecting the ground he touched, Bara could sense temperatures; in this case, when the dirt had become perfectly hot enough. Had Bara been born to another township, one that didn't rely as heavily on farmers as Zasse did, she might have been cast aside as a weakling and probably doomed to some dark fate.

As it was, however, Bara was an exceedingly well-respected farmer in their little village, and she and Jenothii worked together almost exclusively in the root fields.

"That's all for this patch," She said, blowing a strand of curly black hair from her eyes before carefully placing the last of the roots in the basket. Jenothii straightened at her words, groaning as his back gave a magnificently loud crack.

"I'm getting too old for this, I think," He joked, though his voice was deep and somber. Bara snickered and strolled over to the next patch of untouched plants.

"Don't let your wife hear you saying so," She replied. "You're going to be even more tired once the baby comes, and that won't give you an excuse to slow down in the fields, either." Jenothii let out another comedic groan, but he couldn't hide a smile of enthusiasm. "When is Mirin due to give birth, anyway?"

Jenothii looked to the sun, which was rising in earnest by then.

"The healer said sometime before Winter." His voice hardened, though more out of irritation than out of true anger.

It seemed that whenever a woman became pregnant during the snowy months, the date given for the expected birth was as broad as possible. It wasn't surprising, Jenothii supposed—the broader the window, the more likely it would be that the child would be *born sometime between autumn's harvest and winter's first snow*—but now that it was him and Mirin expecting, it was grating on his nerves. How was a man, employed as a farmer, supposed to plan a harvest when a birth could come *anytime* before Winter?

Jenothii shook out his long, charcoal grey hair and huffed out a sigh before bending to the newest set of plants.

"It's no matter, anyway. The baby won't come today."

As it turned out, Jenothii was incorrect, for by the time he returned to his home for lunch that day, Mirin was in the middle of a heavy labour.

The same day had so far been peaceful in the warrior training city of Powlle, which lay nestled beside a canyon in the heart of the Air territory.

It was a foggy afternoon, for nobody had bothered to call a wind summoner to chase the mists away, but the Winged legion was out and performing their routines as usual, anyway. They didn't have actual wings, of course, but could rather manipulate currents and pockets of air in such a way that it rendered them able to "fly".

The Winged were the Air clan's primary warriors, and there were many different regiments of them throughout the territory. Powlle's squad was quite large considering the population of the city and closest towns, but that only made sense, as people didn't come to Powlle without being connected to the Winged in some way. New residents typically only moved in if they had interest in joining the ranks, and anybody who stayed was either in the division themselves, or directly related to somebody who was.

The Winged served their clan in other ways as well, including delivering important messages around the country when it was needed, for they could cover ground far faster than any horse, but their primary purpose was protecting Air blood. The battle formations and routines they performed, though necessary for practice, were also great sources of entertainment; and, in a city like Powlle, spectating was a popular activity.

And it *was* thrilling, to watch an entire host of people soar up and above the marketplace in tight formation, or plunge down into the canyon in the distance, only to pop up again to raucous applause.

But Lawre knew that if she watched too joyously—searched the ranks *too* carefully for one particular silver haired male—that it would surely draw unwanted attention. So, instead, she drew a hand across her growing belly, dropped her eyes from the Winged, and continued about her daily errands in the marketplace.

It wasn't that Mhont didn't share her affections; indeed, he had been overjoyed when Lawre told him of the pregnancy… it was just that they were both quite young. Their city was strictly traditional, and going against the grain risked cursing a child and their parents in all future endeavours (unless the child was born with extremely powerful gifts, of course). The social norm was not that a man and woman must be married to have a child—indeed, many couples did not wed within the city—it was that sexual relationships of any kind were not appropriate before the age of majority.

Lawre scowled to herself as she paid for her bread and turned everything over in her mind. She and Mhont were far from being children—both had recently celebrated their eighteenth year—and they loved each other dearly; however, in Attina, a person did not become an adult until their nineteenth year. The Winged were the most highly revered members of Air society, as well, so for somebody like Mhont, who had only just joined their ranks, social standing was *everything*. The Winged might be greatly respected, but respect could be taken away, and nothing would wipe the slate clean quite as effectively as an underage pregnancy in Powlle.

It was supposedly Mhont's hope that after their nineteenth year, he and Lawre could make their relationship public knowledge—but Lawre knew it would be too late by then. The baby would have already been born to a juvenile mother, and unless the child was gifted immeasurably, they would be marked forever by it. By associating with Lawre and the baby, Mhont would only be throwing away any good social standing he might have gained by then.

He said he didn't care, but Lawre did, and she knew deep down, he did as well.

Yet still, under all of the fear and anxiety, she could not deny that she also felt a grudging kind of excitement, as well. She'd gotten pregnant in very early Spring, and that meant her birth window extended through the harvest. Obviously most autumn births were not prophecy births… but still, the possibility of being part of the story that had been told to her since she was a little girl was intoxicating.

And, if the baby did happen to be one of the Promised Four, Lawre and Mhont would have no more worries, for a child of prophecy would be celebrated above all else, especially something as simple as an infraction of societal expectations. Losing the babe would be an unimaginable cost, of course, but the parents would be renowned as heroes in their own way, after giving it up for the good of the nation.

If Lawre had to admit it, even *with* the threat of losing the child hanging over her, the idea of all of her problems and supposed-transgressions being forgiven in an instant painted quite the pretty picture. It could be that she hadn't fully considered what losing a child might do to a parent, but it helped her through the long evenings.

All that said, if it turned out the child *wasn't* one of the Promised Four, just like all of the other autumn babies before it, Lawre would be stuck as an underage mother to a baby that would be shunned for its entire life.

And yet, right as Mirin went into labour over in the Fire clan, Lawre's basket of goods fell to the ground of the marketplace as the first contraction of her own labour hit, as well.

The Winged sent their fastest messenger to the neutral palace soon after.

And, as the sun dipped lower in the sky on the same day, Yarren of the Earth clan was walking up a well-travelled ridge that stood a reasonable distance away from his family's estate. Most of the Earth territory was wreathed in strong trees and plant life, but there were also a good assortment of rocky hills and mountains, especially as one drew closer to the neutral border. The community of Altikvo was located within such rocky foothills, and the majority its residents preferred hiking and harvesting the alpine resources to toiling in fields and forests, as many of their clan brothers and sisters did.

Nobody else was out hiking that evening, even though the path had been crowded earlier in the day, since the town's foragers had been out in full force to capitalize on a bountiful mushroom harvest that had sprung up overnight. Yarren didn't mind the solitude, though; in fact, he'd sought it out. He'd needed to get away from his family unit and take some time for himself. He loved his kin, of course, but the differing political views around the dinner table could occasionally spark exhausting and heated discussions.

These discussions had only increased in frequency and potency since Yarren's wife Freyja had gotten pregnant, and he'd had enough of it.

The family had never fully accepted Yarren and Freyja's pairing, since she was from a far lower caste than they were. Freyja's family was mostly comprised of people who could influence only the most basic of the earth's properties; plant growth direction, for example. It had never bothered Yarren—and as the heir to the family's wealth and titles, not many had fought him on it when he'd made his true intentions known with his now-wife—but the snide remarks and cold regard had remained. Yarren's father, as well, while still comfortable in his own position of power within the family, was blatantly disrespectful of the two of them. He made it abundantly clear, as often as he could, that he didn't she was a fit match for his son.

That evening, the patriarch of the family had even gone so far as to suggest that Yarren and Freyja's baby would not be welcome, if it wasn't born before the very next day began; because of course, they'd already heard the other clans had charted births that day, and if Freyja went into labour and delivered on the same night, the child would be one of the Promised Four. Freyja's birth window had, of course, covered the large period between harvest and the time when snow usually began to fall, but she'd gotten pregnant late, and the chances of delivering before Winter were slim.

Yarren kicked a stone, sending it careening off the nearest rocky ledge and into the sparse forests far below.

Of course his father would use the prophecy as leverage against Freyja. *If* the child was of prophecy, then *of course* she, as the mother, would become a celebrated member of the family, at last. But if the child was *not*—which was the far more likely scenario—then his father could use it as some half-baked excuse for his increasingly poor behaviour. Yarren wasn't sure if his father would actually disown the child, but unfortunately, he wouldn't put it past him.

In any case, that was the flavour of the discussion around the table that night, so before things could get too heated, Yarren had walked Freyja back to their quarters and then gone out to clear his head.

His father was old, and extremely set in the ways of the ancient Earth folk; in other words, he still lived by the castes related to both social standing and importance of power. Yarren would have been lying if he said he hadn't benefitted from his father's views of power, though, for it was not a fluke that he had been chosen above his older brother to one day inherit the land (A fact that would surely change, should Yarren continue to go against his father's wishes).

Yarren's magic allowed him to shift the tectonic plates under Attina itself; in other words, he could cause earthquakes ranging in power from dull shaking to catastrophes strong enough to bury the country under the surrounding ocean. He rarely used his gift, for it was too unpredictable even at the lower levels, but his family had a nasty habit of ensuring everybody knew what he could do, all the same. They were already a distinctly powerful and wealthy household, and Yarren's gifts only stood to increase their overinflated sense of self-importance. But that didn't mean *he* thought he was necessarily better than anybody else, or that his wife deserved to be alienated because of her own lower tier family. Sure, the perks he gained from rich blood and extremely powerful magic were nice… but was it worth the cost?

Could he choose his wife and unborn child over his family, even if it meant losing all he stood to gain? It frightened Yarren to admit that he wasn't sure what option he would choose when the time came; that is, until one of his family's household servants came dashing up the ridge behind him.

In that moment, his mind was made up for him.

"Yarren, sir!" The strained voice called Yarren out of his thoughts, and he turned to see one of his staff hurrying towards him. "The baby is here!"

Emotions erupted in Yarren's chest at the words; first, disbelief and excitement. Then fear. Then shock—was his child one of the Promised Four?

His already fair face paled, and the hazel shine of his eyes flashed in the evening light as he realized there must be a reason why his servant seemed so ill at ease, rather than happy.

"What of Freyja? When did the labour start?"

"Hours ago, sir, and all done now," The servant gasped, clutching his chest. "You are a faster hiker than I, and you know our horses cannot make this ridge."

"She wasn't expected to give birth for weeks! What happened?"

"Your daughter had other ideas, but sir—" The man stammered, still out of breath.

"*What else?*" Yarren snarled, already hastening past him and down the ridge. *Daughter…*

"Your father—"

This caused Yarren to stop dead in the dust and spin backward.

"What?" He hissed.

"Your father became overwhelmed by p-pride when the child was born," He gasped. Yarren could barely keep from shaking him to hurry up. "When he realized the child was of prophecy… sir, I'm sorry to say that he enacted the old Earth wielders' practices. We could not stop him."

Yarren's entire body numbed in an instant. He could not believe it—could not believe that his father would do such a thing to his own flesh and blood. But somewhere, in a haunted part of his brain, he knew the words were true.

He would kill him.

As he fought off the mental images suddenly assaulting him, Yarren was barely aware of his body while he began fairly flying down the treacherous ridge. Adrenaline and a lifetime of hard hiking aided his speed, and in a quarter of the time it had taken him to get up there, he was back down and hurtling towards his family's large estate. The ground rumbled underneath him, matching his anger, as he lost hold of the leash he usually kept on his immense magic. His usually-tidy green hair streamed out behind him in a wicked tangle, and his face reflected the agony within him as he pushed himself on.

Faster.

Yarren tore past the stone gates that his grandfather had built and carved out, without uttering so much as a word to the guards, and began pounding up the sloping lawns. From the fleeting looks he caught on their faces, they already knew what had transpired, and did not dare to slow him down.

His father had blinded his baby.

Centuries before, the strongest, most powerful (and most unhinged) elders of the Earth clan occasionally underwent the process of maiming themselves. They would claim that one did not need sight of the eyes when one could rely on the sight of the earth, and to fully be able to trust their magic was the true height of power. It had never been a common practice, and even at the time, was highly controversial. The elders in question would explain away their actions by fabricating ridiculous stories of spiritual sightings and elemental connectedness, but even amongst their brethren, the zealots' actions were often viewed as unnecessary and barbaric.

But to do it in the present-day… and to a baby, who had no say in the matter…it went above and well past what Yarren had ever considered to be evil before.

He knew then that the madness of his father's lust for familial importance and recognition had no limits, and Yarren's first stop upon reaching the estate was not his baby's sickroom, but was instead his father's chambers.

The envoy from Altikvo arrived at the neutral palace in the middle of the night, before the first signs of dawn had appeared on the horizon. A substantial discussion regarding the Earthen child's wellbeing was brought up at once, and after much time and consideration, the child was decreed still of prophecy, since the witch doctors of old had not specified that any such thing would interfere with fate.

As the palace staff went to rouse the sleeping delegates, riders were dispatched to each of the clans to collect the children in question; including an extra and heavily-armed party to Altikvo, sent to ensure the babe's safe removal from the family.

Once they were gone, the clan representatives began filtering into the palace's main hall to discuss matters. At first, those in attendance, having been so recently roused from sleep, did not believe it.

"Are you sure?"

"Four children, from each clan?"

"Each to first-time parents?"

"The last one was born on the same day, without question?"

But after checking and rechecking the times and date of all the official records that had been sent in, it was confirmed without doubt.

The Promised Four had come at last.

Chapter 2

Deep blue clouds converged across the sky. In the distance, thunder shuddered through the air like a great lumbering beast, and slowly, the wind picked up. Where it had been calm and quiet mere seconds before, a gentle breeze began to build. Any birds still lingering in the area took to the skies and cleared out as the gale gained strength.

The thunder boomed again, closer at hand.

Directly overhead, the clouds deepened in colour until they were more purple than they were blue, and soon enough, the breeze that had started out so gently, had whipped itself into a tempest. Dust and dry autumn leaves scattered across bare ground in a frenzy as the pressure built. The clouds piled on top of each other, and the first flashes of lightning high above lit up the purpling sky.

Nearby thunder clapped in response.

On a small outcropping of rock, situated above an open expanse of dust and scrub and with a forest of sentinel trees behind, stood four cloaked figures awaiting the coming storm.

One of them, a delicate male named Prinidan, had hair of the purest white—the long strands of it blew in the ferocious winds, yet never seemed to tangle. His long, hooded eyes were grey, but so light in colour that they could pass for silver; and his skin, like his hair and eyes, was extremely pale. The way he held himself perfectly still and watched the storm, as if he was following the movements of every gust of wind like the most practiced tracker, was ethereal. Haunting.

Standing directly beside him was a small-statured female—small but starkly confident—named Amarie. Her arms, tanned from what could only be hours spent outside, were crossed as she faced the storm unflinchingly, and there was a grim light painted across her expression. She had small, rounded eyes of a dusky brown colour, but there were milky scars across their surface, akin to the lightning now flashing in the sky. Her hair, pushed back in a tight knot, was dark brown, but had highlights of mossy green when the storm provided a flash of light.

Beside her stood another female, powerfully built, with a smile to match her considerable size. Her name was Zeraphall. She had skin of a rich mahogany brown, and the ends of her black, curly hair resembled the embers of a dying fire; it was also shaved on the sides and above the ears, with the top and back left free to grow as it would. She was the only one grinning at the storm, and she was doing so as if in challenge, with large eyes of the blackest night.

The last of the group was another male, and his name was Ellion. He was the tallest of the Four, but had an elegant build—long limbed and lithe. He had hair of a stormy blue-green that fell wild and thick around his shoulders, and was braided and twisted around shells and pieces of rope. His wide, mischievous eyes were bright green—the colour of seafoam—and though he looked graceful enough, the air around him felt charged. Wild. As if he was a creature about two moments away from leaping back into the sea.

"This will be a good one," Zeraphall murmured, widening those black eyes of hers. Her voice landed somewhere between a rasp and a crackling hum. "You're not doing this, Prin?"

Prinidan's face was impassive.

"It's not me. The storm is its own tonight. Unless—?" He glanced towards Ellion meaningfully, but the blue-haired male shook his head, braided shells clicking together softly. Anything he had been about to say in response, however, was drowned out in the newest clap of thunder.

It fairly boomed overhead, and sounded as though it had rent a hole in the uppermost heavens.

"It's here." Amarie was the next to speak, and as though her words had broken some sort of floodgate in the clouds, the rain began falling in earnest. Ellion gave her a sidelong glance with a sharply quirked eyebrow, and cleared his throat expectantly. Amarie gave a half-apologetic grin, then fell quiet.

The group didn't speak from then on, and simply enjoyed the show. The rain hammered against the dusty—now muddy—ground, and in a short time, there were little rivulets everywhere, gaining size by the second. The wind increased still further, somehow, until the trees across the clearing and behind them were fairly groaning with it. Branches snapped, trunks moaned, and from somewhere far in the distance came the distinctive crash of deadfall finally giving up the fight.

The Promised Four were taking a well-earned break from studying and practicing, and one of the group's favourite pastimes was observing nature do her own work—for once. When one could control the elements, witnessing them acting of their own accord had a certain appeal, though the temptation to alter what was happening, or to share in the experience in a deeper way, was sometimes almost too strong to resist.

The challenge they set for themselves, at such times, was to not use magic of any kind; to allow their minds and bodies to rest, and to spend a few moments being together. But when such overwhelming power was as much a part of their beings as breathing, it could be difficult to shut it down. It was reminiscent of an itch begging to be scratched; however, they knew and had learned about the power of restraint, and they worked hard to achieve it.

Sometimes, knowing when to hold back was a commanding influence all on its own.

The Promised Four held power previously unknown in the land of Attina, but arrogant, they were not. They played at such things sometimes, as all young adults and teenagers occasionally do, but deep down, they knew that though their strength was unprecedented by anybody but each other, they still had much to learn.

'Learning is a life-long experience,' One of their dearest instructors had said before he passed. 'To cease to learn would be the worst sort of self-sabotage imaginable. One would be better off dead.'

They'd taken those words to heart—all of them had—and it was reflected in their studies. They were hard workers and devoted students, and any of the palace attendants or advisors would have said the same.

So even though the royals had already bypassed their nineteenth year and the age of majority in the realm, they still worked at their studies every day. Those studies could range from political debates with each other and their instructors, to elemental practice, to physical exercise, and anything else in between. It was a daily occurrence.

They were four leaders who had been born into their power, and ruling an empire was a job that was never done. There was always something new to learn. Far be it from them to allow anybody to say they were brash or unprepared and have those statements backed up as fact.

They were the most fit leaders that Attina could have ever hoped for.

—

"Two reps from Air and Water in the council room."

The Promised Four thanked the attendant for the news. It was just another morning in the neutral palace; another day of hearing concerns from the clans, working through disagreements alongside them, and in general running the country.

"I need to ride out to the neutral border today, to meet a trading caravan that was having some issues with highway robbers," Amarie said before her siblings went into the large chambers where the clan reps were waiting. "Does anybody want to come?"

Zeraphall turned, black eyes glittering.

"What, and ride through the aftermath of the storm? No thank you," The Fire elemental said with a wicked smile tinting her words. Amarie scoffed good naturedly at her sister, then turned towards the males, lifting her eyebrows in silent question.

"Do you need someone?" Ellion asked, his voice laced with contained strength. Amarie shook her head.

"No, but I thought I'd offer, if anybody wants a change of pace." After all, she thought, the daily meetings could get tiring after a while.

"We should deal with these reps, then," Prinidan finished, glancing towards the council chambers. "When will you be back?"

"Tomorrow evening, at the latest. It didn't sound like the caravan's concerns will take long to work through."

The Promised Four bid each other farewell, and while Amarie went off in the direction of the attendants' hall to find escorts for her trip, the other three went in to hear what the clan reps had to say.

"Welcome to our home," Prinidan greeted the Air and Water representatives with a nod, and swept his deft gaze over the others seated at the large wooden table. He was careful not to let his gaze linger on the representative from Air for too long, and graced him with no more attention than he did the woman from Water. They might share the same distant bloodline, but Prinidan belonged to no clan. He invited everyone to find a seat with a smooth wave of his arm.

Ellion went so far as to shake ether rep's hand before finding his seat, but like Prinidan, didn't give the Water woman any special attention.

Zeraphall's gaze, on the other hand, swept right over the Air attendant and locked on the Water spokeswoman. She said nothing, but something glittered deep within her dark eyes.

"Regrets from our sister," Prinidan continued. "A matter needed her attention elsewhere."

"But of course, there is no need to apologize, Your Highness," The man from Air said, meeting his would-be clansman's eyes. Prinidan murmured his thanks, ever a gentleman.

The Air rep's eyes, while angular not unlike Prinidan's were, had no distinctive colour to speak of, and the pupils stuck out starkly against the white. It gave him an air of apparent surprise, or even fright. A bird pin on his chest marked him as belonging to the Winged legion—those who were able to command air currents in a close mimicry of flight. Since the Promised Four had come into their rule, inter-clan wars had been scarce, but the Winged remained as well-trained as ever, should the need arise once more.

"Thank you for meeting us." The woman from Water said.

She and Ellion were of the same distant heritage, of course, but they couldn't have looked more different in the moment. Ellion had a touch of wildness about him—perhaps it was the ornaments he braided into his thick hair, or the untamed glint in those bright green eyes—but the woman seemed decidedly tame. It wasn't just that her hair and eyes were muted tones of brown, it was more that she seemed entirely calm and collected.

In control. Bored, even; yet somehow, respectfully so.

Zeraphall's eyes had not yet left her.

—

"Begging your pardon, My Lady…" A deep voice floated over to Amarie as she wrestled a saddle up and onto her waiting horse. She recognized it as belonging to Fron, the stable's newest hire. He was of an age with the Four and from Fire, if Amarie's memory did not fail her. He was untrained in dealings of the court, to be sure, but he knew how to tend to horses, and he knew how to protect what was his.

"What is it, Fron? Speak freely, please," Amarie said over her shoulder with as warm a smile as she could muster while tightening her horse's saddle.

"Couldn't—well… that is to say… Shouldn't someone else be coming too?" He cleared his throat, clearly uncomfortable. "No, I mean—what I mean is… is it safe for you to go alone?" He seemed horrified that he had voiced the question at all.

Amarie's mouth tightened, though she wasn't exactly surprised by his question. She made him wait in silence for a few moments more, then sighed ruefully when she was done with the saddle. The only reason she wasn't irritated by his question was because he was so new to the palace ranks; indeed, this was the first time they had truly spoken together. If a more seasoned employee had asked her the same type of question, Amarie might have taken offense. As it was, however, she couldn't fault someone for honest curiosity—though he would do best to remember her answer.

She turned towards the sound of his voice and put a hand on her hip.

"Do you mean to ask me if I could handle myself, should things turn sour on the road?" Her voice was light and conversational, but in reality, all of her physical combat training was beginning to rumble to the surface of her memory.

All four of the royals had been taught such things throughout their lives, but Amarie had been the one most taken with it. She had trained the hardest out of her siblings, and had retained the most knowledge. Being able to defend oneself without sight or magic was innately special.

And though this was the line that her thoughts were travelling on, Amarie did not intend to start a true quarrel with Fron; however, if he kept asking questions… well, throwing him on his ass into the hay would really only hurt his pride.

"No, Miss. Not like that. I only meant—well how would you know the way? What if you were to get lost and ill-intended folk came upon you?"

Amarie banished the thought of showing him exactly how well she could handle herself, for the time being. There were other ways to put his well-intentioned doubts to rest.

"You needn't fear for me out there, Fron. I know where you're standing based on your voice alone—and if you've noticed, I've angled myself to face you with my back towards where I know the exit is. I can hear that you're carrying a bridle, and what I'm guessing is a length of rope. Were you to attempt to contain me with those items, one of two things would happen." A wide smile flashed across her face. "One; I would slice open your belly, because again, judging by your voice, you stand quite a bit taller than me. That makes me at the perfect angle to—" She swiped out with the small knife she kept hidden in her sleeve. Fron stumbled back a step, though Amarie had known exactly how far off he stood from her.

Her smile widened still further. "Or two, I would simply sever my bonds when your back was turned."

"I didn't know you could do all that," He mumbled after a short time, now sounding far more sheepish than curious. Amarie chuckled.

"Most don't—but we like to keep it that way."

She sheathed her knife once more, then turned back to her horse. She could hear that Fron stood still for a time, watching her, if she had to guess, before finally turning to go.

"Oh!" Amarie said, spinning back and tucking her hands behind her back. His steps paused. "I forgot to mention the third option."

She blinked and cast her awareness out like a net around her, pinpointing the change in Fron's location through the weight and feel of him on the ground. With a simple flick of her head, the ground underneath him hardened and shot up from the earth. He yelped in surprise, but Amarie, chuckling in earnest, commanded it to bring him in to her. The sound of crunching gravel and rumbling dirt filled the stables for a half-second, and then he was deposited in a heap at her feet.

She shrieked in laughter, covering her mouth and apologizing profusely.

"I'm terribly sorry, I am. It was too tempting." She reached for him and was instantly met with his hands as he grasped around to try and find his balance. To her surprise, she found her own grip easily swallowed by his. She helped haul him back to standing, and tried to keep from laughing further as he dusted himself off.

"Did I deserve that?" He asked. Amarie shrugged, putting on her most queenly expression.

"Probably," She snickered, but her smile faded a few moments later. "I do thank you for your concern though, however poorly introduced it was. I will have an escort with me, and we don't plan to be gone long."

The Promised Four were not unfamiliar with misgivings about travelling. It didn't ultimately matter who was leaving—

simply the idea of them splitting up tended to put people ill at ease. Nobody was to blame for these feelings, of course, for even if they were frustrating to deal with, such things were all but hammered into Attinian society. With the fulfillment of the prophecy marking the royals' birth, there also came the great threat, ever-looming.

Whatever it was, it would come in the Four's lifetime, and together, they would have to face it or risk losing everything. This was all they knew of the matter. But it had to be done together.

So, perhaps understandably, whenever the royals split up, it could bring about some speculation, be it about safety, planning, danger on the roads, or almost anything else. Even the royals themselves were not innocent of it all of the time. Separation from each other often nagged at them, in the corners of their minds.

It was ridiculous, they all knew it, but it was what they had been taught. The prophecy had never promised victory, after all—it had only stated that their one chance to defeat the coming evil was together.

—

"Could you have been any more obvious back there, Zera?" Ellion mused, eyes alight with mischief, even though he kept them focused on the small orb of water that he was levitating between his hands. He didn't smile, but the shadow of a dimple showed on his cheek as he fought it down.

The three siblings were lounging around one of the many common rooms of the palace, after having dealt with the reps earlier that morning. Ellion had sprawled his long body across a low sofa, while Prinidan and Zeraphall had both opted for the plush chairs in front of the fireplace—Zeraphall sitting closest to the hearth, of course.

"Obvious with what?" Zeraphall said, feigning ignorance and turning from the low crackle of flames to look at Ellion. Once her attention was elsewhere, the fire flickered and died, considering there was no wood in the grate.

Prinidan met his brother's eye at the same time, though he hid his own smile behind a slender hand. He knew exactly what was coming.

"That poor Water rep probably thought she was in some kind of trouble, getting stared at by a queen like that—did you even *blink*?" Now Ellion allowed the smile to break through, flicking his wrists and causing the orb of water to stretch and change shape above him as he did so.

Zeraphall snorted and rolled her neck from side to side.

"I can't resist a Water woman, you know that." Her tone of voice suggested that if they didn't already know, they probably should have. "It's not my fault. They're the only ones that can quench my fire." Before the words were even out of her mouth, her brothers were covering their ears and shouting their complaints about her choice of language. Zeraphall leaned forward and grinned wickedly at them. "I tell you, Ell. If you and I weren't related, and if you were a woman…"

"NO!" Prinidan howled, beating a powerful gust of air towards Zeraphall that knocked her backwards into her seat with a wave of his hands. "I forbid you to finish that sentence."

Zeraphall cackled in laughter, but didn't bother to rise up from the cushions.

"Excuse me—" The voice of one of the palace assistants broke through the cries of mirth as Ellion shattered and reformed the disc of water, daring it closer to his siblings at every turn.

In a heartbeat, the trio dropped their playful attitudes. The water vanished from the couch and everyone's clothes, and they sat up—kings and queen once more. There was a time to play, and there was a time to lead.

It was rare for an attendant to seek them out so late in the afternoon.

"Yes?" Zeraphall's crackling voice betrayed none of the previous moment's laughter.

"There is another rep—from Fire—waiting in the entry hall."

"What, another one?" Prinidan echoed, turning to look quizzically at his brother and sister. "Why didn't they come earlier, with the other two?"

"I didn't ask her, Sire."

The siblings chewed over the attendant's words for a few moments. Such a thing was quite unheard of. The morning was when official hearings were held—all clans knew that if they wouldn't arrive in time for the morning audience, they were expected seek out lodging in the palace and await the sunrise.

After another few moments of silence, Ellion nodded.

"We'll hear what she has to say—but, less formally. I've had enough of the meeting chambers for today. We'll go right to her."

The others agreed.

"A thousand apologies, Promised Ones," The Fire rep spoke before she'd even been properly greeted. Her skin was charcoal grey, and her long hair was as black as night. "But I arrived late and… and I couldn't wait until morning."

It was only then that the siblings realized she had no escort with her—she'd come alone. Her boots were muddied, and her hair was disheveled, as if she'd ridden through the previous night's great storm.

It looked as though she hadn't even attempted to clean herself up beforehand.

"What is it?" Zeraphall asked, going to her blood kin and grasping her cold hands. In a heartbeat, Zeraphall had warmed them up to a comfortable temperature. The woman thanked her and took a steadying breath.

"I come at the urgent request of one of our high families." Prinidan and Ellion exchanged tense looks. The Promised Four had tried to stamp out the power-based hierarchy in most areas, but sometimes, things were rooted too deeply. The Fire rep continued. "Their eldest daughter—she's sick."

"Sick how?" Prinidan asked, focused. The Fire rep took another breath and brought a fluttering hand over her chest.

"Sick—her gifts… they… they seem to have disappeared."

The words were like a physical blow. Ellion actually fell back a step.

"What do you mean?" Zeraphall asked sharply once she'd recovered, her voice acting like an anchor between reason and panic.

"She wasn't the most powerful in the family… but she had a real knack for putting out flames by sight. Couldn't start them to save her life, of course, but had never struggled with the former. That is—that is, until yesterday morning. After breakfast had been fixed, she went to put out the morning cookfire, as she has always done—and…" The woman shrugged. "And, well. Nothing."

"What, she just couldn't do it?" Ellion's eyes were wide—contemplative.

"Was she tired? Perhaps she'd been practicing," Prinidan asked gently. It wasn't unheard of; in fact, it was quite common. Exhaustion was a troublingly familiar feeling when overusing magical gifts—even the Four knew this. Still though, usually a few scraps of magic remained.

People weren't left with… *nothing.*

"My first question as well, Lord Prinidan." But the woman shook her head. "Though alas, the family claims she hadn't done anything out of the ordinary. Put out the cookfires—that's it."

Zeraphall cursed the spirits, which admittedly shocked the rep; however, her brothers barely batted an eye. She leaned back on her heels and rubbed at her eyes with the butts of her hand. If what the rep was claiming was true… then it was a new problem in the realm.

One that had never been reported before, even before the royals' time.

"And she's been quarantined?" Zeraphall asked. The rep confirmed immediately. Zeraphall hummed deep in her throat, letting out a snapping drone of sound. She glanced to her brothers, trying not to let the worry creep into her face.

"Was there anything else?" Prinidan asked, when Zeraphall failed to say anything more. The rep shook her head.

"As of now, nothing. The girl says she feels fine—no dizziness, pain, or nausea. No accidents. It's just that her power is… gone."

A troubling thought to say the least. If there was a sickness running through the clan and wiping out powers, the implications were too grim to imagine.

"Nobody else has similar symptoms?" Ellion asked.

"None, and the family has continued on with life as usual, since they had meetings this morning too important to postpone. They're some of the foremost trade negotiators in Fire, and they deal with all other clans on the regular."

So, if it *was* a sickness, it had already been spread to the other clans.

"You've given us much to consider this night," Prinidan spoke into the quiet, placing a steadying hand on Zeraphall's shoulder and nodding at Ellion. "We would be honoured if you would stay here at the palace over night as our guest, and break your fast with us in the morning. Perhaps then we can discuss happier things before sending you back to your clan."

"The honour would be mine, Highness. Thank you."

—

Amarie checked her mare's gallop as she and her party neared the border where they were to meet the travelling caravan reporting issues. The road had turned harder packed the closer they'd come to the border; Amarie could feel it under her horse's hooves, and she sensed that they were coming to a crossroads. The wind had died off with the storm the night before, but rain and dark clouds were still scattered across the territory.

She shivered slightly in her saddle, wishing for Zeraphall's gift of warmth.

"Any sign of them?" She asked the scout that had gone ahead as she heard him canter back to the group. She'd cast out her awareness over the land, but there was no telling which party was which amongst those she'd found. The scout confirmed, and told them where they needed to go. Amarie thanked him and clicked her tongue, sending her horse into one last gallop before it could have a well-earned rest.

It was entering late afternoon by the time Amarie and her escorts pulled up on the convoy and dismounted. Her muscles were stiff, but she gave each merchant that greeted them a shining smile. The reception the royal party received was warm, if not a little bit slipshod.

One large caravan seemed to hold most of the wares for sale or trade, and it was the heaviest against the land. A handful of other covered wagons were stationed around the area as well, and they felt smaller and less full. Amarie heard the cooing of a baby being rocked by her older sister in one of them, so deduced those were the vehicles reserved for transporting family or personal goods.

The traders also seemed to prefer sleeping on the ground in erected tents, rather than cramping together in their wagons, for Amarie could feel many such small structures around the camp. She supposed that only made sense. If the weather allowed it, why not sleep under the stars and get a little fresh air?

"Is Nagra around?" The highest-ranked official in Amarie's group asked. "She was the one who made contact with us."

"Glad to see you hurried," Came a voice thick with age and authority. Amarie and her escorts turned towards the voice. Somebody was walking up to them; Nagra, undoubtedly.

Amarie focused in hard, as she always did when meeting somebody new and of influence. Nagra's voice had lent the assumption that she was on in her years, as did the feel of her shuffling gait against the rocky ground. The Earth Queen also noticed that Nagra's footsteps were heavier than their size and points of pressure would have made her originally think, which led her to the notion that Nagra was not lacking in bulk to keep her warm.

"We came as soon as we could," Amarie amended to what the woman had said. It was good for the subjects of Attina to think of the Four as timely and as taking their concerns seriously—but it was bad if anybody thought they would always come at the drop of a hat. Amarie cleared her throat. "We understand your caravan has been having some problems lately." Nagra's voice was grave when she replied.

"In all my years, never has any group of bandits been brave enough—or foolhardy enough—to attack one of my convoys." Amarie felt her weight shift from foot to foot impatiently, and frowned in thought.

She ran through what she had been told about the situation on the journey over. Nagra's power lay beneath the ground, in the roots of the trees and plants—a fellow Earth elemental. With surprising deftness, Nagra could bring those roots up from their resting places and control them, yet somehow never do any lasting harm to the plant they came from. There were others like her throughout the Earth bloodline, but she was one of the most powerful the realm had note of.

"What became of the robbers?" Amarie asked, tilting her head in sudden curiosity. From the weight of the wagons against the ground, it did not feel as though the caravan was empty or light on tradable materials. If the thieves had taken anything, it certainly didn't seem to have been very much.

"With permission Ma'am, I disposed of them proper."

It was not illegal for a merchant to defend their wares from bandits, so Amarie dipped her head in understanding. She knew Nagra was not finished, though, for if she'd simply dealt with them and been done with it, the palace would never have been called in the first place.

"That was the first time," The merchant leader continued, shifting her weight from foot to foot again. "The next time, as well. But that's not what bothered us."

"Go on," Amarie's official prompted beside her. Nagra's body weight shifted again, but this time to the back, as though she was exchanging a glance with one of the traders behind her.

"Please, speak freely Nagra," Amarie prompted.

"Well, you see, Highness. What bothered us most, was that them robbers didn't seem to have any powers at all. Thought I should probably tell you in person."

Chapter 3

Amarie and her officials began to make camp as the moon rose. After such shocking news from Nagra that afternoon, conversation around the merchant's dinner fire had been subdued. Normally, the trading convoys made great company for an evening drink or a song and stories around the campfire. But this was a passive group, and no wonder.

Never, in all of the history lessons Amarie and her siblings had had over the years, was there any mention of people *without* powers. Just… with nothing. No magic. Amarie hadn't believed Nagra at first, of course. She hadn't thought the elder trader was lying, exactly, but perhaps mistaken—confused.

"Is it possible they simply didn't use their gifts?" Amarie had tried after finishing off her bowl of thick, delicious stew. "Or maybe their magic wasn't all that noticeable or powerful in the first place? Perhaps that's why they turned to a life of robbery."

At her words, Nagra had leaned back on her stump.

"Always a possibility I suppose, Ma'am—but at some point, they knew they was gonna die by my hand. If they *could* have put up a better fight, I like to think they would have."

Nagra had spoken so simply, that the bandits had known she would be the one to kill them, that Amarie had found herself slightly in awe, despite the subject matter. Killing wasn't something to necessarily strive for, of course, but the Promised Four had never seen real conflict. They were powerful, to be sure—but young in so many ways. And there was Nagra, a woman well on into her life, that could both command a fleet of mixed clan traders *and* protect that fleet when push came to shove.

It was inspiring.

And yet such a woman was coming to her, to Amarie, with her concerns and fears; looking for answers. Suddenly, Amarie did wish the others had come along—not for protection per se, but the

Four were stronger and smarter as a group. It was second nature to bounce ideas back and forth between themselves and help each other come up with answers.

Taking a breath as her palace escort continued setting up their tents, Amarie replayed all that she had heard and learned of the encounters in her head. Any big decisions about the situation would have to wait until she had briefed her siblings, of course, but she could think on it. Originally, she had been confident that she could deal with the traders' problems by herself; unfortunately, now that it was such a strange and potentially dangerous problem, the others would have to be included in the resolution of it.

Even so, it would be nice to leave the merchants with some parting words of wisdom in the morning, when she and her party left to travel back to the palace.

Perhaps if she slept on it, something would come to her.

Unlikely.

Nagra had seen Amarie's worried expression while they were going over everything, despite the queen's best efforts to hide it, and had explained that if any future robbers followed the same pattern as the ones who had already attacked, they would be fine and there was nothing to worry about. It was the unknown, Nagra said, that had her and the others in the caravan so unsettled.

And it *was* strange—if it was true and correct, of course.

Unheard of.

It opened up a whole host of frightening possibilities, as the unknown often did. Were the robbers part of a new and unannounced clan that somehow didn't have elemental powers? And if so, were they hiding some deeper and more powerful kind of magic? Were they invaders from a different land where there was no magic at all? Or was there some evil at work within Attina that was slowly stripping magic away, causing people to resort to lives of crime to get by?

"All set up here, Miss," Said one of her attendants, once their own tents were finished. Amarie, lost in thought, only gave a quiet nod before turning to the small spit of land where she would sleep.

Without a word, she lifted her hands and called to the sweet song of power within her blood.

Like old friends, the earth answered her, and Amarie was immediately comforted. She sent her consciousness down through the dirt and rocks, greeting the terrain intimately and reminding it who she was. In reply, the ground started writhing as if it were made of water. A second later, a large boulder had risen from the dirt, displacing smaller stones on the surface. With a blink, the rock began rearranging itself to form a hollow cave. The roof was low, and a precise overhang drooped over the mouth so that the inside was all but invisible.

Amarie smiled, feeling more settled and at home than she had mere seconds before. The closest attendant grasped her shoulder.

"Try to get some sleep, Miss. We'll be right outside your door."

—

"Tell us," Prinidan mused over the breakfast table. "How are relations amongst the Fire clan right now?" His near white eyes were sharp, focused keenly on their guest, like some kind of ethereal hawk.

"Mostly well," The Fire rep said, clearly reading into the intent behind Prinidan's question. Her name was Sehnai, and though the leaders of the realm were nearly choked with curiosity after the news she had given, they had resolved to try and discuss less official things over the breakfast table. "The families who hold to the old ways are ever stubborn, though."

"Of course," Prinidan reassured her. "We are young yet—and those traditions run deep."

"That they do," Sehnai agreed. "But even the most prejudice and powerful of families keep it quieter than they once did. You Four are highly respected within my clan, and even those who do not agree with you would not dare to openly oppose you."

Zeraphall's brow knitted together slightly, and she caught Ellion's gaze. People smiling to their faces but snarling at their backs was not necessarily as good of news as Sehnai was painting it to be.

"Would we be well-received in the family's city where the girl lost her power?" Ellion asked.

It was a question worth asking. In some cities, where there were lots of powerful and old families, love for the Promised Four, whose very existence meant an ending of the old ways, was not always apparent.

The Four did not frequent the cities deep within the clan territories often, either. There had been one visit when they were babies, which none of them remembered, another when they were around ten years old, and one more when they were nearing the age of majority. Now that they were adults and proper leaders in their own right, there would undoubtedly be another visit soon enough.

More visibility within the powerful cities could only be a good thing.

"Your reception would be warm enough," Sehnai answered. "Though not too warm, I should think."

"Enough of this grey and official talk," Zeraphall barked, leaning forward and spearing a sausage before offering the plate around. "Let us try to speak of sunnier things."

The morning slid by with talk of Fire festivities, of the clan's preparations for Winter, and of the rising artists within the larger cities' hearts. All clans had artists, of course, but Fire folk were typically adept with painting—one of the more transportable mediums. Zeraphall had one such painting hanging in her room over the head of her bed. The way the paint blended with the scorching and burned marks along the canvas, in that piece in particular, reminded Zeraphall of where she had come from—and where she had still to go.

Once breakfast was over, and they had shared communicable talk for some hours, the royals bid Sehnai farewell. There were no other official clan matters set to be discussed that morning, either, so the three siblings went separate ways until Amarie's return.

Zeraphall went to the courtyard—a place mostly shielded of wind and made entirely of stone and marble, where she could practice to her heart's content, without fear of scorching anything elsewhere on the large property. She wanted to work on fires that held no heat. She had to start the fire and simultaneously leech it of its warmth, all while ensuring that it continued burning. It was a tricky sort of magic.

"Spirits be cursed to the Four Hells!" Zeraphall snarled as she failed time and again, and her blood began to boil in her frustration. With another hiss of annoyance, she scraped a burning hand down her shaved head and took some breaths. "Again," She growled to herself when she was back in control, and sat down cross legged on the cold stone.

Between her hands a spark ignited, which soon became a large ball of flame.

"Now cool down," She whispered, as much to calm herself as to aid her focus. Her black eyes were intense, wide pools of night, as she focused on the ball of fire. She tried to split her attention between the fire and the cooler temperature of the marble below her—really *feel* it. As she did so, she closed her eyes and let the chill seep into her bones; and eventually, the fire in her hands did not feel quite so hot anymore.

Her eyes popped open and she gave a wicked grin.

While Zeraphall succeeded at her experiment, Ellion had gone to the closest lake on the palace grounds, instead. The weather was not warm, but once in the water, he took no notice of the cold. He shucked off his clothes and tied back his thick hair and braids before climbing onto a rock that hung over the water at some distance. He leaned back and looked to the sky, scanning the clouds. There would be more rain that night—Ellion could sense it in the clouds. Hopefully Amarie would be back before it started. He supposed that if she didn't make it in time, he could always ride out to meet her and ensure that the last leg of her journey was dry.

It would be the considerate thing to do.

He smiled to himself, his mind made up, and then dove into the depths of the chilly lake. It hadn't been a deep pond, originally—but with a little help from Amarie, and after a lot of practice himself, the once-shallow puddle had been transformed into something of a natural wonder. It was so deep, Ellion could swim downwards for over an hour and still never reach the bottom. In fact, he and Prinidan were the only ones that had ever even *seen* the bottom. Prinidan was a slower swimmer, of course, but he could bring the oxygen out of the water around him and have plenty of air for the long journey down.

Of Prinidan, while the others went their own way, he retired to his personal chambers.

Set in the highest turret of the palace, the windows (of which there were many) had no glass, and they allowed the wind to howl through uninhibited. If it was bitterly cold, Prinidan would simply cast air shields where the windows would have been, but otherwise he let it come in with joy. There were wind chimes and hollow pipes hung in one corner of the room, as well, and when he allowed the air to travel through them, the sound was haunting and lovely. Prinidan had always been drawn to such instruments, but after he was told that much of the Air clan had similar interests, he took the initiative to hang a few up. It felt nice to be connected to his blood clan in that small way; there, in a place where nobody else would see and think he was playing favourites. He wasn't, of course, and never had, but there was something special about knowing where one came from.

After relaxing for a few minutes, Prinidan alighted to one of the many windowsills. He bent down and scanned the sloping roofs and battlements of the palace, stretching below and away from his tower bedroom. Finding whatever it was he had been looking for, he suddenly straightened and leapt into open space. He free-fell for a few seconds, before gathering up a gust of hard packed air and bolstering himself upward—again, and again.

—

Amarie shared a quick breakfast with the travelling merchants that morning, before they brought her to the scene of the most recently-attempted robbery. It was near the forest lining the neutral territory border, in a shaded patch of road.

"Tell me what you see," She murmured to the member of her staff that gave the most detailed descriptions.

There were marks of Nagra's power everywhere, there—huge rifts out of the earth near the largest trees, where their roots had been displaced to do the old woman's bidding, then replaced again, good as new. There were also wheel and hoof marks where the animals or wagons had quickly changed course, no doubt when the robbers had first set upon them. As the scene was described, Amarie felt out through the ground for any abnormalities, but found none.

She asked to be taken to the bodies, next.

"We've already given them a thief's burial," Admitted the male she'd asked. Amarie sighed grimly; it was no better than the robbers' deserved, of course, but it was still a brutal way to be sent to the afterlife.

A thief's burial, reserved for people who had been found guilty of thieving or other wrong doing, was meant to be as quick and as lacking in respect as possible. All bodies needed to be buried or burned, of course, so wayward spirits would not get locked in Attina, but there was generally no ceremony for criminals; among their own kind, perhaps, but certainly not among the general public. A thief's burial was not even a burial, per se, as it was more of a careful placing of debris over an unhonoured body.

"Bring me to them," Amarie said, her voice hard. She leaned over to her closest advisor as they began to make their way into the trees and muttered softly to her. "Keep your wits about you." For if the robbers truly hadn't had any elemental magic, who knew what other kind of evils lurked about?

Eventually, they reached the makeshift barrows. Amarie sensed most of what lay before them, but she asked for a description of the scene, anyway.

The corpses were piled together, a classic undertaking with thieves' burials, and covered by branches and leaves. Stones had been put on top to hold it down and mark the site. The traders had also dug out a small trench in the earth—not deep enough to be considered a burial, but deep enough that the bodies and their spirits wouldn't get swept away with the first rain.

Amarie moved closer to the barrow, but an attendant pulled her back.

"Don't touch them, Miss," He murmured.

Amarie nodded and tilted her head instead, sensing out where the weight of the bodies and piles of debris were situated. She flicked a wrist, and began shifting the branches and rocks out of the way. By attaching her mind to some of the uprooted plants, she was able to feel where each of the bodies were, in relation to them. She carefully unpacked the rubble until her attendant whispered that the first body was in proper view.

Upon inspecting the bodies, Amarie and her party found that, indeed, there were no distinctive clan marks on any of them at all. None of them had blue or white hair, none had fire-red skin.

"Nothing?" Amarie repeated, feeling a spark of impatience, though trying not to assume that her assistants were missing anything.

"Nothing—except," Her attendant hesitated, and Amarie felt her weight shift as she bent closer to the ground.

"What is it?" She prompted. Her attendant sucked in a slow breath and hummed as she considered whatever it was that she was looking at.

"On his hand—there's a tattoo."

"Clan?"

"I don't think so—none I've seen, anyway."

"Describe it, please."

"It's on the back of his hand—small enough that it doesn't cover the entire hand. It's a circle."

"Fully coloured, like a spot?"

"No, empty and blank."

Amarie frowned. Such an ambiguous marking could have been for anything.

It could have signified that the band of thieves had formed something of a brotherhood, it could have been from a distant family group… as far as Amarie knew, it could have even indicated a mysterious clan stationed beyond the edges of the map. She could only guess.

Upon returning to the main camp, Nagra hadn't been able to confirm if the other group of thieves, the first ones to attack the caravan, had had the same tattoos, or not.

"I didn't look, Ma'am."

"No worries, Nagra. Thank you," Amarie said, though her face was dark. Realistically, there was nothing to go on. Worse still, other than the simple, strange, infuriating tattoo, nothing about them spoke of magic.

Nothing at all.

—

"No powers at all, you say?" Zeraphall asked as Amarie hung up her travelling cloak. She shook her head in response, even as Ellion and Prinidan crowded in.

"That's what Nagra said, anyway."

"Could they have had powers before, and lost them?" Ellion asked.

"You think it's tied to what the woman from Fire told you about?" Amarie asked, frowning. It was strangely coincidental that they'd suddenly heard of multiple instances of people having no powers—especially considering no such phenomenon had ever been noted in all of Attina's history previously.

"It's possible, isn't it?" Prinidan echoed in a level tone. "It would have to be, I think." Amarie shrugged.

"I mean, we checked over the bodies thoroughly. Nothing would have marked them as having clan magic in the first place. Their hair was supposedly hay coloured, almost yellow?" She couldn't picture it, but from what she'd learned, it was a trait seen little and less throughout Attina. "And one did have fair skin, but I asked, and it was not so fair as Prinidan's, and his body shape didn't follow the moulds of Earth or Water. Another had dark skin, but then she also had green eyes." Which would have completely discounted her from the Fire clan.

The royal's faces fell as one.

After plenty of discussion between the four of them, eventually, the subject matter began going in ever shrinking circles. There was only so much fact to go on in both cases, and the rest was only guesswork that became more irritating by the minute. Before tempers could run too high, though, the Four decided to take the matter to one of their retired instructors. He had always encouraged healthy debates between them, and he seemed like he would be keenly up for the task.

They held great love for their past-instructor in their hearts, and as such, had convinced him to live out his retirement there in the palace. He often provided insight or advice when the royals ran into obstacles that they couldn't work around.

"Zeraphall," The old man greeted, when they entered his chambers off a quiet hallway on the main floor. His rooms were large, as he spent most of his time there. Floor to ceiling windows provided much light during the daytime, a pantry was always kept well stocked should he ever want to take his meals in, and a large walk-in fireplace against one wall stood as the main accent of the living space. It gave the entire room a cozy feeling, especially when it was lit, as it currently was.

"Hello, Kyzer," Zeraphall smiled, her face lit with the kind of respect only those who had truly earned it, received from her.

"Not practicing too hard, I hope?"

"Never."

"And Ellion." Kyzer reached up to take the tall Water elemental's shoulders in his gnarled hands.

"Hello old man," Ellion said fondly, bending at the waist to plant a kiss on top of his head.

"Glad to see you haven't caught your death yet, swimming in naught but your skin in all manner of weather." Kyzer's tone turned disapproving, but Ellion's dimples flashed in a wicked smirk as he glided into the room.

"You wouldn't understand," He said over his shoulder. The old professor snorted.

Kyzer was from the Fire clan, or had been, before he'd given up his latter years to train the young leaders of the realm. His skin was more black than it was brown, but in a subtle kind of way, and his eyes were deep red, with a spark of curiosity that not even his old age could dampen.

"Prinidan," Kyzer rumbled, turning from Ellion with a slight shake of his head. "These three aren't giving you too much trouble, are they?"

"I would think something was seriously wrong if they weren't, old friend." Prinidan brought out a slender hand to grasp Kyzer's shoulder, a smile lighting up his pale eyes. Kyzer chuckled as Amarie ducked into the room, as well. Out of the five people in the room, she and Kyzer were the closest in similar height.

"And here is the Earth Queen," The old instructor hummed knowingly, stroking her brown hair and cupping her face as the others crowded around the sitting area in front of the fireplace. For once, Zeraphall did not sit closest to the hearth—that spot was reserved for Kyzer. "How are you, Amarie?"

"Better now, Kyzer. It's lovely to be here with you."

"But I think this is not a purely social visit," He said, turning and taking Amarie by the arm to lead her to the others. "You never come to visit me simply to talk, anymore."

"Not true!" Zeraphall was the picture of hurt. "I was here just last week!"

"Bah," Kyzer said, waving a hand dismissively, but his eyes twinkled. "So, tell me," He continued, patting Zeraphall's knee good naturedly as he settled into his usual chair by the fire. "What brings the Promised Four to my doorstep this day?"

They launched into a full discussion of everything they had learned over the past two days. Amarie forgot nothing, including the strange plainness of the robbers, and the maddeningly simple circular tattoo. Prinidan headed most of the details that Sehnai had shared, with Zeraphall or Ellion filling in anything he missed. Once Kyzer was caught up on the details, they shared a few of their theories as well—but when spoken aloud, each sounded less and less likely.

"And so—you're wondering what you have to do now?" The old man asked, leaning back in his chair and crossing one knee over the other.

"I mean, speaking with the family in Fire is step one, I would think?" Ellion suggested, to which the others considered. "Then informing the country of the danger?"

"Perhaps," Kyzer mused, stroking his chin. "But I wonder—"

The others paused mid discussion and focused in curiously. Kyzer shrugged.

"I wonder if it would be more appropriate to keep this possibility quiet—for now. If it is a sickness, and so help us, the great threat that you were all born to face, I don't imagine people would take warmly to the idea of it being something so unpredictable. I personally have always assumed the threat would be physical—an enemy, something to fight and conquer. How does one fight a disease? I think such a revelation would cause panic in the realm."

"But—but what do we do, then?" Amarie asked, the idea of keeping anything so serious from the population chafing against her spirit. "We need to meet the family, at least—find out for ourselves what Sehnai was talking about."

"The girl from Fire has been quarantined, I take it?" Kyzer asked.

"That's what Sehnai said, yes," Zeraphall confirmed. "But the rest of the family is continuing on with life as usual and dealing with reps from the other clans on the daily."

Kyzer stroked his chin once more, humming to himself.

"So, if it were contagious… its already made its way through the clan representatives," He concluded.

"That's what it sounds like," Ellion said.

"Are we sure this is the first case of its kind?" The old man asked. "Is the girl from Fire the first infected case?"

The royals exchanged a glance.

"What do you mean?" Prinidan asked, finally. Kyzer leaned back.

"It's quite shameful to admit, yes? Losing one's powers?" He asked conversationally, tilting his head to hear their replies. The siblings frowned, looking back and forth between themselves.

"I mean… no. Of course, not—" Amarie started, but her confidence trailed off with her words.

"Maybe, though." Ellion matched his sister's expression. "If a family based its worth in society on their level of strength and magic."

Kyzer hummed in apparent thought, nodding along.

"Would it be so shameful, do you think, that certain families would try to cover it up?" He prompted.

Zeraphall raised her eyebrows.

"You think people have been covering this kind of thing up—or it's been around for some time? And we haven't heard about it before? In *all* of our country's written history?" Her voice was skeptical.

"Anything is possible, clearly." Kyzer opened the palm of his hand, indicating the existence of such a problem in the first place.

"Well… how would we know, then?" Prinidan asked. "If they've been covering it up forever?"

"And why have we heard of so many cases just recently, then?" Amarie echoed.

"All questions I cannot answer," Kyzer said gently. "My job as a fussy old man is to make you think for yourselves, if you remember."

"Well, we're still back at square one," Ellion said. "The only case we can reasonably track is the family from Fire. I still think we need to go and talk to them, try to figure out what's been going on."

All was silent for a moment.

"What if the family came here?" Kyzer asked. The Four paused, waiting for him to continue. "If they all still supposedly have use of their powers, it is probably safe to assume they aren't afflicted by whatever has the daughter so ill-at-ease."

"And if they are sick and merely haven't shown it yet…?" Zeraphall continued. "What if it doesn't always manifest right away? What if they're carriers?"

"By the sounds of it, there's a good chance the other clans have already been infected by it anyway—if it is something contagious, that is, and has only started just now. You can't lock yourselves away from everybody."

"But bringing them here would draw the same suspicion and attention that going there ourselves would," Prinidan argued gently. "And it would be a lot more work for the family. We never invite people here."

"What if you invited others, as well?"

"You're going to have to be more clear, Kyzer," Amarie said.

"A gathering of a few families from each clan. Don't call it a meeting—I agree with Prinidan, that would bring too much attention and would risk the aforementioned panic. Instead… call it a party." He smiled. "Try to slip in some casual conversation about the absent daughter here and there—I can get some of the attendants to mill about with the guests and ask questions as well. I believe your twentieth birthdays are soon approaching, are they not?"

—

"So, we're just making *sure* everybody is infected by this thing, then?" Zeraphall asked skeptically as they left Kyzer's chambers some hours later. "Planning a nice little contagious gathering?"

"We don't even know that it *is* a sickness." Prinidan stroked her shoulder comfortingly. "And if what Sehnai said was true, the other clans have already been in plenty of contact with the family in question—and who knows how many more they possibly infected before the daughter showed any symptoms?"

"And there's always the possibility that the sickness has been around for a lot longer, and we're only just hearing about it now," Ellion said quietly.

"It seems like a bad plan," Zeraphall grumbled as they halted in the hallways that would lead each to their personal chambers. "This is the kind of thing rulers get assassinated for."

"Realistically, it will be good to meet with some of the other well-informed families in person anyway," Amarie added placatingly. "We need to see if they've noticed anything similar in their own families and are willing to talk about it. Maybe the family from Fire isn't the only one ready to admit to whatever this thing is."

"Besides," Ellion said, stretching his long arms over his head. "We've never had a birthday party before."

Chapter 4

The party was to fall directly on the Four's twentieth birthday. Realm-wide celebrations always took place on their birthday, of course, but this would be the first year that anybody was invited to the actual palace to celebrate it.

They'd had to be extremely careful with their guestlist, for though they needed the most influential families to come so they could hear the clan gossip, they also could not be seen favouring any such groups. Typically, the most significant families within the clans followed the old hierarchies—more power meant more respect. The Four and their advisors had worked hard to abolish that way of thinking, at least on the largest scale, and to only invite the families with powerful connections and magic would send the entirely wrong message.

To offset the potential problem, the royals had sat down with their most informed consultants to make the actual list. The neutral palace was large, with plenty of room to accommodate guests, so fortunately, they had a little bit of room for negotiation.

In the end, they'd decided to invite three prominent families and their households from each clan, as well as two families per clan that would be seen as more "every day" by the general population.

They left it up to the advisors to choose which families to actually invite; they were happy with anything, as long as the list included a certain Fire clan family.

—

"I love *parties*," Zeraphall growled as she and Amarie got ready in the former's chambers, although Amarie knew this perfectly well already. Zeraphall had come around to the idea of it, despite her previous misgivings. "The decorations, the *food*, so many new people…" She sighed contentedly, turning her head sideways to ensure that her dark cosmetics were even in her reflection. Her looking glass was a strange piece of architecture, and as beautiful as anything. It had been a group project between her, Ellion, and Amarie, and it was very dear to her heart.

To make it, Amarie had first aligned four slender pieces of rock in a large rectangle, and flattened out a larger piece to fit flush with the back. With a quick blink, the rocks had melded together to form an unbreakable piece. Ellion had then called water into being and filled the rock basin perfectly and entirely full—up to the brim, but without overflowing, and Amarie had arranged a fine sand to float over top of the water in a thick, unbroken layer. Lastly, Zeraphall had heated the sand until it melted to glass. The glass had cooled and hardened once it touched the rock border and had become fixed in place, and the resulting project was a one-of-a-kind mirror pool that could be hung or positioned against a wall and never spill a drop of water or lose its reflective properties.

How Zeraphall loved it.

Amarie grinned as Zeraphall's handmaid finished pinning up her own long brown hair in an intricate, twisting knot that draped over one shoulder.

"It feels beautiful Kiala, thank you. What do you think, Zera?" She asked, running her hands across its length. Kiala clicked her tongue in approval before bustling off to the other rooms.

"You're a vision," Zeraphall replied distractedly, turning to the clothes hanging for her. Her own hair, which she normally loved to wear curly and wild, currently flowed in a long black curtain down her back. She had heated her hand to near burning and ran her fingers tightly down it, which had straightened it, and revealed how long it truly was when not up in its usual tight curls. The orange of its ends shimmered almost red as she moved to her wardrobe, like true fire.

Zeraphall's chosen outfit for the night was a touch more scandalous than her sister's choice of evening wear, but then again, she'd have settled for nothing else. She emerged from behind the screen, and Amarie turned expectantly.

"I look fantastic, by the way," Zeraphall said helpfully. Amarie chuckled.

Zeraphall's dress was the cold grey-black of charcoal, and the fabric was strange and shimmering. When the light hit it, rather than sparkle, it seemed more to shadow. It was floor length, with a slit that ran up the length of one leg and ended at her hip bone; the bodice itself was strapless, and hosted a deep cut that ended below her breast bone. For jewelry, Zeraphall had chosen a heavy necklace and earring pair made of uncut obsidian, and she had skipped wearing shoes entirely.

Once she was good and finished getting ready, Amarie dipped behind the screen to get dressed herself. Her outfit for the party was far more conservative, but nobody would say it wasn't elegant.

Amarie had opted for a deep forest-green dress with creeping brown detailing along the hemline that climbed ever upward in the fashion of tree roots, as described to her by her attendants. On one side of the dress, the hem touched the floor, while on the other side, it rested above her knee. The dress clung to her small frame, but was ample enough in fabric that she didn't feel naked. It had short sleeves at the top and a squared neckline to accent her graceful collarbone and neck, rather than her cleavage. She'd chosen to wear no jewelry, and her chosen shoes were slim green boots that laced up her bare legs.

Zeraphall blew out a breath when Amarie came into sight.

"Exquisite, sweet sister. The Earth clan may destroy itself when you choose not to go back to the territory with them. Or at least any number of males that hear the same thing about their beds."

Amarie scowled good naturedly.

"You *do* know this party isn't just some overwrought foreplay for all of us, right?"

"Maybe not for you, but I'm going on the hunt," Zeraphall countered, sticking out her tongue.

"Put that tongue away."

"How did you know?"

"I know everything."

Zeraphall snorted, and then stretched her arms over her head, the picture of happy calm, but Amarie's forehead knitted together as it often did while she was thinking hard.

"There *are* more important matters at hand here you know, Zeraphall."

"And they will be just as important tomorrow. Come on, Amarie. The party is the first night we'll get to even meet these people. They aren't going to tell us anything sensitive if we hammer them with questions right off. Let's get to know them a bit first, and enjoy that this evening was a necessary step in getting the answers we need." Her black eyes, darker than her dress, crinkled as she smiled. "Show them that even the Promised Four enjoy food, and wine, and—"

"Sex?"

"Four Hells, yes! Definitely sex."

Amarie scoffed at her sister's casual curse, but looped their arms together all the same as they exited the room and went to meet their brothers.

"I suppose *some* revelry wouldn't kill anybody," Amarie reflected quietly, as a deep-voiced guest excused himself from their path and clasped their hands as he went on his way.

—

"How's this?" Ellion asked as he emerged from behind the dressing screen once he was ready, holding his arms out to the sides. Prinidan looked up from his lounged position on one of the couches, swirling the wine in his goblet and taking him in.

"Quite presentable."

"That's it?"

Prinidan's eyes twinkled as he took a long sip of wine.

"What else shall I say?" He asked.

"That I look dashing and irresistible."

"You look dashing and irresistible."

"Thank you, brother."

Ellion had pulled all of his long, wild hair back into a thick bun, but had kept the usual shells and trinkets in place, as he always did. He was wearing black leggings and plain boots, and though he'd left the formal tunic behind, he'd put on an emerald-green waistcoat instead.

He straightened the sleeves of his white undershirt, then went to take Prindan's place on the couch once the latter went to get changed himself.

Prinidan's chosen evening attire was similar to Ellion's, but more formally so. He kept his long white hair smooth and untied, which allowed it to fall freely across his shoulders and back. And, ever the figurehead, he had chosen to wear the formal tunic that completed his own outfit rather than leave it behind, as Ellion had. He wore a pair of silver-grey leggings and formal jerkin, tight fitting to accent his slim frame, with a black shirt that peeked out underneath.

Together, the brothers made a handsome duo.

"We're not going to get much questioning done tonight, are we?" Prinidan asked, absently flicking his fingers across the shoulder of his jacket and smoothing a non-existent crease.

Ellion grinned roguishly.

"Don't act as though you haven't already been drinking wine all evening," He said.

Prinidan winked, knowing he'd been caught, but did not smile.

"Fair enough—but it would probably be in our best interest to practice *some* restraint… wouldn't it?"

"It's a party, Prinidan. We're the Promised Four. This is our first party, ever, and bless the spirits, we're actually old enough to appreciate it. All we *do* is practice restraint. I think it would be in our best interest to *not* practice restraint." He winked. "Just this once."

"It *would* probably do our subjects good to see their leaders interacting with them as equals," Prinidan considered.

"Drinks all around!" Ellion crowed. "I've already told the guards and attendants that the four of us will be in no fit state to rule the realm this evening, and if anything terrible happens, to please wait until we've rehydrated in the morning to tell us." He gave a hearty laugh as his brother steered him towards the door and the party guests waiting beyond.

"I know *three* of us will be in no fit state… Amarie might take some convincing."

"If she wants to run the country by herself all evening, so be it," Ellion said with a final nod.

—

"Ellion, Zeraphall, Prinidan, and Amarie."

As they were announced and stepped out into the main body of the party at last, the gathered crowd clapped and cheered appreciatively. The ballroom and decorations were exquisite, and the main floor was a mass of colours, light, and new faces. Most of the colourful reflections came from a massive chandelier hung low in the center of the room that was full of crystals in all kinds of differing colours, all in some form of red, blue, green, or white. The resulting effect was a gentle rainbow that danced over those standing nearest to it, bathing everybody in its magical light.

There were fountains against one wall, a tribute to Ellion, that danced in ever increasingly intricate patterns. Against another wall was a large fireplace made of black marble for Zeraphall, deep enough that it wouldn't make the room uncomfortably hot for those who were not fire-inclined. The tribute to Prinidan was the ceiling, which was made of glass and provided an endless view of the sky and heavens beyond, and finally, for Amarie, were the gardens outside.

The wall directly facing the garden was made of glass as well, and there were large arching doors that opened directly onto it. With twisting paths and even more fountains, the gardens were like a ballroom all on their own. Trees of all varieties grew in differing sizes along the borders, and rocks in exotic colours lined each and every one of the many paths. Large and complex plants also twisted and flowered up from the ground all over the garden's expanse to create a sweet-smelling canopy overhead, through which the stars could twinkle once the sun set.

In fact, the sun was setting as the Promised Four entered the ballroom that evening. Through the glass ceiling, the clouds were visible, painted in all shades of gold, pink, and orange. Somehow, the chandelier seemed to catch that colour as well, and sent it in magnified perfection across the shining floor for the guests to appreciate.

Across the ballroom's substantial length, there were also small tables draped in white finery, with shining silverware and delicate flutelike glasses from which to drink the many different varieties of wine being served. The tables ended where the main floor began, which left plenty of space to dance and mingle. A band had set up against the only remaining wall, and they were starting the evening with a quiet, yet lively, melody.

There were guards stationed at every door, and twice as many palace staff, who were milling around and offering food and drink to the visitors. Also in attendance were the employees who had been tasked with staying sober and asking subtly probing questions as the night wore on. It wouldn't do to be obvious about it, for if the royals started asking the same questions later on, it would bring suspicions, but a few well-placed enquires here and there would do no harm.

The guests had come with their entire households, and though their own servants and attendants were dressed less formally, everybody at the party was the picture of charm. It seemed that everyone was overjoyed at being invited to share in the beloved royals' celebration, and interclan parties were rarities; at least, ones in such dazzling volume. Each clan was also relatively easy to discern within the larger collection, for aside from some of the more distinctive features, general patterns of formal wear seemed to be popular amongst the various groups, as well.

The Fire clan families tended towards a more scandalous kind of wear—as Zeraphall exhibited with delight. Chalk it up to their heightened body temperatures and not being bothered by cold, though no one actually knew what sparked clan fashion. As a whole, there was plenty more skin showing amongst the Fire folks than in the rest of the groups.

Low necklines, high slits, exposed midriffs; yet somehow, the Fire women managed it with the utmost of exotic formality and grace. The males too, as a whole, tended towards outfits that displayed their own bodies, as well. From vests with no undershirts, to sleeveless tunics, they complimented their female counterparts perfectly. The colouring of choice for the clan seemed to be largely blacks and greys, though there was always the occasional burst of brighter colours from within the crowd.

Those from the Earth clan were slightly less exposing of their bodies, but were all the more decadent in the costs and values of the actual fabric and jewelry they wore. Both the females and males in the clan had opted for jewelry, and most of their dresses and doublets were intercut with gems of all sizes. Diamonds the size of chicken's eggs adorned some of the women's necklines, and cufflinks of increasingly precious metal flashed whenever somebody shook out their arm. Necklaces, bracelets, earrings, and rings were worn made of gold, silver, rubies and emeralds, and here and there were even a few fine blue diamonds.

The Earth bloodline produced people distinctly smaller in stature than, say, those from the Fire clan, but they cut a proud picture none the less. Looking over the ballroom and the others in their finery with nothing short of mutual appreciation, they were the first group to branch out and begin to mingle.

The Water clan folk were the tallest and most graceful in the room, and they had somehow perfected a mix of untamed passion and formality for the evening. The women wore jewelry made strictly of opals or pearls, and some even had headpieces designed of fine pieces of coral in blues, reds, and yellows. The males tended to wear long earrings as well, of equal or even greater quality, though more often than not, only in one ear.

Chosen dress for the Water bloodline seemed to follow the presumed colours of blue, green, or white, but the designs were what caught the eye. Many of the dresses appeared as though constantly rippling, or had hemlines that perfectly mimicked the look of ocean froth or waves. From a distance, indeed, it appeared as though they were wearing water-made-fabric. The men had jerkins and tunics made of comparable fabric, with shirts often worn open to reveal sculpted and tattooed chests underneath.

Finally, from the Air clan, were the most ethereal of the attending guests. They carried themselves lightly across the floor, giving the appearance of hovering rather than of walking. Indeed, many of the woman's dresses (white or grey across the board) were floor length and wide at the hem, so that when they walked, there was no visible sensation of their legs moving at all. The men wore white or grey to compliment the others, but did not adorn themselves much further than that—finding joy in simple elegance, it seemed.

With hair largely of the same colour as their chosen apparel, the Air folks appeared to take pride in *not* standing out, and as such, stood out all the more. They did not try and accent or highlight any of their pale colouring with contrast; instead, they seemed to embrace their subtlety.

"A gathering to make any leaders proud to know their subjects," Ellion called out across the ballroom after being introduced, nodding to each clan group in turn. His strong voice carried without trouble to all gathered there.

"We dearly thank you for joining us, and welcome you most excitedly to our home," Amarie was the next to speak, dropping a formal curtsy and giving a winning smile.

"As you know, we have never had a birthday celebration before," Prinidan said, a smile tugging at the corner of his lips. Many of the clans celebrated the Four's birthday in the comfort of their own territories, as something of a national holiday, but this evening went far beyond that. "We hope everything stands up to your expectations."

A murmur of appreciative laughter rumbled through the crowd.

"So, without further ado," The Fire Queen called, snatching up a wine glass from the nearest attendant. "Let the evening begin!"

It was a lovely change for the royals, to be able to relax and enjoy themselves in the presence of so many people, without having to worry about ceremony. Appearances did still need to be held up by and large, but anybody could understand a night of revelry; especially for a celebrated birthday.

And what a night of revelry it was.

Zeraphall and Amarie strutted right off the podium, the latter arm-in-arm with an attendant, and headed into the crowd. Zeraphall immediately snapped her fingers and caused the low burning fire in the fireplace to ignite with a fury. She grinned triumphantly towards her sister, then began calling on guests at random to share in wine with her. Turning from her with private laughter, Amarie and her attendant went to join a group of nervous clan household staff that were hovering around the food tables.

"No need to wait for an invitation," Amarie said once the scene had been described to her, reaching out to grasp one or two people by the hand in greeting, before taking a plate that was offered to her. "Dig in!" A few of them looked downright relieved at not having to be the first ones to eat, and others simply joined the line.

As the girls joined the fun, Ellion leaned back on his heels and smiled hugely at Prinidan, his bright sea green eyes sparkling in their own mischievous way.

"What shall we do first, Prinidan?" He asked, idly sauntering down the first few steps with his hands in his waistcoat pockets, and turning to glance back at his brother. "Plenty of interesting people here to talk to, I'd say." Ellion always seemed to find the most interesting of people to talk to during large gatherings.

Prinidan beheld his brother, a few steps away, with quiet contentment. Typically, he would have hung back from the action of the party for the first little while and simply observed.

The music from the band was gently floating over the lull and murmur of the party guests' conversations, which were dappled with laughs or playful shrieks every now and again. The sun had finished its decent from the sky, though some of the clouds were still painted in beautiful colour. Beyond the glass wall, as well, the lights in the garden had come to life in the evening twilight, causing beautiful plant shadows to twist and bend through the reflections of the fountains. It would have been just as enjoyable for Prinidan to stand there and keep looking everything over from a distance as it would have been to actually go and join in.

He'd never lived among the Air clan, it was true, but something about their quiet ways seemed like more than simple learned behaviour. It went deeper than that, for he felt it as well.

But that evening was for having fun.

"I'd say we should get good and merry, for starters." He beckoned a server over and offered a glass of wine to Ellion, as well as took one for himself. "We'll have to do our best to catch up with Zeraphall."

The royal from the Fire bloodline had already made a few friends, it seemed.

"How long do you reckon we have until she finds a companion for the evening?" Ellion asked, dimples flashing.

"Not long," Prinidan agreed, running a slim hand down his arm.

"What about you? Has anybody caught your eye, yet?" Ellion asked, pivoting on the stair to look back up at his brother. He kept his voice low enough that the closest guests at the bottom of the stairs wouldn't hear what he'd said. Prinidan shifted slightly.

"You know nobody's caught my eye, El."

His brother lifted his head to the ceiling.

"I know nobody has so far—but this is a party. For us!" A devilish light came into his eyes. "Perhaps you haven't met the right person, yet. No time like the present, Prin."

"I'm not going to meet the right person, Ellion. I have no interest in sex." Prinidan's eyes flicked across the crowded ballroom and back again. They'd had this conversation before.

"But… *never* though?" Ellion's voice bordered on baffled. "I know what you always say, but surely…" He gestured mutely to the gathering throng at the foot of the stairs.

"It's not a waiting game," Prinidan said with practiced patience, lacing his arm through his brother's. They slowly began to descend the stairs, towards the waiting guests. "I don't see a handsome person and think of all the things I want to do to them, the way you and Zera might. I have no interest in that. I never have."

"Alright. I only wanted to be sure." He gave a mock-sigh of acceptance. "But that does leave me and Zera to represent the royals. I swear, we shall not disappoint our noble house in this matter." His green eyes flashed devilishly as he crossed a fist over his chest. "Whoever shall I approach?"

"Don't pretend like you haven't already noticed that group over there." Prinidan nodded towards a group of mixed-clan females that seemed to have developed a particular interest in the Water king.

Ellion glanced over and hummed in thought.

"I don't have any idea what you're talking about, brother."

—

Breakfast was a subdued affair the next morning, scheduled to start a fair bit later than was typical. It was planned that they would take their meal in one of the larger dining rooms, to be able to fit more guests in at a time. The Promised Four would share a table with the family of the girl who had lost her powers, as well as their personal serving staff and household attendants, and the other families would be invited in turn.

Prinidan and Zeraphall met in the entry hall outside of the dining room, and were the first royals to arrive. Zeraphall had one arm slung over a woman from the Water clan as they approached, both of them looking like they didn't get much sleep, but looking quite pleased about that.

"I'll catch up with you later." Zeraphall had already been informed that they would be dining with the Fire family. The woman gave her a private kind of smile before turning to go locate her own house.

"Nice evening, was it?" Prinidan asked, pushing open the large double doors. They were the first ones to arrive in the dining hall, as was custom in the palace. They wouldn't eat until everybody else had shown up, but they were to be the first ones to claim their seats.

"An amazing night." Zeraphall winced in the bright light of the dining room.

"Glad to hear you're still in one piece," Amarie said coolly, arriving with an attendant and finding her place between her siblings. "I wasn't sure if you'd make it out of your chambers alive this morning. I thought maybe you'd have drowned overnight."

Prinidan gave a delighted bark of laughter, and Zeraphall looked at her sister in mute astonishment. Amarie was not typically the one to dish out such playful talk.

"Just because you can only find enjoyment in things of a higher matter," Zeraphall said, sticking her nose in the air and matching her sister's playful tone. "It doesn't mean the rest of us don't like a good romp."

That seemed to be Ellion's cue, for he walked in as Zeraphall finished speaking.

"Amarie doesn't deserve that tone." He flopped down into his seat and downed a generous glass of water, which had sat empty seconds before. "Some of us don't use any excuse we can to have sex, Zeraphall."

All three of his sibling's faces fell into comical mirrors of disbelief.

"You're telling us that you retired to your chambers alone last night?" Prinidan asked, fighting a smile. Ellion blinked in the morning light, and scrubbed a hand down his face.

"I can confirm that the only bloodline in my rooms last night was Water."

"So, you brought back a person or people from Water," Amarie finished with a spirited scowl. "You're too hungover for sneaky world play, Ellion."

"I can neither confirm nor deny that," Ellion said, waving a hand, but when Zeraphall cackled in laughter, he grinned.

"I'd like to believe at least *two* of this country's royals possess even a minor share of couth," Amarie shuddered. "What must our visitors think of us?"

But whatever the others were going to say in response was lost, for the first few people began entering for the meal, then. A few people came that the Four vaguely remembered from the party the night before, but none that had left a lasting impact. Then, the deep voiced young man Amarie and Zeraphall had met in the hallway walked by the former's seat, pausing there for a moment to let an older family member pass.

Amarie inhaled casually, having not yet noticed him right behind her, then stiffened slightly as his scent hit her. The male glanced towards her in the close proximity, and his expression shifted into something that was equal parts delighted and equal parts wicked. Amarie dropped her eyes and blushed until she looked as though she'd be right at home with the Fire clan guests.

"You *did*!?" Zeraphall hissed triumphantly, too loud, her eyes tracking the handsome male as he made his way back to his seat. "Well done, sister. He is certainly a pretty thing."

"No—" Amarie breathed, but Zeraphall wasn't having any of it.

"You most certainly *did*."

"I did not!"

"Amarie," Ellion growled in delighted appreciation.

"What a curious turn of events," Prinidan hummed, then bent to look under the table and around on the floor. "Where is that couth we were discussing? We seem to have misplaced it."

"I *didn't*," Amarie whispered desperately, ducking over her plate. "He just flirted terribly with me all night whenever I was near."

"Then why are you blushing so much?" Ellion whispered, as Zeraphall leaned in, hanging on every word. The first of the Fire attendants due to sit at their table had begun filtering into the room, so the conversation became hurried.

"I—took a walk once I was done at the party," Amarie said. She could hear the volume rising in the dining hall, and was silently praying that she would be interrupted before she had to continue.

"A walk that led you to whose bed?" Zeraphall screeched almost silently, barely able to control herself.

"Not someone's bed. I merely… took a walk down to the stables. That's all," She shrugged, feigning boredom. Her brothers and sister froze at her words, and the latter's mouth fell open in poorly concealed delight.

"Prinidan," Zeraphall barked with a snap of her head. "What's the new stable hand's name?"

"Fron."

At that exact moment, a sharp huff of air that could have easily been defined as a giggle broke out of Amarie's lips. She covered her mouth and shut her eyes in horror, but the damage had been done. By the time the first of the Fire clan's attendants had sat down, the other royals were grinning from ear to ear.

"Good morning," The first one said, and Zeraphall rose to shake their guest's hand heartily.

"It most certainly is. It most certainly is!" She turned and gave Amarie a friendly nudge. "A very good morning indeed."

"Tell us," Amarie said loudly, before the Fire folk now sitting down around them could catch onto anything. "Was the journey here decent? No trouble with robbers or poor weather?"

"No, it was all fine." The matriarch of the family smiled. Her name was Myna, the Four had been told before the party had commenced, and her power was heat transference via eyesight. Not having to touch what she wanted to heat or burn made her extraordinarily powerful.

In the family was Myna and her husband Gynoro, and the royals had been told that three of their four children would be in attendance. The daughter that had been left at home in isolation, powerless, was named Triga. The family was all quite powerful, except for supposedly Triga, who could only put fires out—though it was not a gift to be scoffed at in its own turn. Having the ability to quench a fire was arguably just as useful as the opposite gift, but in a family like this one, the flashier the power the better, it seemed.

The family also had a multitude of personal staff with them, all with lesser powers of their own, though most of them still sounded more powerful than the average household servant.

"We were hoping," Prinidan said quietly, having recovered himself by then. "To discuss Triga. News of her condition greatly disturbed us."

"She did not make the journey, we take it?" Amarie asked, the image of professionality.

"No, she stayed home," Gynoro said, spooning some bacon onto his plate. "It is as we had Sehnai tell you; one day, Triga was fine and putting out the cookfires as usual. The next day…" He waved his bacon in the air, splattering grease on the tablecloth. "Nothing."

Some of the serving staff looked downright disturbed as Gynoro discussed it, and the youngest of the family's children had actually teared up.

"Were there any precursor events that may have caused it?" Ellion asked casually, trying to act as though the subject matter wasn't quite so serious, but his eyes were bright with worry.

The more information they could squeeze out of this family, and the quicker they could do it, the better. There were a few palace staff hovering around the table as well, poised to listen and take note of the reactions of the rest of the table as the topic was discussed.

"An emotional shock—perhaps some kind of… injury?" Zeraphall prompted following Ellion's words; as she spoke, however, she trailed off and her eyes narrowed at something across the table.

After a heartbeat, she blinked a few times, as if clearing her head, and refocused on their guests. Her siblings noticed her lapse in attention immediately, though, for they were too familiar with each other to miss much of anything. Prinidan glanced at her and lifted a pale brow in question. His sister didn't reply, but gave a minute shake of her head.

"No, nothing like an injury," Myna said, replying to Zeraphall and having not noticed the silent exchange. "Our children all follow the same general schedule; lessons in the morning with their tutor, elemental practice before lunch…" She trailed off, looking to the eldest daughters, who were twins.

"And after lunch we complete our household chores, then have free time until dinner," Claimed one of them.

"Nothing had changed recently, with Triga? She hadn't been acting strange or shirking her duties?" Ellion continued.

"I mean, not really. No more than normal," Said the other twin. "She spends a lot of time with the staff, but that's not new." She looked towards the household guests and smiled politely, as if both acknowledging them as well as making it clear that they weren't expected to contribute to the conversation.

"There was *something* strange." The little boy who had teared up at the mention of his sister's problem spoke up. His name was Lyam, and the Four had been told that his power was the ability to call flames into existence and sustain them.

"What was strange, dear?" Myna asked, with the tone of someone humoring a child.

"I wanted to make a fire to cheer Triga up before we left," Lyam said, fiddling with his shirt collar. "But she was mad she couldn't come to the party. So—so," He paused, looking to his mother with wide, red eyes. She nodded gently. "So, I made her a fire and sent it under the door of her room, but she yelled at me, and then my fire went out."

A beat of silence followed his words.

"You mean you were upset that she yelled at you and you lost hold of the magic?" Gynoro asked softly, recovering first. Lyam shook his head.

"No, I had it—but it went out."

The Promised Four exchanged glances with the family. Myna shook her head in confusion and looked to her husband, but he seemed at a loss for words, as well. As he fumbled for something to say, Zeraphall suddenly sat upright in her chair, wire straight.

"Pass the potatoes," She basically yelled, and pointed across the table at a plate of roasted potatoes in front of the Fire household's staff. The other royals turned towards her, each equally surprised by their sister's blunt change of topic, and the rudeness with which she'd made the request.

A different plate of potatoes sat on her other side, easily within her reach.

"Zeraphall, just—" Prinidan tried, gesturing to the plate closest to her.

"No, I'd like those ones, please," Zeraphall said, boldly interrupting her brother and pointing at the farther plate once more, as Amarie leaned to Ellion to get an explanation of what was going on.

The attendant in front of the potatoes glanced to his masters uncomfortably, looking for confirmation, but Myna and Gynoro hurriedly beckoned him on. The Promised Four got what they desired, no matter what it was. The servant frowned in silent confusion, but picked up the plate anyway and reached across the table.

Zeraphall did not even make a grab for it, but instead waited expectantly until the servant had stretched across the table to try and pass it to her. She was barely even looking at him.

"For *goodness'* sake, Zeraphall," Ellion muttered furiously, breaking off from his whispered conversation with Amarie and grabbing the plate from the poor attendant. He all but threw it in front of his sister. "What's gotten into you?"

"Sorry," Zeraphall said, slightly breathless, as if coming back to herself. "I must still be reeling from last night's events." She spooned some potatoes onto her plate, but her siblings noticed that she did not eat even one of them.

Chapter 5

"Do you care to explain what that was?!" Prinidan asked, exhibiting a rarely-seen emotional outburst. He'd rounded on Zeraphall the moment they had bid their guests farewell for the morning and retired to Ellion's chambers to have a conversation. "We're trying to foster *relationships* here Zera, to gain their trust and get information—not alienate and confuse them!" Amarie crossed her arms as he spoke, looking distinctly unimpressed, and Ellion's face was grim.

Zeraphall sat down on one of Ellion's many couches as Prinidan finished, and exhaled heavily, as if she'd been holding her breath.

"That attendant? The one who passed me the potatoes?" She shook her head, taking another steady breath. "He had a tattoo on his hand."

Amarie's eyes widened, and she clutched Ellion's forearm.

"The same one? The empty circle?"

"Yes."

Prinidan and Ellion's cold expressions cleared, and Amarie all but jumped in excitement. The siblings gathered close to hear Zeraphall's explanation.

"He caught my attention when I realized that he didn't fit in with the others at the table. Fire clan blood makes skin tone anywhere from black and brown, to tan and red, right? Nothing paler than that—nothing."

"And he didn't—?" Amarie asked.

"His skin wasn't tan," Zeraphall said with surety. "I thought it was at first and discounted it, but then he moved into some better light. It *wasn't* tan. So, I asked him to pass me the potatoes so I could get a look at his hands."

"Are you sure?" Prinidan echoed, loathe to jump to dangerous conclusions. Zeraphall nodded in earnest, having already jumped to them herself

"So, what does that mean, then?" Ellion asked, running a hand through his hair, disheveled as always.

"It means that the robbers with no powers and Triga losing her magic—even temporarily—are connected events. It's *not* a sickness," Zeraphall replied. "Something is going on."

"Get Kyzer in here," Amarie finished.

The decided course of action was to learn as much about the house attendant with the tattoo as they could; though it would be difficult, for not only would they would have to do it without raising suspicions, they would also have to get all sleuthing done before the guests were scheduled to leave the palace in a few days' time.

"Work the kids—they seemed to know more about Triga and her schedule than the parents did," Zeraphall offered, as the royals and their closest assistants sat and discussed the matter.

"Can some of you try to get his guard down—perhaps go out of your way to be extra friendly?" Amarie asked.

"I'll head that off, Ma'am," Replied one staff member.

"Somebody should talk to Myna and Gynoro and ask them about their own staff, as well. Make it seem like we still have nothing to go on and are simply sending out feelers; who do they employ, how long have they employed them? That kind of thing," Prinidan said, lacing his fingers together.

"Please keep in mind that the tattooed man could be dangerous," Ellion added. "All we know is that it could link him to a group of people that don't have powers." A shiver went through the group. "Try to keep your wits about you."

Over the following day or two, the Promised Four and their staff put the plan into action. Amarie had her handmaids offer to treat Myna and her daughters to a morning of palace pampering—massaging them, rubbing fine and expensive oils into their skin, brushing their hair. Zeraphall offered the same to the other guests, so nothing would seem amiss. The hope was that the women would happily chatter away as they relaxed, sharing gossip and swapping stories between themselves.

The handmaids had been instructed to listen to everything with keen ears.

Ellion and Prinidan planned a hunt, and invited as many people as they could—including Gynoro and some of his staff, though not the man with the tattoo. This was intended to separate him from some of the people he was most familiar with, but the motive was easily disguised.

In the meantime, the palace staff began getting to further know the people they'd met at the party, under the guise of being let off their duties in honour of the celebration. They were instructed to host a small party of their own, supposedly a secret, and held under the cover of darkness in the generous staff housing built off the main palace. Servant-invites only. The wine would be flowing, and hopefully, tongues would be loosened.

Even the palace children were tasked with a duty, though they weren't explicitly told what they were trying to learn. While supervised, they spent their days playing with Lyam and the other visiting children—talking freely, as children do.

Most of their efforts paid off, and with only a day to spare.

It was learned that Triga had somewhat of a softer heart than the majority of her family, and spent much of her free time with the house staff at the family's estate. She aided them with cooking and extra chores, and seemed to take great pleasure in hearing their stories. They could confidently say that she had not been acting any differently in the days leading up to the situation, and they knew her well. Many of the staff had been in the house since before she was born, so she was almost as much their daughter as their own children were—though unofficially, of course.

That was the case with the long-time staff, anyway; however, the family had hired on a host of newer employees in the recent past, as well. This included the man with the tattoo, which was discovered with a subtle bit of digging. A bit more prompting had yielded the knowledge that the man had been hired right around the time Nagra's caravan would have first been attacked by robbers.

One of the older twins had also revealed, after a bit of relaxation and a few glasses of spiced honeyed wine, that Triga had taken a special interest in one new staff member in particular, which the handmaids were hardly surprised to hear. Whether it was romantic or not, the sister couldn't (or wouldn't) say, but there was some kind of familiarity there. A closeness that went beyond a simple everyday association between worker and employee.

Miraculously, some of the other families had been willing to offer up that they'd noticed similar things within their own kin in the recent past, as well. Some had discounted it, for the powers had returned in due course, but some others remained afflicted and had not felt up to mentioning it. But with gentle prodding, and some helpfully placed rumors, a few of the guests had started opening up. None of the newly uncovered cases had been quite as blatant or seemingly well-timed as Triga's, but as Kyzer had surmised, the issue of losing powers was not so rare after all.

Whatever it was, it was wider spread than the royals had first imagined; however, they still only had one definitive lead to go on.

The tattooed man.

Fortunately, the man himself had agreed to visit the staff-only party, and as luck would have it, it had turned out to be the most fruitful venture of them all, thanks to one palace employee.

The tattooed man had apparently kept to himself at first, but with a few well-timed glances from some of the more outgoing staff, he'd opened up. One had seemed to catch his eye in particular, a woman named Hella, and she had ensured that the wine had continued to flow to him in copious amounts. At one point, he'd even suggested that the two of them go off somewhere alone to continue their conversation. She communicated exactly where the two of them would be if things should turn sour, with a few subtle nods towards the other staff.

Hella herself had been entirely sober by that point in the evening, and the man with the tattoo had been decidedly not; so much so, in fact, that he did not notice her own clear-headed state. Hella had taken the man to a grassy clearing in front of a small network of ponds. The moonlight was reflecting on the water and the crickets were chirping, and under different circumstances, it would have actually been nice. The stranger was handsome enough, after all; aside from the unsettling fact that he didn't look like he belonged anywhere.

There were no visible clan markings on him. He was distinctly *other*.

In any case, the determined palace staffer had encouraged him to sit down and offered him the bottle she'd brought along. She'd leaned into him at all the right moments, giggled at his jokes whenever the situation called for it, and even allowed him a few small private permissions she deemed to be acceptable in the moment.

By the time he had apparently been convinced that she wasn't up to anything, he had brushed her fire red hair from her ear and whispered softly. Hella admitted the thrill of his mysteriousness had not been lost on her, and for a moment, she fell to the mercy of his breathy words tickling against the skin of her neck.

"Can I show you something?" He'd murmured in a husky voice, his strange amber eyes devoid of any kind of magic.

"Yes," She whispered, her breath coming rapidly. She knew in the back of her mind that she did not want the encounter to go too far, but with him whispering to her, smelling of cloves and cinnamon and mystery, her resolve had faltered.

"You're from the Fire clan, aren't you?"

His question had caught her off guard, for she was clearly from Fire, with reddish brown skin and flame-like hair, but it also reminded her of what she was doing. She'd scolded herself internally, then nodded as if she trusted him.

"What's your magic?" He'd asked, drawing her to him, stroking his hands down her back as he spoke. Hella had barely contained a shudder as he had done so—but something about him was curiously hard to resist.

Only the thought of poor Triga at his mercy had kept her head clear.

"Minor combustion," She'd said, leaning into his touch and telling him the truth, for what harm would it truly do? "By eyesight—only small, flammable things."

"Watch," He'd then breathed, his teeth playing at his lip for a moment before he released her and turned to the dry grass beside them.

For a moment, nothing had happened—and then Hella had felt a jerking pull within her soul, as if ice had been dropped into her blood. She gasped, though not at the sensation; it wasn't painful, just uncomfortable. No, what had made her almost cry out was the sight of the grass catching fire, seemingly of its own accord. It burned and smouldered, but the heat wasn't intense, and after the dry patch was charred, the flames didn't jump to the wetter grass surrounding it.

It was her power in action, undoubtedly. She knew it like she knew herself.

"How—" She gulped, but whatever strange and demonic hold he'd had on her was released, and she felt the flame within her gutter back to life.

"That's my own secret," He'd drawled, and had pulled her drunkenly to his lap. He laced his arms around her back and held her fast. "Fire calls to me," He sighed into her, burying his face in her long hair. With her own face not in his view, Hella hadn't bothered to conceal the disgust and horror that had suddenly come over her. Such a violation… her *power*. "I'm useless with the other elements…" He continued.

"Where did you come from?" She'd whispered deeply into his ear, having found it easier to disguise her voice than her expression. Here was a drunken fountain of information—if only she could properly tap it.

She'd run her hands through his hair then, grabbing hold and tightening her grip, as if his show of apparent power had won her over.

"There are hundreds of us," He said, his slurring voice turning husky. Whatever she was doing, it was working. "Four different factions to match the four elements."

"Why have you come?" She'd asked, pushing him backwards with her hands until he was bracing himself up in the grass with his forearms, gazing at her with half-lidded eyes.

"To—" His words had cut off suddenly as Hella shifted her weight, as if he was losing the ability to form coherent speech. "Rule."

His eyes had rolled back then, and he'd submitted to the pull of alcohol-induced slumber.

"You shouldn't have taken it so far." Prinidan's words, though quiet, rang with authority. Ellion, beside him, nodded fiercely.

"Nonsense, it was my choice," Hella said, tossing her hair. "If I'd had to lay him to get the information for you and for our country, I would have." Her eyes were hard and determined, but the royals winced all the same.

"Though I agree with my brothers," Amarie murmured. "We still can't thank you enough. The information you've given us is invaluable." Her siblings murmured their agreement.

The guests were set to leave at daybreak, and Hella's store of information had come at the perfect time.

"What are you going to do now?" Their attendant asked.

"We're going to go and speak to Myna," Zeraphall said grimly. "I believe one of her staffers will be staying for a while longer."

—

It turned out that the tattooed man's name was Rog. Myna had been confused and slightly affronted when the royals had insisted he stay on to work for them there at the palace.

"Why?" She asked, and Amarie felt Ellion tense slightly beside her.

"Some information has come to light, concerning Rog, and it would be in the realm's best interest if he stayed here." Though Amarie picked her words carefully, Myna's eyes still sparked. Her husband took her hand placatingly.

"Don't we get to know why? What information is it? Is he a criminal?" He asked.

"It's about Triga," Prinidan said grimly, silvery eyes locked on her parents' faces.

"Explain yourselves," Gynoro demanded, which was, admittedly, quite a presumptuous way to conduct himself around the Promised Four. "Did he hurt our Triga? Is that why she lost her powers?"

"From what we know—no," Zeraphall now filled in. "Our intel suggests that he has done no harm to anyone." An indulgent stretching of the barest truth, for taking the essence of somebody's soul had to be considered harm of some kind, at the very least.

"And anyway, from the sounds of it," Ellion put in quietly. "Lyam said Triga got her power back, somehow."

"He's young." Myna shook her head dismissively.

"But he knows his gifts, darling," Gynoro said to her. "If he says the fire was put out, but he did not lose it—then I believe him." After that, the conversation followed the same pattern for a time.

It was frustrating for the Four to have to withhold pertinent information from their subjects, and it was grating on their nerves. They had always been quite transparent with the population of their country; but unfortunately, Kyzer was right. If word got out about whatever Rog was and what he could do, before a plan had been made to confront it or before they truly understood it, panic would undoubtedly ensue.

Eventually, Myna and Gynoro accepted the royals' decree. The palace offered to compensate them for whatever Rog's paid salary had been thus far, but they denied payment.

"I know you're not telling us something," Gynoro said as they prepared to leave. "But I accept that. I must believe you have your reasons. But promise me one thing."

"What's that?" Amarie asked.

"If it was this Rog person that had something to do with our Triga's affliction… make sure he can't do it to anybody else."

—

"Are you sure you're even comfortable with this, Hella?" Zeraphall asked quietly. The women were preparing in Zeraphall's personal chambers.

"Fire calls to him—he said so himself. And frankly, he liked me. I'm the best candidate to talk to him. If he takes my gifts again, realistically, nobody will be in any real danger. But if he took *your* powers, Lady Zeraphall, well… things would not turn out so nice, I think. No. It has to be me."

The fire in Zeraphall's blood sparked in indignation at the idea that *anybody* could take *anything* from her against her will, but she held back her retort. They didn't know what they were dealing with, and though it irked her to admit to any sort of supposed-weakness, Hella was right.

"We have other Fire attendants here," Zeraphall said instead, but Hella shook her head.

"He was almost blind-drunk to tell me what he told me. I doubt somebody else will get as far as I did."

"Alright—but please, *please* keep in mind that the moment you're uncomfortable, we'll have someone standing by to aid you in whatever it is you need," Amarie said. "Do *nothing* you're uncomfortable with—clear? You talking to him is only to give him a conceivable reason for having been made to stay behind. He is not our prisoner, not yet; we can't keep him here if he refuses to stay."

"I can get more information out of him." Hella checked herself one last time in Zeraphall's reflective looking glass. "I know I can."

—

"Rog," Hella called to the figure standing by the large front doors of the palace.

Rog was in the entrance hall, looking slightly confused after the last of the party guests had left, including his own house. He and Hella crossing paths at that moment was made to seem accidental, but was in reality well-timed and meticulously planned. Right beyond the corner of the entrance hall, three of the Promised Four stood hidden, listening hard. Zeraphall had been told to stay behind, for they didn't know what Rog could do yet, and keeping her (and her magic) away from him seemed like a good idea.

Rog turned at the sound of his name, fixing Hella with his penetrating, yet perfectly ordinary, stare. His face reflected first surprise at seeing her, and then pleasure, and then finally, it landed on suspicion.

"Do you mind telling me why I haven't gone back to the Fire territory with the rest of the household I serve?" His voice was deeper in sobriety—cold, but not cruel. Hella took a breath to steel herself against it.

"Forgive me for not asking first," She said, halting a few paces from him. "But after the other night, I—well, I called in a few favours."

"Favours?" Rog repeated, closing the distance until there was but a foot of space between them. Hella cleared her throat.

"Well, we have a household here that needs staff, too. And frankly, I wondered if it wouldn't be that big of a shift for you—to stay." He didn't reply, but Hella's part was played flawlessly. She looked, for all the world, like a woman caught in the early throws of admiration. At his continued silence, Hella allowed a crease to form between her eyebrows. "Unless—unless there was something else—some*one* else—that you wanted to return to, back there?"

Hella and the royals were trusting that Rog had been too drunk to properly remember the point at which their previous encounter had stopped. Without outright saying so, it was Hella's job to make him believe that they'd been together in the most intimate way, and that frivolous promises had been made.

"Nothing like that." The suspicious light in his expression dampened slightly. Hella made a quick mental note; either he and Triga had not been romantic after all, or he was lying.

Was that the difference? Sexual tension?

Hella would have been lying to herself if she'd said she hadn't found him alluring, the other night; until he took everything that made her who she was, of course.

She would have to dig deeper about Triga.

"So—what, then?" Rog continued. "I work here at the palace now?"

Hella nodded softly in response, giving a little shrug of apology. But suddenly, he was upon her, his hands around her back as they had been the other night, pulling her to him. She put a hand against the planes of his hard chest, if only to try and keep herself steady.

"Are you a sympathizer of the cause?" He murmured to her quietly. Hella withheld a frown of confusion.

"Yes—?" She tried, mentally flinching and hoping it was the answer he was looking for. He pulled away and held her still, staring into her eyes.

"Brilliant woman." He set her hand over his heart. "I had no idea how I would place myself here in the palace without raising suspicion." It was all Hella could do to not let her confusion and concern show on her face. He'd *wanted* to end up there? Had they played into this strange and dangerous man's hands?

Prinidan and Ellion had tampered with the air quality and temperature directly between themselves and Hella, which meant that they caught every word that was said—and they were just as confused as their staff member was.

"It was the least I could manage," Hella breathed, easily heard by the royals hidden behind the corner. "After the other night. I—I had my own selfish reasons for wanting you to stay, of course—other than the cause."

"But the cause comes first," Rog said, a hard and determined light coming into those hauntingly ordinary eyes of his. Hella nodded again.

"Of course."

"How did you even hear about it?" He crooned, attempting to lace his hands together against her back.

"Not here," Hella whispered, lifting a finger to his lips and looking around as if she'd heard something.

Amarie booted Prinidan out from behind the corner just in time.

"Oh—Hella," He called and strode up to them, instantly professional and slightly aloof, as if his sister hadn't shoved him. "Perfect. Zeraphall needs something in her rooms. I don't know what it was, I didn't ask. She sounds like she's in a state."

"Of course, Highness," Hella said, dipping a bow to Prinidan before turning back to Rog. "I am one of Miss Zeraphall's personal handmaidens." As of earlier that day. "Whatever it is, I need to go and see to it. You *do* remember where the servant's quarters are, don't you?" Rog smiled.

It was merely by good foresight that there had been a room emptied and prepared for him not fifteen minutes before.

—

"He *wants* to be here?" Zeraphall asked once the five of them were safely in her rooms and they had updated her. Amarie and Prinidan were on the couches, Ellion was pacing by the door, and Hella was sitting in front of the reflecting mirror again.

"He made it sound as though I'd just solved a terrible puzzle for him. He said he'd had no idea how he would have managed it on his own," Hella growled in frustration.

"Well, that's a bit strange," Zeraphall said, massaging her temples.

"There's another thing, as well—" Hella blushed a dark red. "I—that is to say, he—he may have some kind of hold on me. Or had."

The Promised Four snapped to attention.

"Your power again?" Ellion asked, but Hella shook her head.

"No, not that. It's… he was drunk enough the other night that it was easy to convince him we'd slept together. But—but I think I might have actually considered it, before he'd taken my power. He has an unsafe and fascinating way about him," She shifted, and the royals exchanged glances. "But—but what I'm wondering is; *could* he have stolen my power otherwise? Is the connection the secret—romance, tension?"

"Nobody will confirm whether he and Triga were romantic or not," Prinidan said slowly.

"And though he denied it, it could explain why he came onto me so strongly," Hella mused. "If he wanted to form that connection in order to steal my magic, I mean."

"Or he's just another rutting male and that has nothing to do with it," Zeraphall said skeptically. "Though if it is true," She added with a laugh. "I suppose I'll be perfectly safe around him."

"I agree with Zera, though—it's too involved of a theory to take a chance on," Amarie said. "We should operate under the idea that Hella's feelings, however fleeting, had nothing to do with him taking her gifts."

"Alright then—let's work with what we know, for now," Ellion suggested. "We know he can steal powers from the Fire bloodline, but he claimed that he's useless with the other elements. Do we trust him?"

The others confirmed, more or less. Zeraphall mumbled something under her breath that sounded contrary to the group opinion, but Ellion continued anyway.

"Okay. So, we can probably safely say that *he* was the reason Triga lost her magic, and from the sounds of it, she only *just* gained her powers back when the household left for the party—Rog with them. So why did he let her have her magic back?"

His siblings and Hella could only shrug their ignorance.

"He only held my powers for a few moments," Hella said. "Is there a time line on it?"

"Well, it sounded like Triga had been afflicted for some time," Prinidan added quietly. The others frowned.

"Proximity?" Amarie suggested. "When Triga stayed behind, Rog got too far away to hold the magic any longer?"

"That could be," Prinidan said.

"There is also some *cause* he's a part of," Zeraphall reminded them. "With hundreds of members, supposedly. And their goal is to—rule?"

"That was all he would say," Hella confirmed.

"But we know the palace is exactly where he wants to be—and?" Ellion prompted.

"And he has a matching tattoo to the robber with no power." Amarie's hands closed to fists at her side.

"It would make sense for the robbers to be part of this same *cause,*" Prinidan said. "And the reason they didn't exhibit any powers could have been because the elements they were adept with weren't present in Nagra's caravan."

"Both times?" Amarie asked, frowning.

"It could happen," Prinidan continued.

"He asked you what your power was, didn't he Hella?" Amarie asked. She nodded.

"But he said Fire calls to him," She added.

"So maybe they have to know what a power is, before they can steal it," Amarie suggested.

"That could be a good theory," Zeraphall mused. It wouldn't keep her safe from him in that case, for her power was *everything*—but it was a start.

"We need more information." Hella shook her head determinedly. "I'll go and speak to him again; gain more trust. He wants to be here—but why? Is the throne of Attina under real threat from this *cause*?"

The Promised Four exchanged subtly uncomfortable glances, as they regularly did when large-scale threats were mentioned. Was this the O*ne*?

"But Hella." Amarie shook off her own discomfort with the idea. "Do you feel… *safe* with that? Comfortable? Who knows what it will take to get him to truly trust you? After all, there *are* other ways to make a person talk—ways that would be far less enjoyable for him." For a moment, a dark and feral power flashed behind her otherwise calm expression.

Hella held up her hands.

"Peace, My Lady," She said. "If I have the blessing of the Four—I will do whatever it takes to gain his trust and figure out why he's here."

"Even—?" Zeraphall hedged.

"Even that." Hella was truly a woman set in her opinion.

"I don't like it," Prinidan said, his usually calm-voice cold and biting.

"With all due respect, my Lord," Hella continued. "It isn't your decision."

Chapter 6

Over the coming days, Hella began spending more and more time in the servant's quarters with Rog, though she'd also been given new accommodation in the palace proper. She was still filling in the role as Zeraphall's handmaid, as well, so there was plenty of opportunity to fill the royals in on all that she was discovering.

"He was hesitant, at first," Hella said one evening while she massaged oil into Zeraphall's scalp and hair. Amarie was standing nearby, listening intently. "Whatever this cause of his is, they've trained their members to be *very* careful. Too careful. He and I drank together again, the night before last—he far more than I—and yet he didn't let anything else slip. Not even a word of it."

"You've found out nothing else?" Amarie asked, scowling not at Hella's words, but at the situation.

"Not about the cause, at least. But he is starting to trust me, of that, I'm sure. I asked a few questions about his gift—or lack thereof—and he actually did give me some answers. Whether what he told me was true or not, I don't actually know, but it's something." Hella shifted, putting down the container of oil and drying her hands on a nearby length of cloth. "He confirmed our guesses were correct—beyond sensing blood type, he *can't* read what a power is; unfortunately, that doesn't affect his ability to steal it at all." She rubbed a hand down her face. "When he takes a power, I assume he figures it out through trial and error."

"So basically, the same way every Attinian child has to first learn and discover how to use their own natural gifts," Zeraphall growled into the silence.

The other two nodded.

Once Hella had left to the servant quarters some time later, the Four met to have a quiet discussion.

"The scout network came back with no new leads," Ellion sighed, glowering into Zeraphall's looking glass as he spoke.

Over the past few days, the palace had sent out legions of spies and other forgettable folk into the realm to test the waters and see how the population was faring; whether there were whispers of a strange new cause sweeping the nation, or perhaps of a terrifying sickness.

"A report came in from Water about another merchant group being robbed. A few traders were killed and the robbers got away—still nothing taken, though," Prinidan said, lacing his fingers together and studying his hands.

"Do you think it was more of *them*?" Amarie asked in clipped tones. Her brother shrugged.

"Who's to know? It's possible."

"Are they truly robbing these caravans for items, then? If nothing was taken? Or are they after something else?" Zeraphall asked. Amarie gasped.

"Powers," She picked up, squeezing her sister's shoulder. "It was never about the items. Large groups of people are the attractant, and so far, they've merely happened to be traders. That would make sense, wouldn't it? If these are people with no elemental gifts of their own," She continued. "They're going to be drawn to our citizens and their powers like flies to sugar."

"So, they *are* robbers—" Ellion chimed in, eyes sparking wildly. "But of magic, not of trade."

"And if that's the case, I would be willing to bet that some of the survivors of this most recent robbery lost their gifts," Zeraphall barked.

"How can we confirm it, though?" Amarie asked.

"Maybe we need to send a proclamation out to the realm about the thieves," Prinidan suggested. "Ask anybody who's had a gift taken to come here and report to the palace."

"But we're in the same boat we were in before—we're just a little closer to shore, now," Ellion said. "We know *roughly* what's happening… but not on what scale, or how to stop it. What if we send out that proclamation and thousands of people show up here?" He gave his siblings a hard stare. "For now, I think it's best to keep doing what we're doing with the detectives and the scouts. Hopefully Hella can get Rog on her side soon, too."

"I don't like withholding information from the country, though." Amarie rubbed her temples.

"Neither do I," Zeraphall added.

"But until we find out what we're dealing with," Ellion continued, looking at each of them in turn. "I think it's our best option. What would we say? *'Trust no one. Thieves are after your souls'*?"

"No that won't do," Prinidan admitted. "Besides, I suppose some stealth wouldn't be a terrible idea." Ellion nodded along. "Who knows how far these people have already penetrated into Attina? Perhaps if they don't know we're onto them, it will work in our favour. Having legions of unpowered people flocking to our doorstep wouldn't exactly be inconspicuous."

"We haven't even considered what will happen if they *have* been stealing powers and holding them, if possible, for years. They could rise against us," Amarie said.

The others exchanged dismayed looks.

"I don't like how they're so active all of a sudden," Zeraphall whispered. The others shook their heads.

"Me neither," Ellion said. "It reeks of *preparation.*"

—

Hella's next informational report was one of mixed emotions—there was good news, and there was grim news.

"He told me more," She said, closing the door of Zeraphall's rooms tightly behind her. The Promised Four were already there waiting for her. "I think he trusts me now." Her voice was hard and blunt.

"Did you bed him?" Zeraphall asked, even more bluntly. The others flinched, but Hella didn't seem offended.

"It was the obvious move in our supposed relationship," She sighed, brushing down her skirts.

"You can be done with this anytime," Prinidan said, taking her hand and leading her gently to a chair. "*Anytime.*"

But Hella shook her head, as always.

"It was a good lay, unfortunately," She fixed them with a hard stare. "One of the best I've ever had, if I'm being honest."

The royals looked back and forth between one another, unsure of what to do or say. It was good that Hella didn't seem to regret the decision… but enjoying such things brought about new complications. What if she developed true and protective feelings for Rog? What if her word became tainted by those feelings, or worse, her opinion of what the royals were doing to try and gain information from him?

She groaned and leaned back in the chair, closing her eyes, and the royals focused in.

"Romance has *nothing* to do with Rog's ability to take powers, though let me tell you, he found it quite entertaining when I asked," Hella began. "And as we guessed before, he can *only* sense bloodline; not the type of gift, or its strength. I asked after that, and he told me the people in the cause all follow the same general mold that the people of Attina do. There are more and less powerful thieves among them. Rog is rather low powered in consideration— and even though he can sense who is from the Fire bloodline, he has no idea how strong they are until he tries to take their magic and either succeeds or fails. For example, he wouldn't have a chance of taking your gifts, Zeraphall."

"Damn right," She interrupted with a growl, but Prinidan put a steadying hand on her shoulder and gestured for Hella to continue. This information was priceless.

If what Hella was saying was true, then the cause had stolen at *least* enough powers to form theories about the different levels of their own strengths and abilities. It was not a comforting idea.

"It was strange when he explained it to me, though," Hella went on. "It's as if he understands the elements on a more intimate level than many other people do; more than I do, at least. You've no idea how bizarre it feels to have your soul, in essence, explained to you by someone who arguably doesn't have one." She shuddered. "Anyway, the way he explained it was like this; he said that the waters of some powers are too deep and wild within their masters for the people of the cause to swim across. He told me to picture a huge, dark lake in the middle of a storm. Dangerous. Impassable. You wouldn't need to do more than put a foot on the shoreline to know it was hopeless. But other powers, he claimed, are like a calm pond; welcoming and safe. Those are the ones he can steal."

"Did you ask him about yours?" Ellion asked.

"He explained mine like a clear, shallow pool," Hella said uncomfortably. "He had easy footing within it, and could see the closest shoreline with total confidence. It was only a matter of focus to dip his feet in and begin walking across."

"Can he hold them indefinitely? Steal a gift permanently?" Zeraphall asked in dangerous tones.

"I don't know. I haven't asked him outright, yet."

"Anything else?" Amarie asked.

"I'm not comfortable asking about the cause so bluntly, yet. He thinks I'm a sympathizer, which means I should already have a basic idea of what it is. I've only found ways to ask subtle questions—clarification on information I supposedly already know, that kind of thing." She sighed again. "I did find out that his words the other night weren't purely drunken stupor, though. There *are* hundreds of them—he made it sound like they were everywhere. He said it was easy to blend in and prove themselves to any given clan, because they can quickly steal magic, make a show of power, and then return the gift before anybody is the wiser."

"I thought you felt it when he took yours," Ellion said.

"I did—but I didn't know what I was feeling. His power is unnatural and evil. I'd never have imagined anything like that was possible, and I certainly didn't guess that what I felt was my power being sucked away. It wasn't until he lit the grass that I knew what had happened. I imagine anybody that he stole from would simply feel under the weather before the sensation passed—they wouldn't know anything was amiss, unless they tried to use the gift at the exact same time."

"Like Triga." Prinidan's silver eyes flashed in understanding.

"Exactly like Triga," Hella confirmed. "I haven't asked him much about her, but I can imagine that he took her power to fit into the family, and then just didn't return it quickly enough before she tried to use it again."

"And if she was immediately put into isolation, with no chance to try again—" Amarie said.

"—then nobody would have known she had it back after Rog returned it," Zeraphall added.

"You're brilliant." Ellion's gaze locked onto their staffer. "We have a place for you in the scout ranks when this is all over."

—

"Something's changed."

Hella had all but dragged Zeraphall into her own chambers from the breakfast table, and it was only the two of them there; the other royals were elsewhere in the palace, perhaps still asleep. The Promised Four hadn't had any news from Hella in over a week.

"What are you talking about?" Zeraphall asked, placing firm hands on the woman's shoulders and trying to calm her frantic state. Hella shook her head hysterically, gripping her queen's hands tightly.

"Rog didn't elaborate. He said there had been a new development, and to expect big things for the cause." She ran her hands through her thick flame red hair, eyes wide and wild.

"We need to find my siblings." Zeraphall was already halfway out the door and calling for the guards.

"When did he tell you this?" Prinidan asked sharply, once Zeraphall and Hella managed to track them all down. If he was irritated at being dragged out of his airy chambers so early in the morning, he didn't show it.

"Some time ago, now." Hella twisted one long piece of hair around a finger and looked out the window. The sun was beginning to rise. "Before the morning's breakfast was cooked and served. I came immediately, but couldn't find Lady Zeraphall."

"Did he tell you what happened? What changed?" Ellion asked. The wildness that usually followed so closely at his heels was even less held back as he paced the room. It looked as though he hadn't slept a wink; in fact, he looked ready to go to war.

"He didn't say, he didn't say!" Hella practically shrieked.

"'*To rule'*. That's their goal, right?" Amarie echoed what Hella had reported to them weeks before. "So… are they coming to attack the palace? Maybe something changed that will allow them to move against us?"

Her question caused the others to go still.

"That could be," Zeraphall whispered. "They could be coming for the thrones—"

"Or us," Prinidan remarked levelly.

"How many of them could there be, realistically?" Ellion asked, returning to pacing. "They've never attacked before, to the realm's knowledge."

"Maybe that's what changed," Hella suggested. "They finally stole enough powers to form an army."

"Lock down the palace so we can prepare." Amarie reached out to clasp Hella's shoulder. "We'll need to inform the clans—"

"Not until we know that Rog's word holds weight," Prinidan interrupted, his expression set.

"What are you talking about?" Zeraphall said, turning to scan her brother's face. "They need to know immediately, don't they?"

"We shouldn't mobilize our country's armies without positive cause," He replied. The other royals took a beat to mull over his words.

"Prin's right," Ellion said, and Zeraphall exhaled with a bone-deep kind of exhaustion.

"Well, what do we do, then?" She asked, her tone clipped.

"We can bolster the defenses here—fill our own staff in on what's happening," Amarie suggested. "If the cause's goal really is to rule, it's safe to say they'll be coming here to the palace, anyway." The others murmured their agreement. "Even still," She continued.

"We could dispatch riders to the scout camps and inform each unit leader, to be on the safe side."

"That would prepare them to inform the clan armies, if we decide there *is* a true threat to the general population," Ellion agreed.

"Exactly," Amarie said. "The scouts are already stationed within most major hubs, aren't they? Informing the scout leaders is the quickest way to get the word out to them, if need be."

"That'll work," Zeraphall muttered grudgingly, and their brothers nodded.

"It's the best option we have until we know more, I think," Prinidan said. "Remaining cautious and ready to act, but minimizing fear and panic within the nation."

"Hella." Ellion turned to her. "Go back to Rog. Get his guard down. We'll send in other elements to neutralize him and take him to the dungeons. I have a few questions for him."

—

Riders were sent out to the various scout camps a short time after the Four had left Zeraphall's rooms, but there was one large unit stationed on the far border of the Earth territory. It was decided that it would take too long for a horse-back rider—or even one of the Winged—to get there in any reasonable amount of time, so Prinidan opted to go himself.

"I can be back before nightfall today," He said, as he and the others swept through one of the palace's many stone hallways. "I'll get some information from them as well, while I'm there."

"Fly fast," Zeraphall said, and the others murmured their own sentiments. Prinidan nodded and, without any more preamble, exited the front doors of the palace not five minutes later.

And with a skill that not even the next-strongest Air elemental alive could hope to match, Prinidan packed a great mass of air below him with a single flick of his wrist. He alighted high into the crisp air like he weighed no more than the morning mists, and within moments, had angled his shoulders towards his destination. If he squinted into the horizon, still dark as the sun was fresh in its ascent, he could just make out the shadows of the distant hills where the neutral territory slowly bled into the Earth lands.

Prinidan glanced back to the grasses only once, at his siblings on the white marble steps of the palace. Amarie held Ellion's arm tightly against her chest, and Zeraphall raised her arm to him in a single wave. It always felt strange, for the siblings to be separated from each other; and even stranger, in the face of something so unknown.

But Amarie was right. The scout leaders had to be informed of what was going on. It was the surest possible way to get the word out to the country, while simultaneously keeping things as quiet as possible for the time being. So, Prinidan set his jaw, and focused on the air building below and behind him.

He pitched forward in the air, and within moments, was lost to the distant skies.

With grim focus, the other royals turned on their heels and began preparing the palace. If Rog's cause truly was planning to attack the castle, they could strike at any moment.

While Zeraphall and Ellion began informing the staff of the situation and working to get them organized, Amarie ducked down the front steps to go and bolster the forest that bordered one side of the palace grounds. It had been some time since the woods there had been strengthened and tended to, but Amarie was confident that it wouldn't take her long.

Still inside the palace proper, Zeraphall and Ellion gathered all of the palace attendants into one of the great halls, and split them up depending on bloodline. The activity had never been done in the neutral palace before, and it was clear that some of the staff were uncomfortable with the segregation. It went directly against everything the Promised Four stood for, after all, but the royals made it clear that it wasn't up to their own preferences, either.

"We believe there is a group of people coming to the palace who have the ability to steal elemental magic," Ellion spoke loudly to the gathered staff. "There is no telling what a large amount of them will be capable of."

The attendants that had helped gather information on Rog had already suspected that *something* was wrong, of course, but having it confirmed by the royals set the entire crowd to muttering and shifting. It was clear that some of them didn't believe their king's seemingly preposterous words.

Zeraphall held her hands up in a calming gesture.

"We have no intention of letting these people gain the throne or secure a hold on Attina, but we need your help," Her crackling voice, though low, somehow rose easily above the attendant's dull murmuring. "From this point onward, you are to travel in groups wherever you go. In every group, there is to be a minimum of two different elements at all times, each represented by at least two people. Preferably, there will be one stronger-gift, and one weaker-gift, of each. These thieves can only steal one type of magic, and they cannot sense which gift is strongest."

"Our hope is that no group will be completely stripped of magic, and if the thieves *do* manage to get one or two of our gifts, the remaining folk can stand up and fight," Ellion said.

"Lumping all of our strongest citizens together no longer makes sense," Zeraphall added regretfully, as the crowd's attention shifted back to her. "The stronger we are, the more strength we have the potential to lose."

—

The morning grew colder as Prinidan left the Earth border far behind him, a fact that was made no better by the speed at which he was travelling. He threw up a small shield of air in front of him to buffet the bulk of the oncoming chill, but time was of the essence, and he wanted to remain as aerodynamic as possible.

He'd come across a pressure system earlier on that had required some skillful taming to break through and had wasted precious minutes, but once he had gotten past, he'd let it close up behind him again without a second thought. If he had been an ordinary member of the Winged, he would have been foiled then and there—for if an Air elemental could fly, they could not also tame the skies, and vice versa.

But Prinidan was king for a reason, and even with the setback, he made good time.

The ground below him sped by in a comforting blur of green and grey as he soared over the sweeping forests and rocky fields of the outer Earthen lands. He passed by some single houses and a few small hamlets, but nobody was yet out in the fields that morning, and he passed by without notice. The biggest settlements still lay deeper within the territory, though, and he soon realized that he would not remain unseen for long.

It would be nearing midday by the time he flew over the first of the major Earth hubs, and there would be more than enough people out and about to notice him, then. Normally, something like that would be fine. As it was, however, if minimal attention was the Promised Four's goal, then the Air king swooping above the Earth citizen's noontime meals wouldn't be exactly inconspicuous.

He sighed, and glanced up to the misty morning clouds high above.

"Alright then," He muttered reluctantly, and twisted into a reverse dive. In a breath, he shot up and into the cloud line and disappeared from view.

It was freezing up in the clouds, of course, and utterly soaking to boot. The moment he ascended, Prinidan was already dripping. His long hair fell and plastered to his back in a sheet of wet, white silk, and his vision blurred with the sheer volume of the condensation. Fortunately, as he was no longer visible and would not attract undue attention, he flexed his hands and blew a great murky path for himself above the lowest level of mist. He took care to leave a thin line of cloud cover between him and the ground, and with a hearty curse to Ellion and all of his watery ilk, he sped on.

After another few hours or so of sailing high above the ground, Prinidan dipped down through the clouds, as he had been doing periodically, and caught sight of a flat expanse of rocky land in the distance. The royals didn't often visit the outer stretches of the territories, but Prinidan had memorized the maps of his country, and had more or less made educated guesses of where he was as the day had gone on. His estimation of timing had been a little bit off, based on where he came out of the clouds, but he had a good idea of where he was all the same.

The flat land now before him marked the end of the highly populated middle areas of the Earth region, and if Ellion's sources had been correct, the scout camp lay in proximity to the next small village that Prinidan would come to.

By the time midday had arrived, Prinidan had spotted the village, and by his altitude alone, had been able to detect the makings of a camp some way off from it. He propelled himself closer at speed for a time, then when he was within distance of the camp, he let go of the air below him. Going into free fall, Prinidan bent forward until his outstretched arms were pointing directly at the ground some hundred feet below, and fairly shot through the skies. The temperature warmed considerably as he closed in on the earth at breakneck speed, and right as he came within a few feet of the ground, he sent a great blast of air underneath his body and flipped to an upright position once more.

The wave of air slowed him with a great lurch, and the dry ground and dust scattered below him in a frenzy. He waited until his feet touched the ground to drop his hold of the wind completely, and only then did he acknowledge the beginning of fatigue slowly creeping into his blood. He would have enough stamina to fly back home, of course, but the royals were still only human, no matter how powerful they were. Using elemental gifts could be tiring, if done in excess and without rest.

Prinidan took a steadying breath all the same, and smoothed his hands down his long white hair to ensure that not one piece of it was out of place. Once he was settled and felt ready to meet the scouts, he lifted his chin and began walking across the rocky ground, towards the outskirts of the site. He was some way off from it yet, as he'd needed enough room to slow his quick approach without the risk of hitting the camp with hurricane-level gusts, but it wouldn't take him long to cross the distance.

By the time Prinidan had approached the camp proper, the dust had made itself quite at home on his clothes and across skin. The dry terrain was at odds with what he'd seen of the Earth territory when flying over earlier that morning; all of the lush forests and rolling cliffs had given way to pockmarked soil and empty ravines. It left no mystery as to why the majority of the Earth children flocked to the center of the territory. They could grow forests from ash and sustain hearty fields better than anyone, of course, but it seemed even they avoided areas that were so heartily devoid of life.

Prinidan kicked a stray pebble and sent it skirting across the ground, then halted. With a quick spin of his hand, he directed a small burst of air to flash across his body and rid his clothes of all debris. In the matter of a second, he'd gone from a dusty traveler to the unruffled, ethereal Air King once more; and not a moment too soon.

"My lord!" Came the voice of a scout, from the direction of the nearby camp. She was of Air blood herself, and she stalked towards him with meaningful steps. Her eyes and hair were almost the exact same pale shade as her skin, and she dipped her head in a bow as she approached. "To what do we owe this pleasure?"

"Unfortunately," Prinidan said as brushed a hand on her shoulder and released her from her bow. "I don't come with happy news." He gestured to her, and they began walking back to the camp together.

"I'm sorry to hear that." Her eyes were trained on the people milling about the tents. "Though our ranks will be happy to have you, regardless."

When the two of them closed in on the camp and the rest of the scouts, the woman that had greeted him darted away to fetch the camp leader. Prinidan waited, greeting the few people clustered around him and sharing a few quick words.

The camp was simple, to be sure, but was not in any way ramshackle. It had all the look of a place that had purposely traded comfort for mobility and ease. The tents were certainly large enough, but the canvas they were made up of was thin and lightweight. Around the spacious cookfire, there were mats for sitting on and eating, rather than tables and chairs. A few horses were set up in a small copse behind the tents, but rather than a stable or corral, the animals were secured on long lead lines.

"King Prinidan," A man that could only be the scout leader said as he approached, giving a quick but humble dip of his head. He was tall and lean, but with powerful shoulders and a straight back. His blue hair and green eyes told of Water heritage, but he wore his hair close-cropped, a style not often seen in the realm. The brown planes of his face were weather worn and set in a determined expression, but was not in any way harsh. "Greetings. I am Fehran, and I have the lead of this unit. I hear that you have ill news from the neutral palace."

Prinidan nodded gravely, and launched right into his account of the details.

"We have gained wind of a coming danger to the realm." His voice thrummed through the air, powerful and confident. "Word was sent to the other scout locations early this morning, but as you and your outfit are the farthest from the palace, I came myself, in the interest of time."

"So, it is quite serious." Fehran's deep voice turned calculating, and Prinidan nodded again.

"Serious enough that we felt the need to warn the scout leagues in all haste. Prepare yourselves for battle, and be aware that we may soon be sending the order to inform the elders of the cities within your range."

"You're not telling the clans?" Said a man from within the crowd of gathered scouts. Fehran hissed something at the challenge, but Prinidan waved him off.

"Not as of yet. Our source of information was questionable, and we want to avoid nation-wide panic if we can. We must make sure the threat is real before word gets out. I'll send the order at the first sign of true danger."

"Nation-wide panic?" Another scout repeated. "Why? Who's coming?"

"A group of people who have the power to strip our magic from us."

His words hit like punches to the gut, and silence ebbed around him as he finished. The scouts were better-trained at holding their tongues than the staff at the palace were, but even though they weren't muttering amongst themselves, Prinidan had no false illusions that they believed him outright; after all, it was unheard of.

"It is most likely that this threat will hit the palace first," Prinidan continued into the silence. "We have reason to believe that me and my siblings are the prize—or at least, the thrones we sit upon. Even still, if and when this information proves to be more than warmongering, we want the clans to be as informed as possible."

"How can they do such a thing?" Fehran asked, clearly too curious to stay quiet any longer.

"We don't know, exactly. But there is a good chance that you will not realize what's happening unless you're expecting it, or until it's too late. Be vigilant. Trust no one unfamiliar." His eyes were all but burning—white hot. "We believe this society of thieves will host no clan markings, to the point of absurdity. You will know them if you see them. They may also have a tattoo somewhere on their body, perhaps their hand, of an empty circle." He looped his finger through the air once.

The scouts began shifting, no doubt committing the description to memory, and a few of them exchanged uncomfortable glances. Prinidan's curiosity peaked, but Fehran spoke before he could question them.

"We've already heard talk of people like that when the locals are deep in their cups," He said abruptly, catching Prinidan's eye. "They've been spotted here in Earth and in—" He glanced to the others, who confirmed the location. "—and in Water, as well."

"When did you hear of this?" Prinidan asked sharply.

"Some weeks ago, now. Haven't heard anything since."

Prinidan swallowed his curse that they hadn't sent word to the palace immediately. It wasn't their fault, not truly. Who would have suspected that the curiously-bland strangers were, in fact, magic thieves infiltrating the entire country?

For that was what had happened.

With Rog and whoever else had been with him in Fire, with Nagra's multiple reported attacks on her caravan, and now with even more information coming in from the other territories, the verdict was all too clear.

They were here.

"I need to hurry back to the palace," Prinidan said, mastering the ache in his blood at recalling high levels of magic so swiftly. He lifted into the air a few feet, but did not allow even a stray breeze to ruffle the gathered scouts. "Stay vigilant," He repeated, eyes scanning over the people below him. "And test your magic whenever a strange feeling comes over you. Trust *no one*. You may be hearing from the palace sooner than later."

"Rightly so, Lord," Fehran confirmed.

With a final nod, Prinidan shot skyward and began speeding back the way he had come with all haste, no longer worrying about who might look up and see him as he went.

—

As Ellion and Zeraphall were back in the palace organizing the staff, Amarie was making her way purposefully into the border of the trees, allowing her mind to guide her. She did not stumble. As she walked, she noted the positioning of the trees and budding flowers, as well as the roots and new life that had grown since the last time she'd been there; how the dirt and rocks had shifted minutely and left small rifts behind them, which areas were getting the most sun, which were stunted in their growth.

She was, in all ways, within her element.

The forest around her served as natural protection for the back half of the castle, and it had also been the perfect place for Amarie to practice her magic as she'd grown. She could bend dirt and stone as well, but there was something innately special about being surrounded by trees. She let loose a sigh, and brushed a hand against a passing trunk, feeling at peace despite the risk of what was coming.

She'd had to learn how to navigate the majority of her life without sight, of course—court meetings, conversation, nearly all forms of self-care—but her gifts had matured into something powerful as she'd aged and now, when in a place surrounded by natural life, she could form a highly accurate map of the area within her mind. She would not stumble when she could feel and sense the approaching root, and never would she mistake the footsteps of an enemy for the creaking of a tree branch.

It was a gift within her gift, and valuable beyond worth.

Amarie walked on, contemplating things, until she came to a deep portion of trees and all sounds from the busy palace behind were blocked out. Closing her eyes, she then sent her powerful awareness through the ground like a beacon. In seconds, the entire forest knew she was there, and she greeted it with profound joy.

The calm of the forest wrapped around her in a tight embrace, and she inhaled contentedly. For a few moments, Amarie allowed herself to stand still and listen, feel, and smell. There, a few birds were chattering high above her in the treeline, and there—a small animal had just taken off at speed through the underbrush. The many conifers' scents were rich and sharp in the morning chill, and the ground was still slick with dew. Amarie smiled to herself, then bent and buried her hands into the still-cold dirt.

Pure Earthen power spread out from her across the ground, mimicking ripples over a calm lake. Amarie gritted her teeth, and the ripples grew in size and number, though they were not destructive; in fact, they were exactly the opposite. All around the little clearing, the trees and bushes began filling out as the power spread, and though it was nearing the beginning of winter and the forest had already thinned, it suddenly appeared as though it was the middle of spring. New growth sprung up everywhere there was room, and hearty branches began creaking outward and upward from the trees, seeking the sun and already weighed down with healthy foliage.

Amarie knew such fresh growth wouldn't overwinter very well, but she also knew that the palace had a real need for the extra layer of protection. All the same, she vowed to come out once in a while during the colder months and ensure the plants were doing alright.

"No sense giving you life and then letting you freeze," She mumbled, flicking her head and causing a surprisingly mature tree to spring up from the ground across from her.

Any clearings through the forest within hailing distance of the castle were winked out by the thickening foliage. Amarie felt as the smooth dirt and stone of each worn path was taken over by her presence. She flexed her hands in the earth, speeding the process. Everything was alive and growing.

Massive boulders crawled slowly to the surface of the ground, hefted by the power of the Earth Queen's mind alone, and became stuck fast between close-growing trees and other rocks. Fallen logs became slick with moss and were hidden by abundant undergrowth—fairly begging to twist unsuspecting ankles. The packed dirt fell away from the roots of some of the larger and driest trees, leaving them in danger of toppling and crushing any passing beings. On and on Amarie's influence went, until what had been a reasonably untamed pre-winter forest mere minutes before, had become an unearthly tangle of dark woods and impenetrable greenery.

Finally, she straightened up.

As she did so, she staggered slightly and had to rest her hand on a nearby trunk while she caught her breath. Such a show of power was not to be taken lightly, and though it was exhilarating, beautiful, and absolutely *right…* it could also be taxing.

"Lastly," Amarie said after a few minutes' rest, pushing off the tree and standing tall once more. "A bit of spice for our unwelcome guests."

At her words, the underbrush that now covered the forest floor began developing wicked spikes and thorns. The new growths were hooked, barbed, and unforgivingly sharp. Amarie smirked as the needles soon became slick with a clear pus that, if an unsuspecting intruder were to prick themselves with, would cause flesh to rot and die away.

Once satisfied, Amarie turned and followed the single path she'd left through the trees as it wound its way back to the palace. Generous growths of poisonous fungi and plants sprouted in her wake, and she ensured that they were all full of more lethal powders and venoms. With a smile, she filled them each to the brim, leaving them ready to burst with even the slightest provocation.

She made a mental note to inform the palace staff not to enter the forest until the threat had passed.

—

After Ellion and Zeraphall had split the palace staff and any lingering guests into the discussed groups of element and strength and sent them all on their way, the siblings headed towards the dungeons. Rog had been neutralized and brought down to a cell by two staff from Earth and Air as soon as Hella had left Zeraphall's rooms earlier that morning. The thief hadn't fought against the guards, and had supposedly gone along without much complaint.

Zeraphall only accompanied Ellion as far as the entrance to the stairs that led to the dungeons, when her brother held out a hand to stop her.

"Better not risk it," He said, clasping her shoulder with a firm hand. "You probably don't want to get too close."

Zeraphall rolled her coal-like eyes, but eventually conceded that he made a good point; after all, they didn't yet know how strong Rog truly was. He'd *claimed* to Hella that he wasn't a particularly powerful Fire thief, but if that hadn't been true, and he somehow took hold of Zeraphall's powers, there would be literal hell to pay.

"Fine," She growled, glancing down the stairway anyway. Ellion gave her one last pleading look before she finally stalked away from the archway, her chin in the air. "I'll go find Amarie, then."

Ellion gave her a quick nod of understanding, then turned to take the stairs two at a time. The fading sounds of the shells clinking in his hair as he descended into the darkness followed Zeraphall on her way out.

The air in the dungeons was chilly, though it remained so even in the height of summer, which made it the perfect place to store food, as well as prisoners. With Ellion and Prinidan nearby, the air never became overly damp or stale, which both ensured that the food wouldn't rot, and that any prisoners being held there wouldn't get sick. The lockups rarely hosted captives, but the royals believed in being prepared for most anything.

Ellion reached the bottom of the stairs and passed by the many cold food pantries without glancing at them, keeping his eyes ahead. He moved on through the low-ceilinged space until he came to the beginning of the lines of cells. They were clean, if not a little bit dark, and were a far-cry better than some of the holding pens that could be found in the clans proper. The cells were situated on each side of a straight walkway, lining the path one after the other, until they arrived at the wall on the far end.

In the middle of the row were the two guards standing side by side, Air and Earth respectively, with their backs to the bars. Ellion dipped his head dismissively as he approached, and without a word, they guards took their leave.

The king advanced on the bars that the staff had been guarding, until Rog came into his sight. The man was seated at a small table, and though he was chained down, he seemed irritatingly at ease. Ellion hadn't seen the man up close since the meal when Zeraphall had first discovered him, and he'd almost forgotten how… *plain* he was.

Hauntingly ordinary eyes pinned him down, and they filled with smug light.

"Zeraphall didn't want to come and say hello?" Rog asked, his voice a smooth baritone. "I felt her, you know. Up there, with you." He flicked his chin at the ceiling, indicating the halls and palace above. Ellion bared his teeth, but Rog only chuckled. "Worry not… Her magic runs far too deeply for me to touch. By all means, bring her down." He waved a chained hand, setting the metal to ringing.

"Not happening," Ellion said, fighting to keep his voice level. Rog hadn't stolen Zeraphall's powers when he had been in previous close-contact with her, but the fact remained that the royals knew almost nothing about the thief's abilities. It was not worth the risk. The prisoner merely shrugged in reply, the picture of nonchalance.

"Suit yourself," He let loose a sigh that set Ellion's teeth on edge. "To what do I owe the pleasure of your company, Water King?" His voice was gratingly self-satisfied.

"I come for information and answers." Ellion's voice settled somewhere between a whisper and a snarl. "Where are your people materializing, and where do they intend to hit? What is the cause? Who do you serve?"

Rog held Ellion's gaze for a moment, then leaned back in the chair and began sucking at his teeth in a discourteous manner.

"It seems my woman has a rather loose tongue." He didn't appear to be entirely surprised that Hella had sold him out, but a slight tilt grew at the side of his mouth, revealing where his temper lay hidden, no doubt just beneath the surface.

"We know everything you've discussed with her."

"Well, then you know that you're too late," Rog said, tapping his tattooed hand on the table. "The cause is already well situated within Attina—it's only a matter of time, now."

"Until what?" Ellion growled.

Rog gave him a conceited smile and merely leaned back a little further in his chair.

"Until lunch time, I expect. Will you be bringing me my meal, then?"

"Excuse me?" Ellion asked, his irritation rising in a growing wave at Rog's arrogance. The thief chuckled again.

"I think you'll find that my tongue isn't as loose as Hella's, and I don't believe you have what it takes to make me answer you. I don't think you could stomach it. We all know how hard you and your siblings work to unite Attina into a happy, peaceful little country." His eyes darkened. "But being *good* can only get you so far, little fish."

Without deigning to give him another response, Ellion stepped forward until his chest was pressed tightly against the bars. As quick as breathing, he allowed the genetics of his body to melt down to their basic water form (a gift that his father had been adept at, though he only knew vague details). His general shape held and then easily reformed as he walked forward and slipped through the spaces between the bars.

Once on the other side, he instantly solidified, and bent until he was but an inch from Rog's face.

"Until what?" He repeated.

—

"What happened?" Prinidan asked as he joined up with his siblings a few hours later, sensing immediately that something was off. All thoughts of his own exhaustion were forgotten. He'd only arrived back at the palace from his hurried flight a few minutes earlier, and it was nearing late evening, but he scanned the other royal's faces vigilantly. They had gathered in Amarie's rooms.

Ellion was the one who caught his attention first, seated on one of the sofas by the fire. His eyes were distant, fixed on something that the others couldn't see, and his jaw was set. He gave a tight nod, feeling Prinidan's expectant gaze on him and glancing over.

"Ellion went to see Rog," Zeraphall said. She was leaning against the wall beside the fire, gazing into its depths thoughtfully. "Convinced him to talk. We waited until you were back to discuss it."

Amarie was beside her brother on the couch, her hand clutched in his and her face full of quiet understanding. She'd already been filled in on his appearance and the basics of what had happened earlier that afternoon. Prinidan gave a low and empathetic groan, crossing the carpeted stone to sit across from his siblings. He landed on the couch with an audible thump, the only indication to his tiredness, but nobody paid it any attention.

The royals had never faced true combat before, and wartime practices, like making people share information that they didn't want to, were new and unexplored areas for them. They'd always been aware that they might eventually have to stoop to such things, but to have done it alone for the first time would have been terribly difficult.

"Can you talk about it?" Prinidan asked. Ellion met his gaze defiantly, which Prinidan took to mean that he could. "So, what do you find out, then?"

"Members of the cause refer to themselves as the Vague," Ellion started, giving Amarie's hand a squeeze. "They're a whole people group that are born without elemental powers. None."

Prinidan sucked in a breath through his teeth, and exchanged a worried glance with Zeraphall. The idea of it still seemed so strange.

"A faction of them have lived here in Attina for many years—hidden away, emerging only to conduct business and never in large numbers, to avoid attracting attention." Ellion's eyes were still cold. "What he told Hella was true; there are different levels of strength within their numbers that reflects what type of gift they can steal. I also found out that their thievery isn't exactly permanent. They *can* hold onto the stolen magic pretty much indefinitely, but the original person would get their power back in full if the thief was to be killed or *made* to let it go."

"How are they made to let it go?" Amarie asked.

"If they die," Ellion replied. "Or if they're greatly distracted. He classified 'distraction' as *'anything strong enough to pull and hold the mind's main focus'*. I imagine pain would do it, if it was bad enough. Maybe strong emotions or surprise… that kind of thing." He grimaced. "Apparently, they can also choose to let the magic go whenever they want, so threats would probably work too…"

"So why are they here? Did you find out why they've finally come out of hiding?" Zeraphall asked.

"The Vague has recently decided to make a true play for the rule of the realm. Rog seemed to think they would hit here at the palace first and foremost, but he wasn't privy to much about it other than speculation." Ellion sighed. "He'd been sent on a different mission to Fire, to gather intel specifically on Gynoro and Myna's household. Apparently, the Vague was aware of how powerful their family was and wanted somebody on the inside. It was only by way of Rog's sloppiness that Triga's missing gift was discovered at all, after he'd gained entry to the servant ranks."

"That makes it sound like the Vague has information on the strongest clan families," Amarie said. "Could they already be established in the cities?"

"That was more or less confirmed by the scouts I spoke to," Prinidan offered, chewing his lip.

"What about separation?" Zeraphall asked, her eyes widening. "Can they hold the magic at a distance from the original owner?"

"My next question as well. And yes," Ellion confirmed. "Once a gift has been stolen, as long as they actively keep hold of it, the thief does not have to remain in close contact with the person they stole it from. Distance doesn't matter afterwards; however, if they let a specific gift go and want it back, they need to be near the person to steal it again."

"So, in theory…" Amarie started. "The Vague could send in their most powerful members to steal high level magic from the clans—"

"And come here to the palace and hit us with full force," Ellion agreed.

Chapter 7

Over the following days, Attina prepared for battle.

Official decrees were sent out to the scouts and all major clan cities, telling the people of the realm to be on high alert. Nobody had known what the great threat would be when it finally came—if, of course, that was what the Vague proved to be—but there were protocols in place in every major hub in case of invasion by enemies.

By and large, unfortunately, the protocols relied on the citizens using their gifts for both defense and offense. No army from outside of Attina would be able to stand against a population of angry elementals; unfortunately, against a threat like the Vague, their powers would do more harm than good.

Each clan had militaries as well, of course, but because there was the sudden need to diversify which elements were represented in any given location, the royals had to face the budding reality of intermingling the population.

They set their most experienced advisors and generals on the arduous task, and oversaw as much of it as they could reasonably manage. People were handpicked based on power and strength alone, with no thought given to societal standing or family bloodline. The Promised Four knew that there would undoubtedly be kick-back from some of the prouder clan members, the most prejudice ones that wouldn't want to mix with people of a different element, but their list of options was running worryingly thin.

The palace itself also opened up for any Attinian residents who had nowhere else to go in a reasonable amount of time; for example, the realm traders and messengers that rarely stayed in one place for long. It was decided that anybody who sought haven within the neutral castle would be given food and lodging, but would also be expected to fight if it came down to it, and they were physically able to do so.

The royals also went to work on heightening the defenses around the palace, and steadily worked their way out across the neutral territory as they went in all directions. With any luck, they'd have enough time to continue their work and build a veritable stronghold in the center of the realm that any of the four clans could flock to if things became dire.

Amarie would disappear into the trees for hours at a time, and would eventually return from an even wilder wood than she'd gone into. Steadily, the trees and growth began to grow in longer and longer distances from the palace itself as the days wore on.

Prinidan would take Ellion with him, and the pair would alight to the highest peaks of the palace to call and sustain wicked weather systems. Ellion would ensure the clouds were thick and heavy with rain and snow, and heighten the moisture in the air surrounding the palace in a great sweep, while Prinidan built air pressure above and increased winds below.

The kings did not allow the storms to mature into tornadoes or hurricanes, but they ensured that the systems remained right on the brink. If the time called for it, they would release their holds and let it go, but until then, a tentative calm was maintained.

Ellion also flooded all lakes and ponds near the castle proper, sending the waters far across the grounds and creating an untraversable swamp. The farther he strayed from the palace walls, borne aloft by speeding waves, the farther his swamps, lakes, and rivers stretched.

Zeraphall went to work on the palace itself. She had to be careful, for her gifts, if not carefully checked, could be devastating. The palace's outer walls were made of thick rock, so that was where she started. Zeraphall heated pieces of rock until they were near melting, then sculpted them into wickedly sharp edges and points before letting them cool again. In so doing, she all but ensured that nobody would be able to scale any portion of the building, or gain passage to the upper levels, without their knowledge.

Zeraphall also had Amarie line the few remaining paths leading to and away from the castle with huge boulders and massive piles of gravel. It would ensure that any invading parties would have to travel in a near single file line, but Zeraphall could also heat the rocks to molten lava at a moment's notice and boil anybody nearby, if it came to it.

In only a few short days, the palace had been transformed into an elemental stronghold.

This was what the Four had been born to do.

—

The question of whether the royals should attempt to defend the largest Attinian cities in the same way they had the palace and surrounding area was brought up at one of their daily conferences; however, all of the intel they'd been gathering suggested that the people of the land had already done their own work. This was fortunate, for the time it would have taken even Prinidan to travel to every clan city, let alone do anything in the way of defensive strategies once he arrived there, would have been far too costly.

But the people of Attina were no fools, and were well-versed in their magic.

The water levels were rising steadily in the Water territory, and the Air lands had apparently become a nearly-impassable war zone of storms and pressure systems. The Earth clan had strengthened their own borders in much the same way that Amarie had, and pockets of the Fire territory had become quite deadly due to the sheer amount of heat that they were now putting out.

The clan members didn't all have the same gifts, though, and neither did any visiting people from other bloodlines, but this ensured that the territories did not become completely locked down by their most powerful citizens' magic. It was a deficit by way of defense, but there was no way around it, and it wasn't all bad. The royals had no interest in allowing people to be ostracized from their own homes and territories due to differences in ability.

For example, the Fire territory couldn't become wrapped in unending fire, for not everybody there would survive it. The Water clan could not simply sink their territory under an ocean, for then most of the clanswomen and men would not be able to breathe.

Everybody, the royals included, tried not to think about the fact that the Vague could very well be living and working alongside the clansfolk, documenting who exhibited the highest levels of strength while protecting their lands, and preparing to strike with a vengeance.

The first group of refugees arrived to the palace later that day, and were none other than Nagra and her trading caravan. They brought with them all kinds of traditional clan foods and wares they'd picked up along the way, which the overworked palace staff were quick to descend upon. Over the next day or so, more people showed up at the palace, including other trader groups, single merchants, travelling healers who wanted to help, and a few lone messengers and scouts.

The Promised Four did their best to keep up with the throng of newcomers alongside their staff. It was tiring and busy work, and probably not the best use of their time, but all had agreed that it was a better option than letting their citizens wander around in the various territories, alone and undefended.

Worrying reports also started filtering in from the larger cities in the country. It seemed that more and more high-level powers were disappearing from their owners' grasps. The Vague were coming, there was no use denying; and yet, the kings and queens still had no idea when or exactly where they planned to attack.

"So… are we just sitting around and waiting for them to hit?" Zeraphall complained to her siblings one evening. "Just… letting these refugees slowly deplete our patience, resources, and energy as time goes on?"

"Zeraphall," Prinidan chastised gently, giving her a measured look. She snarled a challenge under his gaze.

"Well, they *are*," She said, folding her arms. "Today I had someone ask me where Lady Zeraphall could be found, because she'd apparently requested an audience with them specifically, because they were *oh so* important."

Amarie hid a tired smile behind one hand.

"The Vague are all but invisible. What else can we do but wait?" Ellion asked, massaging his eyes with the butts of his hands.

"Burn the guests."

"Zera!" Amarie whispered, somewhere between a laugh and a groan. Her sister threw herself backwards into the couch beside her and finally lay quiet, seething in silence.

"I think we should keep doing what we're doing—maybe go talk to Rog again?" Prinidan added with a shrug. "It's far from ideal, but Ell's right."

Unfortunately, the Promised Four did not have to ponder the issue for much longer, for later that very night, the palace was hit.

—

The evening sky darkened as if it were midnight, for it was choked and clogged by flying bits of debris and dust that were blanketing the grounds without mercy. Tornadoes, large and small, raged back and forth across the lawns and hammered against the palace itself. Beyond the haze of dust and spinning wind, great fires had started as well, sending bits of flame and burning wreckage flying through the air.

The Four were in the dungeons pressing Rog for more information, hoping against hope that they could come up with some sort of plan based on what he told them, but screaming from above soon reached their ears. Rog grinned through the mass of blood in his mouth when he heard it, and the royals took off running.

Before they'd even arrived on the main level of their home, they could smell the smoke and dust. Prinidan and Zeraphall fairly galloped up the remaining stairs. The Air King ducked straight down the hall and began pounding for the front doors, currents of air already whistling along his body and gathering in his hands, while the others skidded to a halt in front of one of the high windows.

The grounds of the palace lay before them, choked in raging winds and quickly spreading fires. Everywhere they turned, destruction reigned. Despite the late hour, there were many people out on the grounds, already attempting to either tame the storm, or get to safety.

Amarie could feel the plants she'd cultured already starting to go up in flames some way off from the castle, so she redoubled the strength of the forest's roots as best she could from the distance, and commanded them to take on as much water as possible. Ellion, beside her, stretched out a water laced hand over the grounds.

At his command, the clouds above broke and a torrent of rain began falling in sheets. His eyes, usually more green than blue, shone with the depth of the fiercest ocean as he became one with the storm. He funneled the rain exactly where it needed to go, aiming for the hearts of the different blazes. With lifted arms and his head thrown back, he simultaneously commanded the storm and called more water up from underground to meet it. He had to be careful, though, for if he quenched too many fires too quickly, the boiling steam would be just as dangerous for all those standing by as the flames themselves would have been.

He bared his teeth and the muscles in his neck flexed as he *pulled* the waters up from their winter resting places within the earth to meet the swamps he had made across the grounds of the castle. A roaring sounded in his ears and blotted out all other sound as he began to direct waves across the lawns, sending them slipping and rushing towards the flames even as the rain pelted down from above.

Beside him, Zeraphall went to task as well, waving and twisting her arms, her eyes alight with heat. Whatever Ellion hadn't already drowned, she was quick to smother. Her hands grasped and flowed in front of her, as if she were a great conductor, and before long, the fires began receding.

Unfortunately, the raging tornadoes had picked up plenty of burning debris, and try as she might, Zeraphall could not get a handle on the spinning columns of flame as they began building on each other and spreading fires on their own. She swore, but for some reason, she couldn't quite manage it. She had no idea why, but there wasn't much time to consider it, either.

Without another word, she climbed out the window and leapt onto the sloping roofs.

Her feet ignited as she went, and within seconds, her skin was hot enough that it melted into the stone wherever her feet landed. In this way she did not fall, and was able to quickly make her way to ground level with makeshift melted stairs.

Amarie, still beside Ellion back inside, decided to take a different approach. With her brothers and sister focusing on the palace grounds and everybody there, the forests would continue to burn unchecked. It would only be a matter of time until the palace's entire back end was open to attack, and the spirits only knew what kind of forces lay on the other side of the trees.

"I'm going to the forest." She grabbed her brother's shoulder in a quick goodbye.

"Amarie," Ellion said breathlessly, his head turning towards her but his eyes still bright and unfocused, lost in the storm.

"The trees are burning too fast. It's our only defense on that end, Ell," She said firmly. After a quick second, Ellion nodded.

"Can you make it out there on your own?"

Amarie confirmed that she could, then called to a nearby attendant to rush her to the front doors. The moment her bare feet hit the grass outside, she was off and running. The dust was so thick outside that she could barely breathe, however, but she dispersed the clouds closest to her after taking a moment to get her bearings. If she'd had more warning, she could have cleaned out the entire grounds, for she could feel the dust coursing through the air relentlessly; unfortunately, that would take more time than she could afford.

Hopefully, the people fighting outside would be smart enough to cover their mouths and noses before they suffocated.

After securing her own breathing, Amarie was then disturbed to find that it was difficult to focus on and avoid the twisting winds and spreading flames, for they were ripping the earth up and sapping the life from the plants faster than she could sense it. She burned her bare feet quite a few times before her mind calmed enough to take control of the situation. Once her thoughts had finally caught up with her, though, she found her stride within the earth itself. If she paid close attention, she could feel the dirt either heat up from above, or begin to break free from the ground in the wind. In this way, while simultaneously angling her feet towards the distant forest, she stretched out her influence and began destroying the fire and wind's fodder as she went.

By upturning the earth and burying all flammable and dry materials before the flames could reach them, Amarie could ensure that the fires wouldn't spread out of control before Zeraphall had arrived. Turning over the earth, too, would help minimize the dust in the air before Prinidan could get there. Her siblings were more than capable on their own, of course, but if Amarie could help, then she certainly would.

By the time Prinidan set foot on the grounds, having left his siblings standing at the windowsill, he was white with anger. He was not like Zeraphall—he wouldn't race around the grounds, spitting and snarling as he fought off their attackers—no, his anger was a silent thing.

He said nothing as his eyes roved across the lawns, sizing up the largest tornadoes; he said nothing as he began calling them to his own command; and he said nothing as he focused in on the closest Air thieves and suffocated them where they stood. In a few silent seconds, the two biggest tornadoes—the ones that had been reaching swirling towards the palace and beginning to rip up the bricks and stone—had folded into visible tempests that circled around their master, and a whole host of enemies had collapsed to Prinidan's power.

He gave barely a shudder of recognition before slowly rising into the air, leaving the corpses of those who would stand against him, on the ground. With his arms at his sides, his snowy hair whipping around him, and his pupils lost in the glowing silver of his eyes, he looked every bit a vengeful god. It took nothing more than a quirk of his head before he was moving through the dust-choked air above the battleground below, and nothing more than a blink before the tornadoes began changing course, back towards the thieves who had created them.

A few small hurricanes and pressure systems cropped up as well, as the thieves moved and spread out across the palace grounds, but Prinidan tackled them with the same silent confidence that he had the tornadoes, and it was not long before the worst of the storms had been restrained.

There were refugees fighting on the ground, as well, but few had the strength to make a true difference, and none of them could command their Air gifts as well as Prinidan. They provided some help, though, for as the Air King sailed off through the skies, some of the Water and Fire folk began going up against the flames, instead.

They did their best, but even still, it wasn't until Zeraphall arrived that a real change came about.

As she strode through the flames, absorbing the fire as she went, she took in the scene before her. A little girl with molten-red skin was busy fighting a blaze away from the dry stables, and some of the palace staffers were working together to beat a mass of flames back the way it had come.

It was a good effort, but there were many and more fires that had to be addressed as well, since the burning tornadoes had done their damage.

With her teeth bared like an uncaged demon, Zeraphall began stifling the burns in their tracks, while also sending out drums of her own power towards a point of great heat that should not have been where it was. She could not tell how many Fire wielders were rising up against her, but she could sense that they were all standing in more or less the same area, generating enough heat to catch her attention.

Foolish.

Not wasting another second, Zeraphall filtered all of the heat that she had absorbed into the ground, directly underneath where the thieves undoubtedly stood. The nearby pebbles melted to magma, and a few howls of pain came up from behind a particularly thick wall of fire that stood some way ahead. Zeraphall grinned, and sent a fresh wave of heat right at the source of the sound.

A ball of burning matter, loosely and sloppily packed, was hurled at her from behind the wall of fire in an attempt at defense, but she split it open with a look, and cooled it to rock with a blink.

"Enough," She hissed, her voice cracking like a fire-laced whip.

She cut her arm upwards in a sweeping arc, and every one of the remaining fires—of which there were few, after Ellion and Amarie's efforts—winked out like they were nothing more than candles.

She did not show even hint of exhaustion as the wall of flame disappeared from ahead of her and she descended on the thieves.

Ellion let out a cheer from within the castle as the flames were stifled, but his victory-cry was cut short as a massive boulder shattered against the wall of the castle right beside him. He fell back from the window, grunting in pain as the wall was blown wide and he was showered with pieces of rock. He rolled to the side, barely escaping more grievous injury, and crawled back to the opening to get a better look.

Below him, on the other side of where the bulk of the flames had gone out, were a mass of who could only be the Earth thieves. Ellion only caught glimpses of them as they moved back and forth in the torchlight of the palace, before they hurled boulders at the walls anew.

Had Amarie already finished with the forest? Ellion turned and spared a single glance down the great hall, where she had rushed off with the attendant. She would be the only one who would be able to properly combat Earth thieves.

Ellion was whipped back around when, as if in answer to his silent question, a massive, ground-rattling earthquake suddenly rocketed through the halls of the palace. The ground shook so hard that he heard the earth groaning as it swayed and ripped apart under the castle floor. Many of the walls shook and crumbled, and outside, the attacking Earth thieves fell to the ground.

For a moment, the cacophony of the battlegrounds outside silenced as every single person, Vague and Attinian alike, were thrown to their knees by the might of Amarie's great power.

Ellion staggered back to his feet once the quaking dissipated and the noise of the battle had started up again. Whatever group of thieves had tried to get the upper hand on Amarie had just received the punishment of a lifetime.

Using the distraction of the enemies outside as they tried to right themselves amidst the still-receding earthquake, Ellion set off at a run towards an unoccupied window. A few more boulders shattered against the window where he had stood seconds earlier, but as soon as he found an opening, he took it. He dove through the free window as if he were leaping into the deepest lake, and twisted in the air to try and avoid any oncoming attacks from the thieves waiting below.

A rock clipped his shoulder on the way down and threatened to break his focus, but then a wave from the swamps rose up at the last moment and lifted him well above his enemies' line of fire. Up and up the wave ascended, until Ellion was able to jump off and secure a position on the top level of the palace roof.

He landed on steady feet and surveyed the lawns of the neutral castle. A great rift had been torn into the ground from the strength of Amarie's earthquake, and much of the closest swamp waters had spilled into the now-gaping chasm. It wasn't bad news, however, for though the land was left relatively dry in the swamp's absence, the crack in the earth would stand to protect the entire back end of the castle.

Silently praising his sister for her ingenuity, Ellion lifted his arms.

The remaining water in the swamps began churning furiously, and in moments, started rising up to swallow the Earth thieves still attacking the walls. Some of them could swim, of course, but not when the water had an agenda of its own. Ellion did not allow himself to so much as grimace as he commanded the water to take hold of the kicking feet of the Vague members and pull them down below the surface.

He held each person under the waves until they no longer struggled, then moved swiftly on to his next targets.

Moments after the brutal earthquake had thrown everyone outside to the ground, Prinidan caught sight of his brother perched on top of the castle walls, presiding over the small ocean that had grown out of the swamps at ground level. None of the attackers were foolish enough to approach the water's edge, and any who *were*, were quickly pulled under by Ellion's immense control. On his other side, Zeraphall was going to task against a small force of Fire wielders, and their battle was so fierce that it was lighting up the grounds.

With a cold expression, Prinidan turned in midair and began blowing holes through anybody that his siblings weren't already seeing to.

The fighting continued on in much the same fashion, with varying levels of strength and endurance from the opposition, until dawn approached. Finally, however, when Prinidan, Zeraphall, and Ellion met up and held each other in brief embraces, there were no more free assailants left to be seen on the palace grounds.

"Amarie?" Zeraphall asked, stretching her sore muscles and scanning the others on the field around them.

"I haven't seen any sign of her." Ellion shook his head. "Except for obviously—" He gestured to the chasm beyond the palace, chuckling dryly.

"I'd assumed she was fighting in the forest, or with one of you," Prinidan said. Ellion's chuckle faded as his exhausted mind came to the same realization.

"Not with me." Zeraphall frowned.

As one, the siblings turned and hurried to the edge of the chasm that now lay behind the palace. Prinidan leapt into the air to help the others across, and together they ducked into the darkness of the wild trees.

They had not gone far, however, when they hit the first of Amarie's traps.

Zeraphall leapt out of a fierce tangle of bushes, cursing so violently that her brothers came dashing to her side. Her arm was in bloody ribbons from the thorns, and the pus that Amarie had so carefully concocted was already sending sparks of near-unmanageable pain across her damaged skin. She barely avoided panicking as, almost before her very eyes, the wound began atrophying.

"Get it off!" She snarled, igniting a hand and swiping the flames down her skin. The pus bubbled under the sudden heat, but even as it boiled, it continued to spread against her arm. Thankfully, Ellion reacted almost as quickly as Zeraphall herself had, and had soon pulled water up from the soaked forest floor. He placed his hand above her wound, and directed a powerful jet of water to funnel down his arm, towards the injury.

Zeraphall moaned as the cool water hit her and washed the remains of the poison away, and her dark eyes fluttered closed in relief. When her arm was clear, she reopened her eyes and fixed her brothers with an assessing stare.

"Ouch."

From that second on, Zeraphall burned (and contained) a path through the thickest parts of the trees for them. She had absolutely no interest in reliving such an experience. Her arm was tender, but thankfully, with the poison having been cleared out so quickly, it was mostly just scratches from the thorns themselves.

Prinidan chose to walk behind Zeraphall once they travelled deeper into the forest, for they had started coming across a lot more plants and growths that were also, undoubtedly, poisonous. As the many various mushroom caps and pustules burst in the flames, he would siphon the powders and spores away before they could reach the trio.

Eventually, the three of them came to the sure epicenter of Amarie's earthquake. Fissures in the forest floor spread out at all angles from one single point, like a star of destruction, and the closest trees had been split wide.

"Look here," Prinidan hissed, worry building in his stomach as he stepped beyond the closest border of trees and disappeared from the others' view. The destruction seemed to carry on past the trees. Zeraphall ducked to follow him at once, but Ellion hesitated for a moment, chewing his lips and tracing the scene once more.

Did the point of the earthquake indicate that Amarie had put up a good fight? Surely, if such a blast had been planned, it would have stopped any attackers in their tracks; however, she was nowhere to be seen. He had a nasty feeling that the scale of the quake indicated something else entirely.

His attention was pulled when Zeraphall shouted from the other side of the trees, and he leapt over the last of the brambles. His siblings were standing as if frozen.

Destruction.

The forest beyond had been obliterated.

Sweeping off into the distance was a jagged line of uprooted trees, smashed boulders, and great gouges stripped from the earth. A path had been carved out of the ground itself, zigzagging north until it eventually dipped out of sight.

Everywhere the royals' eyes fell, they saw evidence of utter chaos.

Huge old-growth trees had been ripped from the ground and thrown, sometimes hundreds of feet, before they'd crashed to splinters against the ground. Massive craters marked where the deep roots of the trees had been before being pulled free, and the displaced trunks littered the path as it stretched into the distance.

Zeraphall pointed out that the rocks nearest to them had mutated unnaturally and been thrust out of the earth in deadly spikes. Each point reached higher and higher into the sky as they went on, marking the path like the broken teeth of a great, slumbering beast. The points of them were so sharp that they glinted and sparkled.

Prinidan shot into the sky, using such a powerful gust of air that Ellion had to fight to keep his balance back on the ground. From the air, Prinidan's keen eyes traced the path of destruction north, on and on, until even he lost sight of it. He could see evidence of further earthquakes along the trail, including more fissures in the dirt, sink holes, and gigantic boulders that had left their own gouges in the ground as they'd been dragged from their resting places. He could all but picture Amarie running down the line of devastation, destroying the earth as she went. But if she'd been running… why hadn't she run back to the palace? Prinidan rocketed back to the ground, landing without a sound, and was met with his sibling's anxious stares, but nobody said a word.

They didn't have to, for they all knew the truth.

Amarie was gone.

Chapter 8

"Where did they take our sister!?" Zeraphall had Rog by the throat, the muscles in her arms like stone. Fire ringed her hands, and the smell of burning flesh was filling the cells.

Prinidan and Ellion stood by, their faces set in hatred and fury. Neither made a move as Rog choked and gurgled in his pain. Zeraphall screamed at him again for an answer, shaking him, but her own anger was too great, and the thief blacked out from pain. Zeraphall swore and fairly threw him to the ground. She turned and stormed out of the cell, the air around her shimmering with waves of heat. Her brothers followed close by, but didn't dare get too close for fear of burning.

"He does *not* die," Ellion snarled at the lines of healers nearby as the three of them swept towards the far stairs.

The royals had descended on Rog first, but coming up with nothing, had set upon the rest of the prisoners captured in the battle. Somehow, they were all holding their tongues. A few had already died, one to Zeraphall's wrath, and two to Ellion's, but the others continued to refuse to speak a word. They'd been at it all morning, and into the afternoon, now, but still, had gotten nothing.

Leaving the dungeons behind, the siblings tore into the council room back on the main level of the palace, where a mass of staff were gathered. They didn't need to utter a word before the gathered attendants were clamouring to give them answers.

Kyzer was in attendance as well, but he did not offer up anything as the royals stalked in. His face was grave, and lined with exhaustion. It seemed he was taking news of Amarie's disappearance about as well as her siblings were.

"The Winged have made contact with a few of the scout networks already," Said one man, waving a piece of paper.

"No groups of unfamiliar people have crossed over Fire's borders—they're sure."

"The dispatched riders and the Winged are tracking the path Queen Amarie left in the forest as we speak, Highnesses."

"What do we think—broad term?" Prinidan asked into the cacophony, and the staff quieted instantly at the sound of his cold, commanding voice. An older woman from Earth sat up in her seat.

"If a large body of people could hide anywhere for as long as you claim the Vague has, we're in agreement that the neutral mountains would be a good candidate for location."

The neutral territory hosted a fabled mountain range that stretched throughout its length, deep and long. It was exceptionally old, and almost entirely unexplored. It had remained so due to brutally harsh weather conditions and the terrifying elemental beasts which roamed its peaks; humans weren't the only ones that had been gifted by the spirits long ago.

The magical beasts were said to have been herded to the mountains by Attina's ancestors, and left to remain and flourish there, out of sight and out of mind. They were deadly at best, but there were even rumors that some of them were intelligent enough to hold a grudge against the humans who had banished them there.

Prinidan swept from the room without another word and disappeared down the hall towards the dungeons once more.

"How long ago did we send the riders up the path in the forest?" Ellion asked, resting his hands on the table and arching his shoulders.

"Some hours ago," Replied a small man.

"And how far did you direct them to go?" Zeraphall asked.

"They should be back soon, my queen."

Prinidan finally did succeed in getting the answers that his siblings had not been able to, but he wasn't proud of how he'd done it, and the remaining prisoners were in no state to give him anything more. Memorizing what he'd heard, he then rejoined Ellion and Zeraphall in the staff chamber. He was only able to catch the tail end of what was being said, but from what he gathered, Amarie's path went on in a more or less northerly direction, until it slowly fizzled out and became harder to track, though it seemed to be heading towards the distant mountains.

"I can confirm that the Vague are somewhere within a mountainous landscape," Prinidan said from the doorway, repeating what his victims had told him. The staff and his siblings turned to him.

"Which mountains?" One person asked.

Prinidan met the other royals' gaze for a moment before replying, expressing to them that he had more he wanted to say, though it was not the place for it in front of so many other people.

"I don't know."

"Well, mountains rule out the bulk of Water completely; their only peaks are the ones that border the neutral territory. We can have a search team out there today," Ellion said. "Fire does have mountains, though obviously they're mostly volcanoes. It was confirmed that no large groups of people had passed over the Fire border recently though, correct?" The staff who had made the claim were quick to nod their confirmations.

"Withdraw the bulk of the scouts from Water and Fire," Zeraphall said. "Send redoubled efforts to the mountains in Earth and Air. We'll send one Fire team out to the volcanoes just in case, and anybody left over can go to the mountains between here and Water."

"What about the neutral mountains?" One woman asked.

Zeraphall's eyeline didn't change, and Ellion's hand tightened in its position on the table.

"That's where we'll go," Prinidan finished.

—

Though it felt wrong to rest before setting out, the royals had not slept at all the night before, and had expended great amounts of energy fighting off the Vague that had come to the palace.

So, once they were safely within Zeraphall's cozy rooms and preparing to sleep, Prinidan told them what else he had discovered from the prisoners.

He'd uncovered that the Vague hated powered folk, down to their most basic instincts. They'd been in Attina for generations, perhaps since the beginning—but they and their ancestors had gotten no magical blessings of any kind. They resented the spirits for choosing which people to bless and which to leave out, especially considering the well-known legends of the elemental beasts.

Even the animals had gotten magic.

Currently, the supposed plan was to capture and hold high-level power wielders. From there, the chosen Vague members would simply pass and share the gifts among themselves. If they had an extremely powerful Air elemental in holding, for example, whoever had need of the gift at the time could go down with the original thief. That thief could then return the magic to its rightful owner, and the new thief could steal it all over again, before the poor prisoner even had a chance to fight back.

"And if they had *us* in holding…" Zeraphall said slowly. Prinidan nodded gravely.

"But realistically…" Ellion leaned forward on the couch. "How many of them would be truly strong enough to strip us of our gifts?"

"That's not all," Prinidan said grimly. The others turned. He ran a pale hand through his hair and sighed through his nose. "There's a chance that this was all a setup to get to Amarie."

"What are you talking about?" Ellion said.

"When I confirmed that they're somewhere with mountains..." His voice was even flatter now, and his face was tortured. "Some of the prisoners *hinted* that capturing Amarie would all but ensure that we personally came after her, as well as provide them with some insurance in the meantime. I pressed them… and it sounded like the general belief was that they needed her out of the way first for their plan to work."

"Why?" Zeraphall asked.

"They basically confirmed that wherever they took her was an Earthen stronghold—mountains. If they'd taken anyone else and left Amarie powered and on the hunt instead, they'd have no hope."

He rubbed his eyes. "So, from what I gather… this attack was meticulously planned to distract us. They will attempt to steal Amarie's magic, and if they succeed, they will keep her in a place where we three don't have the upper hand."

—

The next morning, well before sunrise, the siblings hoisted on their packs.

They'd opted to ride as far as they could, and to travel the rest of the way on foot, to preserve Prinidan's strength. He'd offered to go and fly ahead, but the fear that their enemies may indeed be strong enough to steal his magic kept him earth-bound.

A road led north from the palace that was well-suited for horses, so it was this the royals followed. Every once in a while, despite their misgivings, Prinidan would swoop off into the trees to confirm that they were still following the correct route, before returning and spurring them on with all haste.

The royals rode their horses hard until sunrise, and by the time that there was enough light to properly see by, the heights of the palace behind them had long-since been replaced by rocky hills and rolling land. For the rest of the day, they pushed the horses to the limit, knowing that they would not need them long-term, and wanting to cover as much ground as possible.

They travelled on north, up the ever-sloping land, until the temperature dropped and the path became slick with snow. Winter was in full-force at such an altitude, but with Prinidan blocking the wind and Zeraphall providing the group with constant heat, they were perfectly comfortable. Such small showings of power did little to sap the royals' strength.

However, by the end of the first day, the horses were exhausted. Ellion ensured the animals and humans alike had fresh and unfrozen water to drink, and Prinidan set up a semipermanent blockade from the howling winds.

"It looks like the road gets worse from here on out," Zeraphall said, once everyone was comfortable around a small fire, stoking it with an easy glance.

"We'll probably be able to cut the horses loose before nightfall tomorrow," Ellion agreed, squinting into the darkness beyond them. The blackness of the mountains jutting up from the horizon was far closer than it had been earlier.

As the small party turned in for the night, with the fire still crackling merrily away, the moon rose fully and the stars winked into life. For a time, the group stayed awake, chatting amongst themselves, but eventually, they all closed their eyes. Zeraphall opted to take the first watch, but they had no real fear of attack, as they were still within a day's hard ride from the palace.

All the same, though, when a loud hissing sounded and tore through the little camp in the middle of the night, adrenaline ran high.

"What is it?" Prinidan whispered, leaping up from his bedroll and falling to attention.

"Nothing down here." Zeraphall's voice was calm. "It's up there."

Her brothers turned towards the distant mountains and beheld what she was watching. What had been jagged shadows of darkness against the sky when they'd gone to bed, now hosted flashes of distant light. Whether it was fire or something else entirely, they did not know. But whatever it was, it was spreading in bursts and fits.

"It's not a regular fire," Zeraphall frowned, standing up and squinting into the night. "It's not spreading properly. Something or someone is making those flames."

Indeed, once the men cleared the sleep out of their eyes and looked more carefully, they found that Zeraphall was probably right.

"The Vague?" Ellion murmured. Zeraphall frowned.

"I'm—not sure. It could be a Fire thief. But the bursts of fire are large, and whatever is making them is moving *fast*."

"One of the elemental beasts, then?" Prinidan asked, keeping his eyes on the peaks.

"Let's hope not." Ellion twisted his matted hair back into the braid that had come out in his sleep and flopped back to the ground.

"When Zera classifies a mysterious fire as large, it's disturbing at best."

"In any case," Prinidan said, walking over and relieving Zeraphall from the watch. "It looks to be well off in the distance. I don't think we have anything to worry about tonight."

"Unless it comes this way," Zeraphall said gruffly, rolling away from her seated position and landing comfortable on her waiting bedroll. Prinidan waved her off, and in moments, she had fallen asleep.

Overnight, the snow began falling in earnest. It was almost pretty, although with Zeraphall fast asleep and with no opportunity to walk around and get his blood flowing, Prinidan was uncomfortably cold. The best he could do was shield the camp from the brutal wind, and though it did make a difference, it was far from cozy. At least he would not be in danger of dozing off.

He kept his gaze on the far-distant peaks, but whatever had made the fire did not show itself again. And, by the time he roused the others before sunrise, their camp had entirely disappeared under a thick blanket of white.

Zeraphall cursed in discomfort the moment her eyes were open.

"Conflagration! Even the spirits would be frozen out here." She cut her arm through the chilly air, and in a blink, their camp heated up and every flake of snow around them melted away at once. She smiled, but Ellion groaned, having been startled to consciousness by the sudden appearance of a great amount of water. Before he even opened his own eyes, he was already directing the water up and away from them in a great arc, so their camp wouldn't become a half-frozen mire before they'd even broken their fast.

"I think we should hold off on big shows of magic for a little while," Prinidan said quietly, eyeing his siblings as they awoke.

"Why?" Zeraphall asked irritably, her gaze simmering with heat.

"Who knows who's watching?" He replied, glancing around at the many places a small group of people could hide. "If the Vague do have lookouts posted—which I'm sure they do, if they're here, which I think they are—then it would be pretty foolish of us to flash multiple facets of power for anyone to see. Maybe we should pick one piece of magic and stick to it, so we can keep a lower profile."

"Do you actually think they won't know who we are?" Zeraphall asked.

"Maybe not by sight, and probably not at any kind of distance," Ellion murmured, considering Prinidan's claim and tapping his chin. "That's a good point, Prin. As far as anybody knows, we could merely be another unit of scouts sent out to find Amarie."

"It could preserve our strength too," Zeraphall ceded with a slow nod, accepting the wisdom in Prinidan's words.

"It'll slow us down," Ellion pointed out, rolling his head around to glance at their brother.

"But may be more beneficial in the end." Prinidan strode to his pack and began to dish out breakfast.

The royal party rode off from the camp for another few hours after breakfast, making great time once more, but eventually the path became too neglected for the horses to gallop safely on any longer. They continued from that point on for a time, until finally, they removed their steed's bridles and halters and sent them back south.

"Be safe." Ellion ran a callused hand down his mare's sweaty neck. "And please go back to the palace. Don't fall off any cliffs. Don't get eaten."

The horse fixed him with a large brown eye and nickered, before slowly turning and cantering off after the other two animals. Ellion sighed and stowed his horse's gear with the other tack by the side of the road, which was wedged into a small crack in the rocks where it hopefully wouldn't capture too much attention of any lone passersby.

The path ahead led straight on over the foothills and directly to the mountains, but it became less maintained the closer it got to the looming peaks. The landscape on either side of them, as well, become clifflike and rocky as the day wore on. Some of those rocks had tumbled onto the road, either blocking the path entirely or carving out great chunks of the thoroughfare that made even walking hazardous at times.

Prinidan still shielded them from the wind as they went along, but he had to allow some of the relentless breezes to escape his barrier and jostle their clothes. Any visible showing of magic would be what he would have to stick to for the remainder of their journey, if they wanted to remain inconspicuous. The same was said for the others. Neither Zeraphall nor Ellion were doing anything about the snow now coating the path before them, though if they weren't trying to remain inconspicuous, they could have melted it away with a glance.

Eventually, however, they entered into the mountains at last.

Thankfully, their leggings and tunics were made to withstand the weather, and the broad-soled shoes they'd brought along did wonders in helping them get through the worst of the snow, but all the same, it wasn't exactly comfortable.

By the time the sun reached its peak in the sky, the snow around them became near-blinding in its brilliance. Everything was alight with cold, sparkling beauty. The ice crystals in the air flashed and danced as they floated by, and even the sparse trees they passed, covered in hoarfrost as they were, glinted and shone.

It was bitterly cold, but with a bit of sneaky and undetectable heat bending from Zeraphall, they felt no major discomfort.

They had come well within the mountain range by the time sunset rolled around, and finally picked a sheltered spot to camp. Prinidan hadn't risked flying off to check on Amarie's path again since the night before, but as luck would have it, he hadn't needed to. For, once the group had come a good distance into the mountains themselves, they'd rediscovered the lines of destruction, which confirmed their sister had been taken that way.

"Looks like we're not the only ones who chose this route," Prinidan mused, chewing on a piece of hard jerky while seated beside a fire that Zeraphall had gone to great pains to make by hand.

"It's the only way through these damned peaks," Ellion sniffed irritably, squinting up at the darkening night sky. It was mostly hidden by the looming rocks above.

"So did they take her on foot, then?" Zeraphall asked, reaching over for a piece of meat. "I'd kind of assumed they had her in the air."

"I've been wondering about that," Prinidan said. "And I think you're right. Even airborne, this route is the best and easiest way through the cliffs." He indicated the upper levels of the snowy and windblown mountains with his piece of jerky. "*I* certainly wouldn't want to fly over those summits. It might also explain how they abducted her in the first place."

"She wouldn't have felt them coming." Understanding blossomed onto Ellion's face.

"Exactly," Prinidan confirmed. "No way somebody could have gotten the upper hand on her if they'd come at her on the ground."

"So, that huge initial earthquake was—what?" Zeraphall asked. "Her way of letting us know something was wrong?"

"Didn't do her much good," Ellion growled, his face dark. Zeraphall clasped her brother's shoulder. As she did so, heat poured into him.

"We couldn't have known things went sideways on her end, Ell, earthquake or no," Zeraphall said. "We couldn't have. It's not our fault we assumed she was fine and fighting. I assumed you two were fine, too. It could have happened to any one of us."

"I know," Ellion groaned. "But… if they hurt her—"

"We know," Prinidan murmured, tossing his brother a piece of jerky. "We know."

The royals were up before the sun rose, and had only been walking for a few minutes when Prinidan threw out an arm to stop his siblings in their tracks.

"Wait." His voice was hushed. He turned around once, checking behind them at the camp they'd just left, then cast his gaze to the slowly-brightening sky in confusion. His pale eyes unfocused slightly and began flitting back and forth, as they did when he began looking through patterns in the air that only he could see.

"What?" Ellion asked, his palms opening beside him. Zeraphall scanned through the shadows of the rocks around them as well, but came up with nothing out of the ordinary.

"I thought I felt—" Prinidan turned on the spot once more. Ellion was about to snarl at him to spit it out, when a bone-chilling whisper caught the wind and encircled the party.

At first, it sounded as though it was some kind of hiss; then, the sound shifted and matured into something that landed closer to a growl, though it wasn't so much a growl as it was a *rip*. It sounded as though the air itself had been rent by the noise, and was doing its best to fold over and cover it up. Even as the group swiveled to the source of the horrible sound, a blasphemous creature of the mountains appeared before them out of the air.

The animal's face, stationed at the end of a long neck, was wicked and cruel, hosting far too many eyeballs and a red beak with a needle-like tip. The animal was raised up on impossibly long backwards-bending legs, and a set of curved, featherless wings were lifted high over its head. Whether the bird-like thing's skin was blue or white or grey, none of the royals could decide. It was the colour of skin left to bloat and rot in the water.

With a clacking of its beak that revealed many rows of unlikely teeth, the beast turned every one of its bulging eyes onto them. It stretched its skin-covered wings and gave off another *ripping* growl.

Prinidan reacted first, hissing and crouching at almost the moment it appeared, before sending a hurricane-strength blast of air at it. The other royals' ears popped as his power flowed forward, but the beast turned on the spot and disappeared entirely. Ellion swore as Prinidan leapt up and turned in a sharp circle, his eyes searching through currents of air around them once more. For a tense second or two, he searched in vain, before his eyes finally locked on to something invisible to the others.

"There," He gasped a half-heartbeat before the thing appeared once more—directly in front of Zeraphall. She thrust a fist forward without hesitation, and a heavy orb of fire and heat twisted down her arm to shoot through the air, missing the beast by a few bare inches. The monster crowed in pain as the missile passed by and singed it, before disappearing again.

A spike of ice from Ellion missed as the animal vanished.

"Teleportation," Prinidan whispered in wonder, again turning and searching through the air itself, eyes as wide as he could make them. "If we can anticipate—"

It appeared again before Prinidan had finished speaking, bringing the stench of burning skin. Ellion's second ice column made contact, but not before the animal had reared backward and slammed Zeraphall in the chest with a massive, clawed foot.

The Fire Queen was lifted into the air and thrown backward from the force of it, landing in a heap against a face of frozen rock behind. She let out a horrific wheeze, her breath lost entirely, and the now-injured beast spun and was gone again before they could get in another counter hit.

The men rushed to their sister and pulled her back upright.

For a moment, all Zeraphall could do was stand there, doubled over and hacking, while Prinidan did his best to watch their backs. After a handful of seconds that felt like eternities, he gave a quick warning shout. It was all he could manage before the creature materialized once more and closed its horrific beak around his shoulder.

Prinidan let out a bark of bone-deep pain as the creature clamped on and swiveled, twisting him along with it and attempting to vanish once more. The bird itself flashed out of sight, but it didn't let go of his shoulder; before his sibling's very eyes, Prinidan's entire body began shimmering in and out of focus, as if he were being pulled from one plane to the other. His face stretched in pain as he put up a tremendous fight, and then he disappeared entirely.

Forced teleportation.

"PRIN!" Zeraphall rasped into the deafening silence that followed. Ellion stumbled away from her and to the spot where Prinidan had just been. He turned in a wide circle, but kept his eyes planted on his brother's last location.

"It's alright." He tried to speak in a level, convincing tone. "Prinidan is stronger than it is."

"It *pulled* him into that teleportation," Zeraphall breathed, her eyes huge in their sockets. "He *tried* to fight it off!"

"It will be *fine*," Ellion snarled, because he couldn't imagine how they would go on if it didn't turn out fine. With Amarie taken, they were already functioning at a major disadvantage—but with Prinidan gone, they would be at half-strength and would surely have no hope against the Vague.

They were supposed to do this *together.*

Zeraphall righted herself properly, her breath still somewhat ragged, and stretched her hands to the sides. The cold air around her shimmered as fire pooled in her hands, and she bared her teeth.

"The *second* it appears—" She growled, and Ellion nodded mutely. He took up a space beside her, facing the other direction, and called two spears of ice into his hands.

Together, they held their ground and waited in silence.

The wind moaned as it passed over the mountains, and as the sun rose above them, it lit up the snow on the uppermost peaks. Fresh powder was whipped into the sky and sunlight in shining, sparkling arcs, before being blown apart so readily that it wasn't visible anymore. Whenever a breeze filtered around them, the two siblings tensed, sure that their brother was about to reappear.

But it was never him.

They fought against the knowledge that he may never reappear, for as far as either of them knew, Prinidan had never teleported like that before. *Could* he even return to them? Did one return from being forced into another plane of reality? Where had he gone? Was it even possible to recover from disappearing into the air itself? Moreover, they had both seen him get bitten.

How would that turn out? What if its beak or teeth were poisonous?

Right when the remaining royals were about to split under the weight of all the worry, something changed.

The same *ripping* sound filled the area, somehow louder than before, right as Prinidan and the monster reappeared. Ellion and Zeraphall were buffeted by a powerful gust of wind that reeked of decay. It was warmer than the mountain air around them and set the remaining snow to hissing.

As the *ripping* faded, Prinidan and the beast collapsed to the icy ground in a bloody heap—but it was the following silence that was the most unnerving to his siblings. Ellion was there beside him so quickly, it was as though he'd teleported himself, but blessedly, Prinidan waved him off.

"It's done," He croaked, taking great pulls of breath. The would-be bird lay crumpled underneath him. Zeraphall hurried over as well and helped heave him to his feet. "My shoulder," He added with a shudder, arm hanging limply from his side.

Ellion and Zeraphall's eyes fell to his injury. It was deep, and terribly jagged. From first glances, the sharp beak had severed his muscle and sinew alike, leaving a ruined mass of bleeding tissue in its wake.

In the time Prinidan been gone—though none of them could say exactly how long that was—blood had leaked down to stain his chest, and more was falling freely. Their brother's already fair complexion was even more pale than usual, and he was turning greyer by the second.

"I'll clean it as best I can," Ellion offered somewhat helplessly, and began siphoning melted snow through the air and down through the bulk of his brother's cut. Prinidan's forehead knit together in discomfort as Ellion worked.

When Ellion was good and finished, Prinidan swayed on the spot, as if drunk. A piercing headache had bloomed in his head some time ago, and the white light of the mountains was murder on his eyes. He knew the pain was from blood-loss, either in part or entirely, though he doubted being forced into teleporting had helped. After a second or two, he shook his head. It was no good.

At this rate, he was just going to keep bleeding.

"Zera," He said pointedly, turning his shoulder towards her. His sister understood right away, and shook her head violently.

"It's too deep. You'll pass right out."

A *very* fine line existed between cauterization and unnecessary torture, and it was one that Zeraphall had tried and failed to walk along before.

"I'll pass out anyway in a second, I think," Prinidan replied, focusing on each word carefully. His vision had started sparkling around the edges. "I'm dizzy—not well at all." The remaining blood in his veins felt sluggish, as though it were filled with molasses and was taking its sweet time getting where it needed to be.

"*No* Prin," Zeraphall growled, but her voice lacked conviction. "I'm not practiced at it enough."

Ellion moved beside her and placed a steady hand against her trembling arm.

"Falling unconscious from pain now is better than dying of blood loss later, isn't it?" The bronzed lines of his face were grim. Zeraphall groaned when she realized that she could think of no logical counter argument, and reached over to take Prinidan's arm in her hands.

"Sorry."

She didn't give him time to reply before she plunged her fingers into the depths of his wound. The injury was surprisingly deep—her fingers went in all the way up to her palm. Prinidan winced in acute pain, already on the brink of unconsciousness, but Zeraphall closed her eyes tightly so she wouldn't have to watch.

With a flash, her hand was instantly burning and cauterizing Prinidan's injury more effectively than any medic could have ever hoped to. His blood boiled around her fingers before hardening off, and though she only held the stance for a moment, fear grew in her heart.

Was she holding it too long? Not long enough? Was her hand *too* hot, and doing more harm to him than good?

Without ceremony, she fairly ripped her still-burning hand out of his arm, and though Ellion had to support Prinidan's now-unconscious form, the river of blood had mercifully, finally, stopped.

"Oh, I hate that," Zeraphall said angrily, bending over and fighting a wave of roiling nausea as she wiped her brother's blood and tissues off of her fingers. "Give me enemies anytime, I'll burn them where they stand. But that—?" She gagged and gave her head a shake. Ellion had no spare arm to comfort her with, but he held Prinidan still while she fought off her discomfort, lending her as much support as he could with his presence alone.

"He'll thank you, you know," Ellion said. Zeraphall waved him off with a grunt.

When she felt up to moving on a short time later, the two of them secured Prinidan in a makeshift stretcher of sticks and spare clothes from their small travel bags. He was awake, but with a tenuous hold on consciousness, so they convinced him to lay down for the time being. Ellion twisted his hands and cut out a wave of snow from the ground, then commanded the particles of ice to twist and fold underneath the stretcher. With another few flicks of his hands, the solitary wave lifted the cot up and began carrying it along beside them as they set out once more.

As the day wore on and they put more and more distance behind them and the scene of the battle, the siblings eventually had no choice but to leave the slipshod road completely and begin picking their way amongst the icy cliffs. The path itself had turned and continued on into the west, but by the appearance of Amarie's hints, she and the others had kept straight on. Their sister's trail had been quite visible thus far throughout the mountains, but the others worried that if new snow fell, or if the fierce mountain winds stirred up drifts with Prinidan out of sorts, the path she'd left could be lost. As such, they had to stray off of the actual path and begin heading in an almost perfectly northern direction.

Prinidan was far more aware of things as the hiking grew difficult, but the group decided it would be best for him to stay in the stretcher until they were through the worst of it. They didn't need him falling to his death due to wooziness or blood loss; fortunately, however, they could use their own powers to aid them through the most treacherous areas, for if enemy scouts *had* been watching on during the battle with the Air monster, they would have already seen the royals use multiple facets of their powers.

There would be no mistaking who they were now, if there had ever been any doubt in the first place.

But with the loss of anonymity came some gains. It meant that Ellion was able to melt and form trails through particularly deep snow, or use columns of snow and ice to lift them up especially steep inclines. By that point, even Zeraphall felt confident using her magic to melt paths through any troubling cliff faces or boulder fields, if the need came to it.

Hiding made no more sense.

Sometime later, around about midday, Zeraphall pointed out that the lack of directional changes from Amarie and her captors probably indicated that they wanted to be followed. They were using Amarie to lure the other three royals to them, and it was working.

"Wouldn't want us getting lost, after all," Zeraphall puffed, groaning as they hefted themselves up yet another snowy crag, Prinidan's cot following dutifully behind. "Especially since we're doing all the hard work of getting ourselves there and tiring ourselves out."

Prinidan grunted noncommittally. He didn't think *he* was working very hard, but with increased encouragement from his siblings, he'd opted to stay in the cot for a while longer. If he had to admit it, he was still feeling rather dizzy.

"Stay alert," Ellion agreed. "If we must play into their hands to get to Amarie, let's not make it too easy for them."

When the sun dipped past the ranges beyond, throwing darkness over their long second day in the mountains, the trio came to rest on top of one of the many smaller peaks nestled within the larger mountains. More hills rose up ahead as far as the eye could see, but in a showing of good luck, there seemed to be plenty of routes going on from that point that looked far easier than the ones the royals had taken to arrive there.

Prinidan had long-since given up on the cot, and had been making his slow way on beside the others for the last handful of hours. Once at a stop, he was the first to sit down. He took a slow, easy breath, and closed his eyes.

"So, assuming the path of wreckage we've been following *was* indeed left by Amarie, what are we looking for?" Ellion asked, stretching out on the cold rock and cracking his back. "Do we think the Vague have some kind of camp set up?"

"Well, if they're actually taking her to their main living area," Prinidan considered, his eyes still closed. "Then I doubt it's going to be as primitive as a camp. They've supposedly been here for generations."

"With who knows what kinds of stolen magic," Zeraphall put in. "I think they're going to be pretty well set up."

"But they've also gone without notice of the general population all this time," Ellion said. "I know the clans don't exactly take summer holidays here, but there are hunters and nomads to consider. Scouts come out this way too, sometimes. Somebody should have seen something."

"Well then we aren't looking for a village, or anything like that," Zeraphall concluded. "It will be something that could escape notice out here."

"A mountain?" Prinidan suggested, gesturing to the unending peaks. "An underground city?"

"Let's hope not," Ellion finished, before they all turned in for the night.

Once the royals had been moving for quite some time the next day, they began running into difficulties with tracking Amarie's supposed-route. Where there had previously been an obvious path of destruction to follow (hopefully made by their sister's mighty wrath), as time went on, the path began to lessen in noticeability. Sometimes, the group even had to crest a peak before having enough of a vantage point to find the next obvious point of Amarie's influence.

This difficult pattern went on for a time, until finally, the visible trail cut off entirely in the gathering twilight. After searching in vain for long, silent minutes, the trio eventually had to conclude that there was nothing left to be found.

"Where did she go, now?" Zeraphall growled as they stood atop the most recent hill they'd summitted, gazing somewhat uselessly into the darkening surroundings beyond and below.

"I can't see any more sign of her," Prinidan said softly, still peering ahead determinedly. Ellion shook his head as well. The elevation provided them with a decent view of the valley and peaks going forward, but nobody could seem to pick out any further clues.

"So, did she stop fighting?" Ellion asked, raw worry cutting through his deep voice.

"Or was she made to stop?" Zeraphall murmured.

"What—you think they were actually able to take her magic?" Prinidan echoed, eyes widening. He hadn't considered it to be a real danger; after all, Amarie was so strong. To think that the Vague were actually able render *her* powerless was disturbing, at best.

"It's a possibility, isn't it?"

"But why here, now?" Ellion picked up. "Unless—" He dropped into a crouch behind the closest boulder, and the others were fast to follow his lead. "Unless this was their destination, where the Earth thief was lying and waiting for Amarie to arrive."

His words sparked the others into looking over the valley with renewed vigour. Zeraphall even risked igniting a small brush fire in the heart of the valley, but even with the added light, they still only managed to pick out a route that was slightly more worn than the area around it. Was it a roadway the Vague used and had packed down over years of travel? Or was it merely a game trail, and nothing more?

"Shall I fly ahead and check it out?" Prinidan asked, his voice resigned.

Zeraphall and Ellion looked him over critically.

Prinidan had been hiking alongside them throughout the day and keeping up just fine, but even still, he didn't seem entirely recovered. His colouring was still pale, more so than usual, and his silver eyes seemed in stark contrast with the dark circles underneath them. He'd kept up with his siblings reasonably well, but the idea of him already tapping into whatever strength he had gained back was worrying. Before they could discuss an answer, however, Zeraphall's attention was snagged by something in the distance, and her head snapped forward.

"Not necessary," She hissed, straightening out of her crouch. "Look." Behind the next hill and at the base of the following peak rose a truly massive mountain that they simply would not be able to hike in any reasonable amount of time. From it, a glow had grown in the gathering night.

At first, the light appeared to be some lingering reflections of the sunset and the others disregarded it—but with Zeraphall locked onto it so enthusiastically, they soon realized that it was the glow of flame.

"Campfire?" Ellion whispered, placing a hand on his sister's shoulder and staring at the light with wide eyes.

"That's conjured and sustained flame if ever I've felt it."

"So then—" Prinidan started, but his words were drowned out by a strangled gasp, for the enormous mountain suddenly ignited.

The royals were dazzled by sudden flashes of fire being spit forth into the darkness. From the base of the huge mountain, where that steady glow still burned, and all the way up its considerable height, light now appeared in fits and bursts; magical flames, being sent into the night sky over and over. As the flames continued lashing out, an echoing groan that was barely audible over the distance, grew in volume and reached their ears.

It sounded like the far-off shouting and cheering of a great crowd of people.

“It’s a signal,” Zeraphall said. The orange and yellow fire was reflected in her black eyes, until finally, the light died and the mountain went dark once more. “They want us to know exactly where they are.”

Chapter 9

"I'm going to the forest," Amarie shouted to Ellion as the Vague attacked the palace grounds. That end of the palace was undefended, other than the thick woods she'd spun, but by some fated magic that nobody had truly considered, she could feel the trees already losing the battle.

Ellion bid her goodbye and good luck before turning back to the window and commanding the falling rains that were hammering the lawns outside. Prinidan had already pounded out the front doors to grapple with the wind storms, and Zeraphall was now out in the battle, as well.

Amarie made up her mind. She planned to double back from the forest and join the skirmish in earnest once she had cleared the trees of fire, but she had the nasty suspicion that more invaders would soon be making their way through the newly burned paths in the woods, if they weren't already doing so, and she would have to see to them first.

With her attendant in hand, Amarie rushed past countless open windows and the loud battle raging beyond them, heading for the front doors.

"I'm good from here," Amarie barked from the moment her bare feet hit the lawn, leaving her attendant behind and rushing headlong into the cacophony. The burning forests called out to her in earnest, and it was easy enough to head towards them across the ground, aiding her siblings as best she could on her way.

The flames were not as easy to avoid as Amarie would have liked, but by straining her ears for the subtle roaring of the fires as they raced across the pastures, and by sensing which parts of the earth were getting scorched, she did alright. Her feet fell onto ground that was far too hot for comfort a few times, but before too long a time had passed, she reached the closest trees; or rather, what remained of them, for the magical fires had already reduced the front lines of the forest to cinders and ash. Instead of bright slashes of life within the map of her mind, like the trees usually were, all she sensed were shadows and flickers of what they should have been.

With a snarl, Amarie brought her hands together in a mighty clap, and out from her ebbed a wave of power so strong that the closest plants shuddered down to their roots. All plants that her power touched were bolstered and encouraged to quickly draw as much water into their roots as they could hold; and thankfully, with Ellion having flooded so much of the palace lands, ground water was still relatively easy to come by.

All around her the woods and the earth came alive. Plants leaned out of the way of stray lines of fire on the forest floor, great mounds of muddy earth rose up to stifle the wandering embers, and even the trees themselves began swaying and physically bending to the ground, forced to drag any of their burning branches in the rich, wet soil.

Amarie was a queen within her element, and her anger was righteous.

Intruding footsteps caught her attention some way through the trees, where the fires had opened up safe paths through the poisonous mushrooms and undergrowth, and it was there she stalked first. There didn't feel to be many footsteps upon the earth, which indicated a small group of Vague, at most.

So, with her teeth bared and her hair flying unbound behind her, Amarie began darting towards them on silent feet. Through the trees she went, ducking at all the right moments to avoid branches, and leaping over roots that might have tripped less keen-footed people. In a matter of moments, she had travelled deep into the trees. She continued directing the forest to take on water and stifle any lingering flames that had dared creep in, but as she grew closer to the sneaking impostors, she also began a new kind of trick.

Well below her enemies' feet, so deep that they would not be able to detect it, Amarie started spinning her magic. She started low, ever so deep within the ground, and commanded the sands, clay, and dirt to begin separating from each other. She could feel Ellion's immense ground water sloshing around down there—wetting the dirt, salt beds, and limestone—and by shifting the other pieces of matter in ever-increasingly difficult patterns around it, she encouraged the water to begin to churn and roil.

It was quick work, for one as skilled as Amarie, and in moments, the water had carved out a veritable sink hole trapped inches below the surface of where her enemies walked. Just as she broke through the trees and appeared before the strangers like a wraith in the night, she pulled the rocks and any stable ground out from underneath of them. With a hiss of pure venom, Amarie exulted in their shouts of surprise and terror as the ground gave way and they began falling to their dooms. There were a few Earth thieves in their midst—Amarie felt it as they drew rocks and earth to them and stopped the group's fall—but they were nothing compared to her.

Less than nothing.

"You dare?!" She roared, racing to the edge of the sink hole and stopping inches before she, too, would have plummeted into the depths. Heavy breathing, magnified by the walls of the cavern she'd created, reached her ears. She heard angry outbursts, a few curses; some pleading and cries of pain. But she was beyond mercy. "You dare come to *my* home? Steal *my people's* magic and use it to burn down *my* forests?" She shook her head sharply, tracking and annihilating a small boulder that was thrust up towards her. With an aggressive slash of her arm, she wasted no more words, and allowed the earth to cave in on itself and swallow them whole.

Her anger abated and was replaced with fear and something close to revulsion as the sound of the earth crumbling below her feet slowly quieted. She made herself stand still and acknowledge the feeling of many pairs of fingernails and hands scrabbling at the layers of earth and rocks beneath the surface, like tiny gnats within her mind, before finally, all went still.

Amarie soon realized that her eyes were wet, so she swiped a hand down her face furiously. It was not the time for such things.

Not when she felt another group of attackers lurking through more trees close by, burning and killing as they went.

Defending this land had been tasked to her and her family, and she would see it through.

So, with grim determination, she moved on.

It was with such conviction that Amarie went tearing through the enemy lines in the forest, and indeed, that her siblings fought with back on the palace lawns, that none of them realized there might be more at play. Nobody considered that the Vague might wage such a fierce attack with a far more meticulous purpose in mind.

For, high above the lines of burning trees, though well within notice of one such as Prinidan, had he not been otherwise engaged some distance away, there hovered two strangers in the night sky.

They did not bear any physical resemblance to the Winged, though they clearly held similar magic, but were instead, rather plain. The only defining feature about either of them was a curiously blank tattoo on either of their hands—an empty circle.

"You see her?" The female of the pair whispered. Her hair was a drab off-yellow colour, boasting none of the richness that might be seen in the hair of one from the Fire bloodline, and her skin was tinged brown, seemingly from long hours spent in the sun.

The woman's companion, an olive-skinned male with a shaved head, glanced down to the canopy below them. He frowned, unable to identify who his partner spoke of.

"There?" He growled, eyes half-heartedly tracking some movement below the line of leaves.

"Wait until she moves through a burned area—" The woman's voice hitched in excitement as the small form of the Earth Queen moved into the moonlight, stalking her newest victims. "There." Her words came out in a snarl as she pointed down, and without any more preamble, she dove from the skies before coming to rest at a point much closer to the ground.

The male was quick to follow suit, though he was less-inclined with this new power than the woman was, so he wobbled his way down to his partner as best he could. He was glad to be out of the worst of the smoke and dust rising up from the forests and the palace grounds.

"*Silently,*" The woman mouthed to him as he reached her, then began dropping out of the sky a few feet at a time. The man followed close behind, and their descent was so slow and calculated that not even the wind brushing against their tunics made but the barest of sounds.

As Amarie moved off beneath the trees once more, the woman held out a hand.

"Remember," She breathed. "You cannot touch the ground, the leaves, or any of the plants. Do you understand? Not even for a *moment.* Everything will fail if she knows we're coming."

"Yes Ma'am," The man confirmed in a near-silent voice, and they continued their slow way down.

It was tricky, finding a way through the trees without touching them, especially since the night was dark and the air was choked with smoke and dust, but they did their best. Soon enough, they found a way into the forest proper through a particularly well-burned patch of trees. Once below the actual canopy, it was only a matter of keeping alert and carefully bypassing any outlying branches or trees in the path, painstaking work at best, especially since the forest was growing by the minute.

Everywhere Amarie's feet had fallen, there had sprouted new growth. It was growing at a shocking rate, curling and trailing right below the Vague member's hovering bodies. The trees were creaking as they slowly climbed upward, leaves were shivering as they uncurled everywhere the eye could see, and the underbrush around them was set in unceasing motion as it grew and spread. It made detecting the queen's trail quite easy, for it was where the forest grew thickest—but actually following it, without touching any of it, took some careful maneuvering. Fortunately for them, Amarie was not moving quickly, and in this way, careful foot by careful foot, the Vague members flitted in her wake.

When they finally caught sight of her, things became even more tenuous. She'd moved into a thicker patch of trees and had gone still, no doubt listening for intruders. Her hands were out, sensing the life below and around her, and her head was tilted to one side. Whether she'd heard the approaching abductors, or whether she was listening for something else, the man couldn't say.

In any case, with the barest signal from the woman, they gathered more air below them and released it in a great, final burst of speed. As they closed in on their target with their arms outstretched, however, the man's shirt snagged on a pus-heavy tuber and snapped it off from its bush.

Turning with inhuman speed as if she'd been physically tapped, Amarie spun and lifted her deadly hands, giving out a feral snarl. In the space of a blink, the trees began to groan and shift in sudden violence and the thorny underbrush rose out of the ground to meet them like clawed hands, but by then the two Vague were close enough to see the forest-green glow in Amarie's scarred eyes.

They collided.

It was chaos.

One moment, Amarie was stalking out a new band of enemies for her trees and poisons to conquer, and the next she'd felt the approach of a new presence when they touched a nearby branch. She'd turned, ready to encase whoever it was in stone or run their body through with a tree branch, only to have them slam into her and knock the breath from her, far closer than she had mapped them to be. They toppled to the dangerous forest floor, and then with unnerving precision and planning, hooked Amarie under the armpits and shot into the sky.

Amarie felt her feet leave the ground, and her body gave a horrible lurch as she was yanked into the night with enough force and speed to send her organs splashing around inside of her.

"Away," Snarled a female voice near her ear, and Amarie was immediately engulfed by fury and fear.

So powerful were her emotions that the ground below them roared and splintered under the weight of them in a massive explosion. Huge cracks formed in the earth and raced across the forest floor, and the earth actually groaned with the force. Amarie felt a chasm form there and widen, deep—so deep—and tear its way towards the palace.

But she was nowhere near the ground.

With a sickening realization, Amarie suddenly realized that she didn't know where she was. She was in the air above the forest, speeding off and away from the castle at an alarming rate, but without the earth under her feet, she could not *see* herself. She could not feel herself or her enemies on the earth and shape it to defend or attack, for where would she aim? They were airborne.

So, without the power of her magic, Amarie turned to the power of her body.

She thrust her knees up and to the side, clipping one of her captors in the stomach. It was a male, and he grunted in pain. With her knees still lifted, Amarie then twisted and caught her bare foot in some of his clothes and then thrashed back the other way. The resulting wobble was enough to encourage her to do it again. When he seemed to anticipate the attack coming, she instead reached up and dragged her fingernails across the hands holding her. She felt warm blood, but gave them no time to react before she threw her head back and gnashed her teeth. Something entered her mouth—a hand or an arm or a piece of clothing, she didn't know—and she clamped her jaws together as hard as she could before ripping backward.

Blood poured into her mouth, a bitter prize, but she didn't let go.

"Gods!" The woman screamed, and one pair of hands holding Amarie disappeared, and whatever she had bit was torn out of her mouth. The shock of falling when the woman let go was enough to pull Amarie up short, but then the male tightened his hold and she was left to hang. She swung her now-free fist upwards and felt it collide with the warmth of the man's body, earning herself another grunt, but he held fast.

Below her, as she raged, the earth was churning as though made of water. The sound of the forest was all but deafening, even from the sky. Trees were exploding, gravel was cascading unchecked, and boulders were being ripped up from the ground and hurled through the air… Though it did little to help her, since she didn't know where she was in relation to any of it.

The royals had never practiced or prepared for such a thing. They hadn't even considered the possibility of it.

Amarie cried out in rage as the woman grabbed her anew and they increased their speed through the night. She tried swinging her knees again, but the man was prepared for it and jostled her so roughly that her legs flopped out underneath her. Another punch failed, and when she tried to bite them again, she was rewarded with a vicious jab to the eye.

The pain was immediate, an explosion in her mind, so she refrained from doing it again. Her magic, though, was as active as ever; unfortunately, she still couldn't pinpoint herself in the sky.

Even so, she tried her best.

All around her and her captors, rocks and trees began streaking through the air. Amarie knew in the back of her mind that if she hit them with a tree, she would plummet lethally to the ground, but she didn't stop.

Boulders rose and cascaded in all directions, and massive pillars of hardened stone and earth shot high out of the ground and melted back in again, like emerging sea monsters, or javelins looking for a target. She poured more strength, *more* power into her attempts to locate herself in the sky, to fight back, but it was futile. Her hair whipped behind her with the speed at which they were flying, but where they were heading, and in what direction, Amarie had no idea.

When her attempts at earth-level all failed, for the Vague members somehow dodged everything she sent their way, Amarie rearranged her body makeup and coated herself in thick, heavy rock.

The sudden added weight caused the trio to drop down in the sky, but even though her abductors struggled for a moment, they did not release her.

She felt another malicious poke against her eye, but the rock protected her from the pain.

Amarie lifted a stone-encased fist and swung it upward in a vicious arc once more, making contact again, though this time, with harrowing power. The jolt hurtled them further down and sideways through the sky, but they maintained the air currents keeping them aloft, even as they shook her and cursed her name.

"If we drop you from this height, you're dead!" The man's voice roared as she continued to thrash in their grip, more animal than human.

Amarie snapped her teeth and kicked her stony legs wildly, as if possessed, not caring what her kidnapper said. If she did get free, coating the ground in thick mud might help save her and pad her landing, but it would only work if she could figure out where she was before she hit ground.

Details aside, she fought and fought, but it made no difference.

For once in her life, she wasn't strong enough.

They'd been flying for some time, and at speed, despite Amarie's best efforts to the contrary. Below her, her awareness of the ground was still strong; and yet, it was wholly different. No longer could she map out where she was on the earth and what lay around her. Instead, she could now only watch, helpless, as the land rolled away underneath her.

She continued to pull trees from where they lay and scatter them in pieces across the ground, but at some point—she wasn't sure when—she'd kept doing so only to create a visual marker of where she'd been taken, rather than to actually try and get away. With any luck, her siblings would find her path and know which way she'd been taken.

Eventually, though, even the bright spots in her mind that marked trees and grass lands were replaced with the duller, sharper kind of visualizations that Amarie usually associated with rocky land and mountains.

In only a few more minutes, they'd left all trace of the forests behind them and had moved deep into the mountain range. Amarie kept up a constant drag on the rocky floor below, creating as much of a path there as she had in the trees, but eventually she began to feel the first prickles of fatigue.

She'd already been deep in her magic when they'd initially taken her, and from then on, she hadn't stopped fighting; marvelously so. She doubted that the landscape would ever be the same. Unfortunately, it also meant that she had expended a great deal of strength.

So, though every instinct she possessed told her not to, slowly, Amarie let go of the strangle-hold she had on her magic. Her body returned to its natural state, and she greatly lessened the impact she was dealing on the rolling land below. She continued to throw out her mind and forge new position markers every now and then, but it was difficult to gauge how far apart her clues were spaced, since she didn't know where she was in relation to them, or how fast they were actually flying.

Some time later, Amarie wasn't sure exactly how long, the drag of the wind on her face ceased. The land below stopped racing by in a dizzying blur, and piece by piece, Amarie started memorizing their location while she had a chance. It wasn't a perfect map, as her awareness of it wasn't particularly strong, but she took stock of what she could. There were sloping cliffs all around them, and the difference in the altitude and slope of the ground made her confident that they were hovering above a mountain valley.

Beyond the valley, Amarie's mind caught the shadow of a massive slab of rock, its peak reaching up into the sky. Her forehead creased as she honed in on it, trying to make sense of it. Its outside makeup felt natural enough, but the inside of it had her scratching her head. Much of it was smooth and hollowed out, and she could feel the weight of many pairs of feet racing up and down its great height.

"Are they ready over there?" The woman asked. Her voice came out rough, for nobody had spoken in hours.

"I think I can see him, there, on the upper balcony," The man confirmed in an uneven voice.

Suddenly, they were heading straight towards the massive peak. It was so big, and rose up so high in the sky, that Amarie was able to visualize it growing larger in her mind as they approached. The closer they got, the clearer it became. Foot by foot, they gained on it.

It was their mistake, and a foolish one at that. No wonder he was nervous.

The moment the mountain felt fully formed within her mind, Amarie would know that they had come within striking distance of it, and she would bring it to the ground. It would be tight—she would have to dip into her power for more strength than she had ever used before—but she would not fail.

The mountain *would* bow to her, and it would bury her captors as it fell.

Right as she stiffened in the Vague member's arms, preparing to lock them inside the rock for the rest of eternity, she was distracted by a staggering sensation within her; as if her blood had suddenly run cold. She gasped and shuddered, trying to rid herself of the feeling, and thankfully, it passed after a moment, as suddenly as it had come.

To her great fear, however, she realized that the approaching mountain had vanished from her mind.

—

Amarie and the woman had been hovering in silence for long minutes, though it felt as though it had been hours. The man was nowhere to be heard.

When Amarie's power had first dwindled within her blood, they'd continued flying for a short time, though Amarie had no idea where. Whether they were truly heading to the massive mountain, or whether they'd flown past it, she didn't know. For the first time in her life, she felt truly blind.

Eventually, though, her captors stopped midair and held a hurried conversation between themselves, and the man had taken off. The shift from being held by two people to being held by only one wasn't comfortable, but all Amarie could do was cling to the hope that she wouldn't be dropped. She no longer had any confidence that she would survive the fall, for it had become an impossibility. There would be no softening of the ground, no commanding it to rise up and gently catch her. She would plummet down and shatter against the earth—a horribly ironic way to die, after all.

The woman's breath was coming in more laboured by then as well, and they'd started wobbling in the air slightly as they held their position. Amarie began to wonder if her strength would fail her before the man returned; perhaps they would plunge to the ground together. It may not be the worst outcome for such a terrible situation.

Amarie felt lost without her magic. Her very soul felt as though it was aching; or rather, the painful spot where her soul used to be was aching, for suddenly, it felt as though the essence of who she was had been plucked out of her. Was this what the Vague members felt on a regular basis? Utterly helpless, utterly ordinary? No hint of wild magic roiling under their skin? She shuddered, hating the way her body felt—sluggish, cold… unfamiliar.

A few minutes later, a subtle shifting of the winds caught Amarie's attention. She turned her head, seeking out the source of the new sound, and soon heard the man talking hurriedly as he approached.

"He has it, he has it." His voice was a mixture of exhilarated and awestruck. "Bring her in, quickly. They want to meet her." A second pair of hands gripped Amarie under the armpits, and she felt her stomach heave as they dropped out of the sky.

In less time than she'd thought it would take, the trio slowed and pulled up. They must not have been as far away from the mountain as Amarie had thought they were. The two Vague members hurriedly set her on her feet, and she stumbled as the hands released her.

She actually *stumbled.*

She'd never felt the ground under her feet like this before… foreign, and completely separate from herself. Her feet felt as though they had become their own entity, rather than an offshoot of the ground they stood on. It was like walking drunk—or onboard a ship. Nausea rose in her belly, but before she could so much as get her bearings, a heavy hand landed on her shoulder and started pushing her along.

So she walked, tripping all the way, into the unknown.

The winds of the mountain range died as they moved on, and the sound of their footsteps began to echo. They must have moved inside a cave or tunnel within the mountain, and Amarie was thankful for the change in temperature, despite everything else. She could smell a fire or fires burning somewhere nearby that were providing a comfortable heat.

For a time, the three of them continued on in the same fashion, until even the echoes of their feet spaced out—they must have entered some sort of large cavern, if her ears could be trusted. There were more people there, perhaps even a large group of them; Amarie could her smatterings of whispers and muttered conversation. Somebody coughed as they walked in and a hard pressure on her shoulder commanded her to stop.

She did so, and an uneasy silence fell around them.

"Is this her, then?" Came a male voice from somewhere ahead of her. Amarie lifted her chin, hoping she looked fiercer than she felt.

"The Earth Queen," Said one of her abductors.

"Not anymore, it would seem."

The rock below Amarie's feet began shuddering, and she fought furiously against her dizzy inner balance to keep her footing. Then, with a deep cracking and rumbling that she recognized only too well, she was hoisted off the ground. Cool air brushed against her face as she was transported across the length of the cave on a pillar of stone. When she finally stopped, she could hear the sound of the male speaker breathing.

"Here you are." He was closer at hand than Amarie had anticipated. She made no reply and merely kept her chin up, both seething in anger and equal parts horrified. "I… can't thank you enough, for this gift," The man continued, his calm voice crawling down her spine like a pretty, poisonous spider.

"It's not a gift," Amarie snarled, losing hold of her tongue and lashing out like a caged animal. The rustling of fabric and a sudden empty feeling in front of her made her believe that the man had leaned back from her.

"Why such hurtful words?"

"You *stole* it, it's not a *gift*. You and your people are good for nothing thieves, each of you as ordinary as the rest, and without a fleck of power to yourselves. You are *weak*—" Her voice was cut off abruptly as a slap that she hadn't seen coming was administered harshly across her face. She took a shocked step backwards on the pillar, but the rock grew behind her to keep her from falling to the ground below.

Never, in all of her life, had anybody *dared…*

"You will find I do not take lightly to you speaking to my mate with such impoliteness," Came the deep voice of a woman, equally as close as the original male speaker. Amarie turned in naked surprise, searching for the woman that had slapped her, but in vain.

"Indeed," Said yet another woman, this one with honey-laced poison in her voice, and Amarie turned again. "I think spending some time in a cold cell will teach this one when to hold her tongue in the presence of greatness, don't you, my love?"

"Of course," Replied another woman, the fourth and final voice. She had an accent that Amarie couldn't place, and more rustling fabric sounded as she leaned in and whispered harshly. "You are no longer in your own court, little queen."

Amarie gaped.

Three women and one man, by the sounds of their voices, all seemingly seated beside each other in the hushed cave, undoubtedly surrounded by their supporters. Not a family, as she and her siblings were, but lovers, if their words could be trusted.

Amarie's mind began to race as the rock pillar below her crumbled and sent her back down to the earth with teeth-rattling impact. She made no attempt to run, though, and even as a pair of rough hands began hauling her from the throne room—for that was what the cave had to be—her thoughts whirled.

The Vague had their own Promised Four.

Chapter 10

Amarie ran her hands across the makeshift stone bars of the cell she had been deposited in hours before. Clearly, it had been made by somebody with stolen Earth powers, and it was beyond humiliating to be kept imprisoned there. It was a truly sick joke they were playing on her.

And, to add injury to insult, judging by the strength of the wind blowing into her cage, she figured that the pen stood directly across from an open window that was cut into the stone of the mountain, which left her entirely exposed to the wintery elements beyond.

It did not make for a comfortable stay.

She'd initially hoped for a bit more of a sheltered space—perhaps something more befitting a queen or a royal prisoner of war—but it seemed that her wish would not come true. Even though it was bitterly cold and her teeth were set to near-constant chattering, though, it did allow her to make reasonably educated guesses on the passing of day or night, based on the temperature of the world beyond the mountain.

The *very* cold times, when she would go long hours without hearing anybody moving outside her cage and with only her misery for company, she assumed were nighttime. The slightly *less* cold times, when she would get meager meals delivered and people mingled and passed beyond the bars, she could only assume were during the day. Passing the time in this way certainly didn't make for entertaining sport, but she was at least able to, somewhat, keep her bearings.

As it was, if Amarie would have said she'd so far spent about two days in the cage. Perhaps three.

And over that time, again and again, constantly and unrelentingly, Amarie tried to reach the piece of her soul where her power normally sat; the deep place where the Stone of Promise had rooted into her being and set her life on its new, noble course. Any spark, any *hint* at her gifts, and she would grab hold and make these people pay for what they had done to her, and what they planned to do still, but… nothing.

During the times when she wasn't furiously trying to call on non-existent magic, Amarie had explored the little cave where she'd been deposited, looking for depressions or cracks where she may be able to get some leverage; unfortunately, like the cold remains of the power she'd so recently held, there was nothing to be found. She'd more or less memorized the small room during her imprisonment, but she didn't know what good it was going to do. Knowledge of her pen wouldn't help her escape, and even if she did get out—what would she do?

Tumble out one of the open walls to her death, more likely than not. Perhaps she could bring a few filthy Vague down with her when she went.

Her heart ached in her anger and sadness, and she both dreaded and hoped that her siblings were on their way to her. On the one hand, the royals would probably raze the Vague's base to the ground; but on the other hand, to come so close would be to risk getting their own gifts stolen as well, and then it would all be over.

Attina would be doomed.

The fact that they'd brought her to a mountain where she so easily could have taken control showed an immense confidence in their own abilities, as well. It led Amarie to believe that the other three Vague leaders were just as strong as the man who had taken her own gift. If any part of their strategy hadn't gone exactly as planned, she would have crushed them; but they'd been confident in their leader's strength. They'd taken a *huge* risk, but it had worked out exactly as they'd hoped.

Amarie felt as though she had become no better than bait, intended to bring the most powerful people in the realm together so they could be picked off by their enemies, one by one.

Some time during the second or third night, she wasn't exactly sure which, an unlikely roaring sound greeted Amarie's ears.

She leapt up from her half-sleeping position against the cold wall and hurried to the bars, already trying to decipher what exactly she was hearing. The sound boomed and crackled in through the open wall across from her, not unlike the sound that came from the castle fireplaces when the flue dampers were fully opened on windy days.

Was it fire?

Was it Zeraphall?

Amarie's hands tightened on the unforgiving lines of stone in front of her, when a blast of welcome heat washed across her face. It didn't burn—the fire clearly wasn't near her—but the flames were hot enough that, for a moment, the chill of the night air was softened. Any thoughts or hopes that Amarie had of Zeraphall faded, though, as the sound of cheering and celebrating issued out of Vague mouths, both above and below her in the hollowed-out mountain. More belches of fire followed, with consequent booming and roaring, and her enemies continued making such a ruckus that anybody within the mountain range would be sure to hear it.

Perhaps that was the point.

Amarie got another meal dropped through the bars some hours later—breakfast, probably—when an abrupt change came over the mountain. It was a sound; another deep roaring, like the one she'd heard last night, coming from somewhere in the distance. She tuned in, listening hard and leaving her food untouched. The noise was made by something powerful, there was no doubt about that, but she couldn't place what it was.

So strange… mysterious and frightening, and yet somehow, not entirely unfamiliar. Amarie tilted her head against the cool stone and tried to piece the noise together in her mind.

Then the shouting started.

A countless number of Vague members were suddenly running by the cage, and all of them seemed to be yelling something different. Their many pairs of feet echoed loudly off the stone walls and added to the cacophony, and Amarie shrank back from the bars if only to get away from the din. The procession of them seemed endless, for a time, and snippets of conversation floated past as they went.

"Did you see that?!"

"They're here; it worked."

"Spirts preserve us!"

"To your stations!"

The roaring outside was getting louder, by then.

Could it be?

"Bend these bars back." A gruff male voice sounded close by, louder than the rest. "We need to get her to the throne room."

At his words, the stone of Amarie's cage was peeled back on itself and she was all but dragged out. With a powerful shove to the midback, she was then forced to join the tide of enemies, tripping up an inclined floor that she remembered from days previous. Once or twice, she was jostled so aggressively that she lost her footing, but strong hands dragged her up again before she got trampled by the stampede swelling all around her.

Instead of panicking, though, she tried to focus her mind on the sounds still roaring outside.

There was wind, that much was certain. It had come up fiercely and suddenly in the mountain valley, and was building every second. There was a comforting familiarity within the way the tempest moaned and howled, and the way it had come up from nothing; it was Prinidan, undoubtedly. Amarie felt herself smile even as she was dragged down a new hallway.

Seconds later, the sound of roaring water filtered in through the open windows as they went along. It was angry and powerful, like the deepest gorge. Ellion.

And as the stone path Amarie and the Vague were on became even steeper, she realized what she'd heard before that she hadn't been able to place. The sound was deep—impossibly low—snapping and thrumming and *booming* across the stone, but now she knew exactly what it was.

It was Zeraphall.

Amarie took a shaky breath as she and her captors slowed down, nearing their destination at last. They would soon discover whether the Vague's remaining three leaders possessed enough strength to make a difference.

"So, your brothers and sister have come with the sunrise," One of the Vague's female leaders said as Amarie was deposited into the throne room once more. She didn't reply, for she was distracted by the fact that she could still hear the din from her siblings in the valley far below. It led her to believe that the throne room had at least one open wall feature, as well. Such designs seemed slightly reckless to Amarie, especially because the Vague was not native to magic, but perhaps that was the appeal to these people.

The woman cleared her throat sharply, obviously irritated at Amarie's lack of response, and spoke again.

"I'm sure it will turn out to be a lovely little reunion."

Amarie didn't rise to the bait. It was the sweet-voiced woman who had spoken, but though she sounded gentle and even caring, Amarie knew the truth. These people were snakes and thieves.

"I can't wait to feel what they feel," Crooned the woman with the deep voice. Amarie got the sense that the woman was trying to taunt her, but was also speaking the truth at the same time. "To be able to fly on the lightest wisp of air…"

To be able to fly?

Amarie's jaw tightened, but she forced her face into neutrality as she locked away the information. The deep-voiced woman would eventually attempt to take Prinidan's magic.

"Hush, my love," Said the man—the one who held Amarie's own beloved gifts. Amarie recalled that he and the woman with the deep voice seemed to be romantically involved. "We don't want this little urchin knowing all of our secrets."

"She's no threat," Scoffed the accented woman. "She has no magic, and she can't see. What threat could she possibly pose?"

Amarie barely managed to stifle a breath of irritation, finding it difficult to remain aloof and queenly in the presence of such ignorance. The woman scoffed again, perhaps at Amarie's continued silence, and her clothes rustled as she leaned back in her chair.

Fools often took silence for weakness, and Amarie tried to remind herself of that as the Vague's four began muttering amongst themselves when she still refused to speak.

A loud *clang* rang into the silence from across the throne room as somebody dropped a handful of metal objects on the stone floor. Amarie listened in, and was able to decipher the scrape of what she thought might be weapon heads, as well as the subtle flapping of leather wraps being gathered back up.

"So, you truly seek to battle my family?" Amarie finally spoke, directing her voice up to where the leaders were sitting.

"Well of course," The sweet-voiced woman said after a moment. She gave a patronizing little chuckle. "You don't think we'd simply let them take you back, do you?"

"Besides," Said the accented one in smug tones. "They've gone to such lengths to get here in the first place."

Amarie took a stabilizing breath, silently praying to the spirits that their arrogance would also be their downfall.

"You're not afraid?" She asked a beat later.

"Afraid?" The man repeated, slow and suspicious. Amarie shrugged nonchalantly.

"Do you really think you're ready for a fight of this magnitude?" She counted to five before speaking again, letting her words sink in. "Are you strong enough?"

"Kanen took your gifts *that* fast," The deep-voiced woman growled, snapping her fingers. "The other three will not be a problem for us."

Amarie arranged her expression into one of indifference as she memorized the name of the man that had taken everything from her. *Kanen.*

"Enough, darling," Kanen drawled lazily. "We have nothing to prove to this once-queen."

Instead of letting herself descend into fury at his words, Amarie focused inward and tried her best to keep everything that she was learning straight in her mind.

Kanen and Prinidan's would-be thief were mates; in fact, Amarie was quite certain that the deep-voiced woman had even called him that, on the first day she'd met them. She also felt confident that the sweet-voiced woman had called the accented-woman something similar; love, mate, or some such thing.

So how could those relationships be exploited?

Amarie's thoughts stuttered to a worried stop when an attendant breezed into the room some moments later. His boots slapped against the stone hurriedly, starting at one end of the floor and stopping right in front of the leaders.

The royals of Attina had arrived.

—

Arrive they had.

Zeraphall, Ellion, and Prinidan had wasted no time in crossing into the valley and going up and over the last slope separating them from the gigantic mountain. Zeraphall and Ellion were prickling with energy, and most of Prinidan's colour had returned overnight. His eyes, at least, were unclouded and aglow once more.

The moment the sun broke over the far peaks, the royals launched their attack. The few guards stationed outside the carved mountain entrance were quickly blown away or washed out by Ellion and Prinidan, and they continued keeping the path and entryway clear as Zeraphall began spinning some magic of her own against the surrounding landscape.

Magma was a curious thing.

It took some focus to form in the first place—heating the rocks to melting, that is—but once it was done, it took hours to cool. Zeraphall was quite adapt at it, and she could all but ensure that any lava she formed would remain hot and burning for long stretches of time. So as her brothers provided her cover against the entrance to the mountain, she began turning the valley floor to magma.

The surrounding rocks and cliff faces in the little valley were the first to go, sliding off in great chunks and landing in sticky, melted piles on the ground far below. It was only a matter of seconds before they'd broken down into puddles, and as Zeraphall repeated the action over and over again, a great pool began to form. The sound of it was loud and echoing, almost painful, and it only increased.

Newly-heated boulders would crumble or sag into the spreading molten rock with lethal splashes, just to become engulfed and melt in their own time as well. The closest cliff bottoms began to melt away after that, which in turn caused even more rock to tumble into the pool, and the process would begin again.

With a few careful calculations, and the heating of exactly the right pieces of stone along the way, Zeraphall all but guaranteed that the magma would continue to melt its surroundings until a mock-lake formed (and remained) on the valley floor.

It would make escape tricky, if not impossible, for any Vague who escaped the royals' wrath on the inside.

"Let's go," She finally growled, dropping her hands after making one last adjustment to a massive chunk of mountain rock.

"Nothing like burning our bridges behind us," Ellion shouted over the din of the building magma.

Zeraphall sent him a grim smile.

"I leave with Amarie, or I don't leave at all."

"We approach each area with wide eyes," Prinidan said, scanning the darkness beyond the entrance of the mountain. "She *can't* get caught in the crossfire."

"They would never risk that." Ellion crouched low and sent a cover of fog through the arch and into the mountain. "She's their only fail-safe right now. If they lose her, they lose their edge."

"Even still." Prinidan's voice was steadfast.

The others nodded, even though it was rather difficult for any of them to truly imagine Amarie without her powers. Their magic was as much a part of them as their personalities were, and one without the other was nearly unthinkable. But they had to think about it, and cement it in their brains besides, if they were to have any real chance of saving her.

So, as the royals hurried up the path and entered into the rock fully, they had to fight against an overwhelming sense of unease.

Would the Vague use Amarie as a shield? A bargaining chip? Would they taunt the royals, returning her powers for a moment, only to steal them back again when the Promised Four's guard was down?

Once inside the mountain, the tension that the siblings were already feeling got even heavier as they were hit with the strange and sudden certainty that they were up against more than they might have thought. It became abundantly clear, quite quickly, that the Vague had been living there and perfecting their mountain base (with stolen power, of course) for centuries.

The walls of the entry chamber looked as though they had been carved into the grey stone, rather than simply dug out, and the pillars stationed throughout the landing were ornate, with carved pictures and looping designs. There were open walls on either end of the room that provided a perfect amount of light to see by, and the upward-slanted floor was as smooth as glass.

Nothing seemed out of place.

The large room itself was empty, since they'd already dispatched the initial guards, but the siblings could hear noise coming from the long hall ahead that, no doubt, led deeper up the mountain. It sounded as though many pairs of feet were descending through the stone towards them. The three of them rushed onward in response.

Zeraphall took the lead, with Prinidan and Ellion flanking her a few steps behind. They raced up the path for quite some time, and though there were no more windows to confirm, it was obvious that they were leaving the ground and valley far behind.

After a time, they saw that the path opened into a large hall up ahead, and as they reached it, power was already blooming in their palms.

The next room had no pillars, but was just as large as the entry had been, and the floor had the same upwards slant to it. It was ornately carved as well, and there were floor to ceiling windows on either end of the space. Across the room was another hallway that branched up and off through the mountain at the far end, but unfortunately, access to it was blocked. A small group of Vague was stationed directly in the royals' path, and before the trio could even properly register that battle was about to begin, they were sent sprawling by a massive host of cascading gravel that broke away from the closest wall.

Ellion immediately lost his footing and fell hard, and a heavy stone grinded against Zeraphall's ankle; Prinidan, however, leapt high into the air to safety, bolstered by a great puff of air. As he did so, he simultaneously threw his good arm forward and buffeted the closest Vague members with striking accuracy.

One plain woman in the front of the group, who had been twisting a hand marked with a circular tattoo, stumbled against the sudden heavy wind. She lost her focus when she tripped, and the gravel below the royals' feet ceased churning. They didn't wait for her to regain herself before they retaliated, for right as she'd landed the initial attack, three more Vague members had come up behind her.

Ellion struggled up from the ground and commanded a wicked shard of barbed ice to form in his hand as he did so. As the first of the three new enemies brought his hands forward to attack, Ellion threw the spike and skewered him through the chest. The Vague man fell, but any last words he uttered were lost within Zeraphall's fierce battle cry.

Just as Prinidan landed back on the ground and Ellion threw his spear, Zeraphall brought her hands together in a ferocious clap. A bright red light blistered into existence from the contact point of her hands and shot outward in lethal, twisting ribbons. The flares twisted and burned through the Vague members standing in the front of the group.

The brightness of Zeraphall's attack was so fierce that even the male royals were left with damage spots in their eyes, and by the time they'd blinked back the pain and fully regained their sight, their sister had commanded the flares to burrow into the chests of the last of the three enemies who had stepped up.

Zeraphall's targets couldn't do so much as scream before the ribbons had burned holes through their bodies, as well. The remaining cluster of Vague shouted in dismay as their fellows burned and died in the space of a few blinks, and then chaos ensued.

Zeraphall immediately took a large rock to the back of the head, which caused her flares to sputter and wink out. Prinidan was also hit, but this time with a blast of air so hot that he had to throw up a pressure pocket around himself just to stop it. It didn't take long to pinpoint the Fire and Air bandits that were working together against him, but Ellion reacted faster than he could.

With a twist of the Water king's hands, the moisture in the cave banded together and formed a great, writhing column of water. The cover gave Zeraphall a chance to stagger up and catch her breath, and Prinidan to cast aside his shield.

Ellion's eyes fell to the attackers as the others righted themselves, and with a snarl, he commanded the pillar of water to twist and thrust forward. It hit with such force that the frontline Vague members were thrown backward into those behind them. Their feet could find no purchase on the smooth—now soaking wet—stone of the floor, and before they were able to sort out their confusion, Prinidan cleaved the room's oxygen in two.

With a painful *snap* of pressure, he spread the air apart with such unyielding force that the royals' enemies had little-to-no hope of fighting against him. Even the Air thieves, of which there were perhaps two or three remaining, had no foot to stand on as Prinidan swept them aside as though they were little more than flecks of dust in a hurricane.

Out and out, he pushed the remaining attackers relentlessly, until they were all teetering on either edge of the open walls. One or two of them had the good sense to look terrified, but it made no difference. With a growl rarely heard from the calmest of the siblings, Prinidan slashed his good arm in front of him, and sealed his enemies' fate.

The Vague soldiers toppled out of the windows one after the other, left to the fate of the ground and magma waiting far below. Whether or not the Air or Earth thieves were skilled enough to save themselves, the royals didn't wait to find out before moving on again.

Zeraphall, cursing and rubbing the back of her head, fell into step beside her brothers as they swept forward. They didn't run, for preserving their strength was paramount, but they moved on with intention, ready for whatever was coming. Zeraphall's cursing intensified when she found her fingers wet with blood.

"Damn near split my head open with that rock," She spat. "I'll have to close it, or it will keep leaking."

"You'd think your head would be hard enough to withstand a bit of a bump," Ellion muttered, breath coming in heavy. Zeraphall flipped him a rude gesture, then ignited that same finger to begin cauterizing her injury. Prinidan's shoulder seemed to pulse in tandem with her fresh string of curses and he rolled it agitatedly, working determinedly through the memory of the recent pain.

"You'll be a medic in no time, Zera," Ellion grimaced when she was finished. "It could come in quite useful before our time in this mountain is through."

"For all of our sakes, let's hope that's not the case."

"It's going to get worse the deeper in we move." Prinidan continued to roll his shoulder and grit his teeth through the pain of it. Jokes were fine to lighten the mood and release tension after an initial battle, but they couldn't afford to drop their guard for long. "They won't let us get to Amarie easily."

"No," Zeraphall agreed, scanning the smoothed stone before them with a keen glance. "But every step we gain brings us closer to her."

"No retreats," Ellion confirmed. "We give nothing back."

The others agreed.

They hadn't heard any more sounds of oncoming enemies thus far, so they continued following the path upward as it wound through more stone and empty rooms. It was easy enough to track the light of the aging morning as they went, as well, since most of the rooms and caves they passed boasted at least one open wall feature.

Eventually, however, the silence and lack of enemies began to wear on them. It was all too possible that the Vague had secret paths through the mountain that the royals didn't know about, and none of them had forgotten that the keeper of Amarie's powers could be lurking just beyond their sight, hidden behind an inch of rock and waiting to attack.

"Why attack in bits and pieces?" Ellion growled after the tension finally started getting to him. "Why not hit us with all they have from the off?"

"That certainly couldn't be all they had," Zeraphall agreed, glancing back the way they had come. "And now we're higher up the mountain than ever."

"Then where are they?"

"They're probably waiting until we've tired ourselves out to attack in earnest," Prinidan said grimly. The idea that they were playing into the Vague's hands resurfaced and cemented into each of the royals' minds.

Fortunately, the next batch of Vague members that the trio encountered were dispatched quickly—even more quickly than the first had been. And while it did mean that Amarie's thief was still at large somewhere, and that their strength was not being properly preserved, they took their luck as it came.

Branching off from the site of the most recent battle were a few different hallways, but there was one central path that seemed to be better-maintained than the others, and it was this one that the royals took. It was not made up of a smooth and sloping floor—as the other halls they'd travelled thus far had been—but was an actual set of roughly hewn stairs. The surroundings were more difficult to see, since there were no windows, but Zeraphall ignited her hands and lit the way well enough.

Each royal craned their neck back to peer past the glow of Zeraphall's hands, up the stairs and into the impending gloom above. It seemed as though the stairs went on for some time, before finally curving up and away into the mountain.

"I'll fly ahead," Prinidan murmured. "We don't want to get caught on low-ground."

He leapt onto a silent pocket of air and began to glide up the stairs. Not even a breath of sound gave him away. As he approached the end of Zeraphall's wall of light, however, the silence was shattered when he gave a strangled yelp and plummeted to the stairs below.

With an icy, echoing crash, the Air King hit the stone steps, jarring his ruined arm in the process, and came crashing and rolling down until he finally landed in a heap, back at Zeraphall and Ellion's feet.

"What happened?!" Ellion barked, dragging his brother back up to standing and inspecting him for further damage.

Prinidan swayed as if drunk, before Ellion tightened his hold.

"I—" Prinidan gulped, looking at his hands in confusion and dismay. He flexed them once, turned them front and back, and then flexed them again.

There was nothing there.

There was no whisper of wind beneath his skin, no connection to the pressure systems that ruled the skies. He could no longer sense the comings and goings of the air currents around them or outside of the mountain, and the air in the stairwell had become invisible to him. The very air in his lungs had turned foreign and uncomfortable, and it suddenly felt as though he might choke on it.

He looked up from his hands mutely, facing his siblings, as his fear took hold. Zeraphall cursed the Vague to the pits of the four Hells when she realized what had happened, and Ellion couldn't even come up with a word of comfort.

"No more," Zeraphall growled as Prinidan looked down again at his powerless hands. She threw a fist forward, and the light in her own hands spread down her arm and across her body. Instantly, she became coated in magma and burning flame—even her hair suddenly crackled with tiny sparks that danced along the lengths of her curls. Her eyes, usually as black as midnight, glowed orange. She snarled, looking for all the world like a demon of the spirit realm whose only purpose was to drag as many enemies back down with her as she could.

Her brothers stumbled back a few paces, for the heat was so intense.

"More will be coming soon." Her voice shuddered and crackled as it burned. She looked to Prinidan. "What do we do?"

A hesitation opened between the three of them that was just as painful as it was quiet.

"Go on," Prinidan croaked somewhat numbly, but Ellion gave a vicious shake of his head.

"No! They'll be coming for you," He hissed. "We need to stay together."

"I'll keep my daggers close," Prinidan objected. "They can't kill me without losing my gifts, and I'll only slow you two down. The worst they can do is capture me."

Ellion and Zeraphall exchanged an aggrieved look.

"I won't have *two* of my siblings in enemy hands," Ellion said.

"Ellion's right, Prin; we can't—" Zeraphall tried, but their brother pointed up the stairs.

"Go! For Amarie, right? Maybe I can help her on the other side, if they do get to me."

Ellion stood as if stunned, but with another violent snarl, Zeraphall grabbed his shoulder and spun him around.

"Don't lag too far behind," She roared to Prinidan. "We'll clear the path ahead and keep them away from you."

Prinidan only nodded silently, all typical strength and confidence shattered. Even the demeanor that he usually carried himself with—distant, thoughtful, otherworldly—had faltered. Rather than appearing almost spirit-like in his mysterious calm, he suddenly just seemed lost and afraid.

And though he hated to do it, Ellion grasped his brother's shoulder in what he hoped was a reassuring way, before turning to race up the stairs after their sister. He threw a fist forward as he went, and ice quickly coated it. It thickened immediately and began to spread down his arm, growing and crackling as it went, until his entire body was coated—the freezing twin to the hell that Zeraphall had called forth. Mist radiated from him as the remaining heat from their sister brushed through the air.

"Don't lose sight of us," Ellion said angrily, his voice echoing strangely within his frozen armour. This was not a choice he would have made, but Prinidan merely nodded, already hurrying up the stairs behind with his daggers at the ready.

—

Amarie was shunted back and forth as the crowd of Vague members rushed around the throne room. Conversations flowed around her that she didn't quite catch, for everybody seemed to be speaking at once, but she heard her own name a handful of times. She wondered if they were deciding what to do with her—keeping her (and by extension, Kanen's hold on her power) safe, while simultaneously keeping her close.

Well, she realized, keeping her close wouldn't even matter, if it really came down to it. They'd already discovered that the Vague could hold powers nearly indefinitely and over an infinite amount of distance, if they chose to. What good would rescuing her do, then, to *actually* aid the battle? Even if she were to escape all the way back to her chambers at the neutral palace, Kanen would still hold her magic.

So, was rescuing her even in the realm's best interest?

"Well, if the first and second waves of soldiers haven't dealt with them, let *us* join the battle." The Vague leaders' conversation rose in volume, and the sweet-voiced woman's sudden words interrupted Amarie's downward spiral. She shoved her nervousness and anxiety to the back of her mind and tuned in to the conversation.

"And put ourselves at risk? Have you forgotten that I am the only one who holds royal magic? It would be foolish!" Kanen replied quietly. "Why so hasty, Meena?"

Amarie locked the name into her mind without so much as a blink; the sweet-voiced woman was named Meena. She hadn't yet discovered whether Meena would try to take Ellion or Zeraphall's powers, of course, but it was heartening to know that she was slowly figuring her enemies out.

"We wouldn't *be* risking ourselves if we used the steeds," Meena replied in exasperation. It sounded as though they'd been over the topic before. "And you could cover us well enough with the Earth magic, could you not?"

"A good idea in theory," Replied the deep-voiced woman. "But if we enter the battle, what of *her*?"

Their voices turned towards Amarie, clearly watching her as the organized chaos of the crowd unfolded around them. Amarie kept her face carefully blank, as if she couldn't hear their words over the throne room's noisy activity.

"As long as she doesn't *die*, my power will remain intact," Kanen said.

"No, Kanen. We can't dismiss this. We *must* keep her safe—you know that," The deep-voiced woman insisted. "At least while the other royals are sweeping the mountain."

"I agree with Illa," Said the accented-woman. Amarie dared a blink as she memorized another name. The deep-voiced woman, Kanen's mate and Prinidan's thief, was named Illa. She knew three names—she only needed one more. "If the other royals were to get her before we'd neutralized them, it would only complicate things."

"Alright, so we keep her locked up and safe," Meena picked up, her voice as gentle as a poisonous flower. "And once we've ensured they will not reach her, we enter the battle on the steeds."

"At what risk to ourselves—and our steeds, for that matter?" Kanen growled, clearly against the idea of going down below.

"Alone, I cannot hope to contend with the royals of Attina, and if we lose the steeds, it will set us well back. We must have more power behind us *before* we move in."

Amarie frowned. Why didn't Kanen want to fight? Even as the only high-powered individual on the Vague's side, he would surely make a big difference. Perhaps being a coward came hand in hand with being a thief.

"So let us mount the steeds and descend to take what is ours!" Meena barked back. "We cannot gain more power without making a play for it in the first place—unless we all get as lucky as you did, Kanen, and can steal the magic from right here."

"My steed isn't fit," The accented woman chimed in, before Kanen could reply. "We would only be able to mobilize three."

"So, then *we* three will ride, and Rana, my love, you shall merely have to lay in wait for the Fire Queen to drop her guard—" Meena began, but Illa interrupted her.

"If our members do what they've been trained to do, they should be able to handle the royals on their own. We may not need to risk ourselves at all." Illa's deep voice rang out heavily. "Kanen is right. We should hold back."

"Alright, but what if they *can't* handle the situation?" Meena continued. "The steeds are a viable option. How can you not agree? We wouldn't even have to ride them, necessarily—we could just set them loose."

A moment of quiet followed her words, which was undoubtedly so the other leaders could turn over what she was arguing for. It gave Amarie a chance to quickly run over and memorize what she'd learned.

Kanen and Illa were mates; Kanen had her magic, and Illa, the deep-voiced woman, would attempt to take Prinidan's. Rana and Meena were also a romantic item; Rana had the accent, and she would make a play for Zeraphall's gifts. That left Meena, with the sweet voice, who would then undoubtedly try for Ellion.

And, for some reason, Kanen didn't want to join the battle, and it didn't sound as though the other leaders (aside from Meena) wanted to either. This was good news for the true royals, for if Kanen was so loathe to join the battle and use Amarie's gifts, they would have a far greater chance of overcoming the Vague.

"We stay out of it for now," Kanen said. "Let the members attempt to fulfill their duty and protect their leaders. In the meantime, we will prepare our steeds. When the time comes, we can decide whether to enter the battle with them, or send them in riderless. The royals cannot fight forever. Eventually they will tire, and that's when we will make our move."

"So, we're treating our members as if they're disposable in the meantime?" Meena prompted quietly, though Amarie doubted anybody would hear her over the buzzing of the crowd.

"Remember," Kanen hissed in reply. "The goal is not to win this battle as quickly as possible; the *goal* is for us to come out of it with four untouchable powers, and with the royals secured."

"It wouldn't do to risk ourselves unnecessarily and jeopardize the objective, sweet one," Cooed Rana, which earned a stubborn sniff from Meena. "Think long-term here, darling. Think of Attina."

Finally, Meena sighed.

"Alright. We wait until the royals are weakened."

"Then it's settled," Kanen said with a clap. "While we see to the steeds, let us secure the Earthling with a member here, in the throne room. It is the most secure location, and the farthest from the battle. Might I suggest—" It was silent for a moment, as if he was casting around the room. "Ryian to guard her, perhaps?"

"An apt keeper, my love," Illa replied.

"Your Highness," Immediately came a female voice that Amarie hadn't yet heard. Ryian, whoever she was, must have been standing at the ready, nearby. "Wouldn't I better serve our cause by fighting down below, rather than staying here to guard a blind and helpless prisoner?"

Amarie's carefully-blank expression soured at the assumption.

"You will serve the Vague in whatever way we feel is best," Tsked Rana, her accent clipping the words sharply.

"But surely this is a waste of my time—" Ryian stuttered.

"Enough," Illa sighed. "Do not question your leaders. It is your honour that Kanen has dubbed you capable of guarding such a valuable prisoner in the first place. You will thank him and do as you're bid, or we'll find another person to do your job and strip you of your powers in the meantime."

A beat of silence drove Illa's words home.

"Thank you, Kanen," Ryian grunted, earning a snicker from one leader or other.

Heavy footfalls approached, and a moment later, Ryian's strong hand had closed around Amarie's shoulder. She reacted like a snake striking its prey.

She drove her head down to her knees, while simultaneously reaching her arms around to latch onto Ryian's arm. One hand clamped around Ryian's wrist, the other hooked her under the elbow. Straightening and giving a yank that would have sent far larger people tumbling to the ground, Amarie then heaved her hands up and out, which forced Ryian's arm into a painful and unnatural angle. Before anybody knew what had happened, Amarie pulled the wrist and shoved the elbow, and Ryian's shoulder popped loudly out of joint.

Amarie was permitted all of a few seconds to appreciate her own success as her target screamed, before a heavy weight hit her between the shoulders and knocked her to the floor. She dug an elbow out and back, but discovered that it was solid rock holding her in place, and not a human.

"*Enough!*" Kanen snarled as somebody rushed to Ryian's aid. "I will not tolerate temper tantrums."

Amarie growled a string of curses that would have made Zeraphall proud, but then the rock pinning her down pressed even harder. She fought until she could no longer breathe, but eventually went limp. Kanen commanded the rock to squeeze the air from her lungs for a second or two longer, if only to flex his new ability, before finally letting her go.

"Ryian," Kanen said. "Do not be shy with this one. If she acts up, punish her. We only need her to remain breathing."

Amarie heard the grunt and muffled shout of pain as Ryian's shoulder was no doubt put back in place, but the woman recovered far more quickly than she would have anticipated.

"Understood, Kanen," She replied in a strained voice.

Nobody hauled Amarie to her feet; however, she quickly picked herself up a few seconds later when an abrupt hush fell over the gathered crowd. She was only left wondering what was going on for a moment, though, when Illa suddenly let out a rattling gasp.

"I can feel him," She wheezed, her words ringing out over the now-silent crowd. She clicked her tongue, and her voice turned inward—calculating. "Their approach through the mountain is swift." She took another deep breath. "His blood calls to me."

"Yes, Illa," Kanen said in heady surprise, even as Amarie felt a serpent of fear coil around her stomach. "Feel it out. Find him."

Similar sentiments were suddenly being echoed all across the chamber as everybody whispered their own encouragement to their leader. Amarie swallowed hard, barely fighting panic as she waited to hear what happened next.

Illa exhaled heavily a second later, then took a final, shuddering gasp.

Powerful wind whipped out of nowhere and filled the room, sighing against the crowd and rustling their clothes, and though the chamber was open to the elements beyond, it had not been windy moments before. It was the kind of breeze that Amarie knew well, but it was wrong to be feeling it without her brother nearby… so wrong.

Then, as suddenly as it had come, the wind winked out and Kanen's voice rose in a hearty laugh.

"Yes, my queen!" He howled, even as Illa snarled in victory.

"Such power," Illa hissed. "I am the *wind*."

A chorus of awe-filled murmurs surrounded Amarie.

"She's going out the window," Someone nearby gasped, and the whispers grew in volume until the crowd was all but cheering.

"She's flying!"

"But where is she going?" One woman shouted in dismay.

"Aren't the royals coming up through the mountain?" Said another

"She's flying away!"

"What is she doing?" Amarie asked, pitching her voice towards where she'd last heard Kanen, but getting no reply. "Why isn't Illa going below to attack?" She tried again, this time turning to Ryian, who still stood beside her.

"She's slowing down!" Somebody called, and Amarie grit her teeth as she tried to get a hold of the situation without getting overwhelmed by all the different voices cropping up around her.

"Look, look at the clouds!" Said another. "She's stirring them up."

"Rana, Meena," Kanen's voice rang out above the crowd, pulling Amarie's focus back. "Come; let us send Illa's steed down to the battle in her stead."

"But what is she doing?" Meena asked, her voice growing closer. Amarie stepped aside as their footsteps approached, allowing them to pass.

"She's going to bring down the mountain from the outside, isn't she?" Rana asked in appreciation.

"It looks that way, doesn't it?" Kanen replied smugly, his voice mingling with the crowd once more.

Amarie didn't hear anything else the leaders said as they moved away, through the throng of people, and made their exit. She could still hear Ryian close by, but nothing else was said to her as the crowd began to filter out of the room after their commanders. Some people went quickly, still discussing Illa with varying levels of excitement, while others remained for a while longer and conversed in hushed voices.

Finally, though, the last of the Vague members left and Amarie and Ryian were left alone.

In the silence, Amarie became aware of the growing wind outside the throne room's open walls. It had started out subtly—barely there at all—but even in the short time since Illa had left, the tempest had gained strength. The thief would not have the same finesse that Prinidan did when controlling the winds, of course, but the fact that she was already both flying and beginning to call a storm, spoke to some considerable capabilities and power.

Amarie scowled to herself as she readjusted her seated position against the smooth rock wall. Her patience with the entire ordeal was beginning to waver.

The Vague might have already found the remaining royals and be fighting at that exact moment, and Amarie would be none the wiser. Was her family alright? How was poor Prinidan faring in the midst of all the bloodshed without his magic?

Even now, her siblings could be dead or dying, and she would never know.

She grunted and shook her head, chastising herself for thinking in such a way. No good would come of it. There had to be something she could do to distract herself, instead. After thinking for a moment or two, she took a breath to steel herself and lifted her chin to cast around for the sounds of Ryian sitting close by.

"Where do you keep the hostages?" She asked aloud, unsure of where exactly the question had boiled up from, but committing to it all the same. It was a relevant question, after all, for the Vague surely had at least a few once-powered Attinians locked up somewhere nearby; how else would they sap the power and share it amongst their brethren?

"Hostages?" Ryian repeated from across the room. The naked surprise in her voice was the most likely reason Amarie had gotten an answer at all.

"My people; the ones the Vague have robbed over the years. What do you do with them? Surely you don't release them all back into Attina to sound the alarm?" It was unlikely, obviously, for no such alarm had been raised until very recently. "And you can't kill them, of course; not if you want to retain their magic, anyway. That only leaves one option—"

"I'm not going to entertain this topic with you," Ryian said, her voice turning clipped and irritated. "Or any topic, for that matter." Amarie bit her lip. Perhaps she shouldn't have dislocated her guard's shoulder so soon into their relationship…

"You're right. Keeping them nearby makes the most sense." She didn't think that Ryian was going to reply, but even talking to herself was better than imagining the grisly deaths of her siblings. "I wonder how many Vague my brothers and sister will have to kill before enough powers are returned to your prisoners that they can start fighting back."

"Stop," Ryian barked through clenched teeth. Even from the distance between them, she sounded lethally annoyed. Amarie fell back into silence for another little while, her expression dark.

"Well then, what about the Vague tattoo?" She asked not many minutes later, unable to stand the way the silence creeped along her bones and set her anxiety blazing.

"On our hands?" Ryian sounded slightly surprised, despite herself, that Amarie knew of it.

"Right. That's how we first discovered that the events were connected. Why mark yourselves so obviously?"

"Aren't we already marked somewhat obviously by our distinct *lack* of markings?"

Amarie could recall only too easily how the Vague had been described to her: plain; ordinary; unsettlingly unremarkable.

"Do you all have the same body type, as well?" Amarie had long-since memorized the visual descriptions of the clan bloodlines, but she didn't really have a point of reference for the less-physical diversities. For example, though Air folks were said to be pale, it made much more sense for Amarie to focus on the equally-common Air characteristic of having lithe bodies. The same was said for Fire, with their larger physiques.

"No," Ryian answered dully. "Our tones and sizes can range all over."

That didn't exactly set them apart, so Amarie moved on.

"So, what does the circle tattoo mean?"

Ryian sighed loudly.

"It is whole on its own, but empty all the same. We have been taught by Attina that we are the same; until we find magic that calls to us."

She stood up and began to pace back and forth across the room, her footfalls as heavy as ever, but she said nothing else. Amarie tried a few times to engage her, but she was having none of it. So, for another measure of time, all was hushed once more; except for, of course, the sound of the wind howling through the canyon beyond the open walls. Illa seemed to be making progress.

It was getting stronger out there.

"What are the steeds that the leaders were arguing about?" Amarie finally spoke up again, unable to resist breaking the quiet. Ryian didn't rise to the bait, so she tried again. "Are they horses? No, surely not… not in this terrain." She hummed to herself. "Do *you* have a steed?"

"The *monarchs* have steeds," Ryian ground out, as if she could contain herself no longer. "Elemental beasts of the mountain, each suited to an element different than the one its rider holds sway with." Amarie's eyes widened. "Some others in our numbers have trained mounts as well, but none are as strong or as obedient as those that our leaders ride. They make sure of it. Now *stop* talking," She spat. "It's bad enough that Kanen commanded me to stay up here at all. I shouldn't have to listen to you, as well."

Amarie finally managed to hold her tongue as a deep worry sprouted in her chest. She'd heard rumors and legends of beasts within the mountains that were gifted with elemental magic, but she had never truly believed she would have such bad luck as to come across one. The stories about them were bad enough—gruesome tales of horrific and angry beasts—but what if her siblings actually had to fight one of them?

Worse still, what if they had to fight all three?

All Amarie could do to (somewhat) keep her thoughts in order was pray to the spirits that everybody was alright. It was the only remaining tactic to keep her feeling sane, so she did so with a vengeance, over and over again. The steadily growing fear and anxiety within her did nothing to help her tenuous state of calm, but the prayers gave her something to focus on, and they kept her from spinning out completely.

Presently, when Amarie had, once again, started to feel like she couldn't stand the quiet for a moment longer, Ryian's voice rang out and shattered the relative silence.

"Lakon! What are you doing up here?"

Amarie shot up from her slouched position, twisting her head to try and pinpoint who Ryian had spoken to. Unconsciously, she threw out her mind to try and sense the rocky floor and who walked upon it; though of course, she came up with nothing beyond the sound of a heavy pair of feet approaching.

"We have the other one," Came the grunt of a man from across the room. "He's here."

The man's footfalls were suddenly accented by the distinct sound of something, or someone, being dragged across the floor. Amarie refused to flinch as he drew closer to her. A short moment later, the newcomer dumped whatever he was dragging beside her, and before the scent even hit her, Amarie knew who it was—though something was terribly wrong.

"Prin," Amarie gasped through a sudden knot in her throat, immediately beginning to claw across the floor for her brother. She latched on tightly when she finally found him, but he didn't respond to her touch. Her hands fluttered over him for a moment or two uselessly, before she gently drew his head onto her lap.

Still, he didn't respond.

The tang of coppery blood was almost overwhelming, but try as she might, Amarie could locate no injuries along Prinidan's body, even though his torso was soaked and ever so sticky. Ryian's footsteps drew closer as Amarie continued to inspect him, but then their captor fell back and let out a cry of dismay.

"What did you do to him, Lakon!?" She squawked.

Amarie redoubled her efforts to find the source of her brother's blood. After another second or two of panicked searching, she found it; or rather, she didn't find it.

"His arm," She choked out, feeling suddenly as though a great weight was pulling her down into the earth. "Where is his arm?" Her hands traced his shoulder, which had some kind of injury that felt as though it had been stitched or recently cauterized, but below that, there was nothing.

Nothing but open space.

Heat sprang to the surface of Amarie's skin at the realization, and when her fingers hesitantly brushed the weeping, bloody stump below his shoulder, she leaned over with a sudden and unyielding urge to vomit.

When she was finished, she straightened back up. The ringing in her ears ceased after another second or two, and she was able to listen in as Ryian and Lakon discussed Prinidan in furious tones.

"*Unharmed,*" Ryian spat, followed by the dull sound of her pushing someone in the chest.

"*Alive*," Lakon shouted back. "And he is!"

"Not for long, you fool, he's unconscious from blood loss! Illa will *flay you* if he dies!"

"Then you'd best cauterize it, Ryian," He bellowed in response.

"Excuse me? You do not command me."

"If he dies, Illa will plummet from the skies—all because of *your* negligence. I would be more than happy to inform our leaders of your lapse in judgement. Kanen will be quite interested to learn why his mate is dead, I'm sure."

Amarie barely staved off panic. Time was running out while they argued. Her hands closed around Prinidan's injury, trying to staunch the flow, but she could feel the hot blood leaking past her fingers. Her brother was still breathing, but he was clammy, and his breath was coming in shallower by the second.

After another tense second, Amarie felt a sudden heat growing nearby.

"Move," Ryian snapped, stepping closer. The heat increased as she did so.

"Be careful," Amarie wheezed, letting go and fighting off a fresh wave of dizziness as her brother's flesh began crackling beside her.

"Get her away." Ryian's teeth were clenched, and Amarie felt a heavy pair of hands close around her shoulders and drag her to a standing position. She didn't bother fighting back—the focus needed to stay on Prinidan.

What felt like an eternity later, the smell of burning skin and muscle lessened some, and the crackling finally stopped. Amarie had sagged against Lakon as he held her, but when the room became silent once more, she perked up, waiting for answers.

"For now, he'll live."

Lakon released Amarie, and she immediately felt her way back to her brother. She found him and dragged herself closer, taking his head as gently as she could and resting it in her lap once more.

Her poor, dear brother…

"Remind me why you took his arm and risked him bleeding out on the trip up here?" Ryian whispered.

"He tried to take us on *unpowered*," Lakon said darkly. "But he had a sneaky dagger hidden in his boot. Stuck Hagor right in the belly."

Even as Ryian sucked a breath in through her teeth, Amarie frowned. Only one dagger? That didn't sound like Prinidan. He almost always carried the twin blades somewhere on his body; in fact, it had been him who had taught Amarie to keep her knife concealed on her person at all times—the knife that, of course, she'd misplaced sometime between the battle at the palace and being abducted.

But Prinidan's knives were like an inseparable pair. Perhaps he'd already lost the other in the skirmish when Lakon and the others set upon him.

"His fighting arm was all but useless anyway—something with his shoulder, you can still see it—and it was nothing to get the knife out of Hagor and hack off the offending limb once he was stuck in the rock," Lakon continued.

"The Vague takes appendages as punishment?" Amarie stuttered, hands laying across Prinidan's chest protectively. "Even from royal prisoners of war?"

"The Vague does not recognize dominion," Ryian growled. "Only power." She paused for a moment or two before continuing. "Stuck in the rock?" She repeated, her voice angling back towards Lakon.

"Brannon got an Earth gift from the latest group," He confirmed. "Called the rock up to hold this one's feet like it was nothing."

Amarie's eyes went wide once more. The *latest* group? Were the Vague bringing in clan prisoners and stealing their powers on the regular? All intel the neutral palace had received had led them to believe that citizens losing their gifts to the Vague was quite rare; indeed, so rare that there were no records of it.

But perhaps it was more common than anybody believed.

Amarie shuddered.

There hadn't been any mass reports of people going missing throughout the realm, she was positive. Any large number of people disappearing would have surely been cause for alarm, unless they were only being taken one or two at a time and over an extended period, she supposed. But would the population of Attina truly keep something so serious from their sovereigns?

Just as Amarie's thoughts were threatening to spin into an exhaustion-fueled maze, a deafening clap of thunder boomed through the throne room. The sound tore unforgivingly at her ear drums, and she screeched in pain. It echoed up and down the valley, louder than anything she had heard before, and by the time it blasted through the open walls of the chamber once more, it sounded as though it had been magnified ten thousand times over.

"Gods save us," Ryian shouted over the noise. "Is Illa trying to deafen us all?!"

"She's brewing quite the storm out there," Lakon called over the sound of the echoing thunder as it slowly lessened in volume. "It's going to be a powerful weapon by the time she's done."

"She could stand to save the thunder until it's needed," Ryian spat, rather disrespectfully.

"How *is* the battle going?" Amarie shouted from her place at their feet. She couldn't resist at least *trying* to get some answers. If Illa were to unlock the secret to wielding Prinidan's powers to their full extent, the others wouldn't stand a chance.

"You can mark it that I want to know as well," Ryian said in grudging tones, when Lakon didn't reply.

"We couldn't get a hold on the demon bitch," He said. "Her power runs too deep; or Rana was too weak to take it."

"Such talk is blasphemous," Ryian hissed in shock. "Rana must have simply been too far away."

"No, they were in the same cavern as each other; I saw it. Rana tried to take the magic, and she failed."

Amarie's breath caught. Not even the Vague's strongest Fire thief was powerful enough to make a mark on Zeraphall. There was hope, after all!

Her sister's gifts were lethal, *especially* in the wrong hands.

"Well then what of Water?" Ryian growled.

"No telling, yet. He's a slippery eel, that one. Meena hasn't yet gotten close enough to make an attempt."

Ryian hummed over the news for a short time, then curtly dismissed him. He obliged without complaint.

Amarie bent her head back to Prinidan as Lakon's heavy footsteps faded down the hall, and took a few breaths. The news from the battle was, surprisingly, not all bad. If Ellion could only keep away from Meena, they might be alright.

Granted, Kanen was still lurking somewhere down below with Amarie's magic, and Illa was undoubtedly figuring out more of Prinidan's with every passing moment, but perhaps their desire to stay out of the actual battle would keep them at bay. If that were the case, Zeraphall and Ellion might stand a fighting chance against the steeds and any remaining soldiers.

Amarie sighed, keeping her hands busy by stroking Prinidan's once-soft hair as the storm steadily built outside. All there was left to do was wait and see what happened. The prospect grated against her nerves more than she cared to admit, but what else could she do?

Prinidan was breathing.

She chose to focus on that. That's what mattered.

All the same, and try as she might to ward them off, unwelcome tears sprang to her eyes as she traced her brother's feverish skin above the hack line. She had to hold her breath to keep from falling apart entirely, and it was only because of this, that she heard Prinidan give a shallow, wheezing gasp.

"What was that?" Ryian said instantly from the center of the room, her ears alarmingly keen. Amarie heard her clothing and armour rustle as she no doubt turned to look at them. Without missing a beat, though, Amarie fabricated her own loud wheeze in a close mimicry of Prinidan's, choosing to disguise the sound as something between a gasp and a wail.

"Oh, dear Prinidan," She cried out, as loudly as she dared, and placed her hands over her brother. After a second, she heard their captor give a dismissive sniff, but Amarie could spare Ryian no more attention. Prinidan had just taken another shaky breath.

In the following quiet, two near-silent words escaped his dry throat.

"Dagger. Boot."

Chapter 11

Amarie felt her blood run cold as the whispered words faded in her ears.

Prinidan, lying on his back in Amarie's lap, was feeling extremely disoriented, but even from the bare few moments he'd spent fighting his way back to consciousness as the group spoke around him, he'd understood the importance of staying silent. With a pain-riddled grimace, he tried to squeeze Amarie's arm… but something was wrong. The muscles of his hand weren't responding to him properly. After another second or two, however, his sister shifted minutely, and dipped her head in the barest nod.

She'd heard him.

Feeling relieved that he wouldn't have to try and speak again, Prinidan then began to cast his eyes around the room to try and get his bearings. A thick, foggy haze had settled over his eyes, but if he squinted, he could manage.

The chamber was large and high-ceilinged, open on either end like the ones he had seen down below, and in the middle was a woman with her back to them. There was a dais with four chairs on the far side, and even from a distance, Prinidan could tell that the chairs were ornately carved—had he perhaps been taken to the Vague throne room?

He glanced back to the woman, but a wave of dizziness washed over him at the same moment, and to avoid retching on the floor and ruining any chance they had of stealth, he closed his eyes. The sudden, clammy feeling that swept through his body was all too familiar, for it was the same sort of wooziness he'd felt after his fight with the Air creature.

But when had he suffered more serious blood loss?

He tried to recall what had happened directly before he'd woken up there in the upper chamber, but a dull and insistent pounding in his head kept him from pinpointing any particular moment. He remembered losing his magic in the stairwell, as well as the cold and hopeless feeling that had overtaken him since then.

Zeraphall and Ellion had put up a vicious fight, and he recalled the deep shame he'd felt at having to stand by, doing nothing, while his siblings went ahead and risked everything. But even without his help, the duo had eventually cleared the chamber, only to be set upon by even more Vague members before they could move on. They'd all been so busy, in fact, that none of them had noticed the men who crept up from behind, up the stairwell they'd only just ascended.

Prinidan could remember gutting one of them with one of his daggers, but the rest fell into haze after that. The pounding in his head increased as he tried to bring more memories to the surface, and in seconds, he succumbed once more to unconsciousness.

The shift in her brother's musculature was easily noticeable to Amarie.

One moment, he had been holding himself tensely in her grasp—as if ready to try and spring up at any moment—and the next, he had gone limp again. She chewed her lip as Prinidan settled more deeply against her, forcing her heart rate to slow and her breathing to come in evenly. She understood what she had to do, and what was needed to get there. And though it felt entirely impossible, she began to work up the courage to do it.

Slowly, silently, *so* carefully, Amarie began to shift Prinidan so she could access his boots. She knew he'd already lost one dagger attempting to fight off Lakon and the other men, so that left her to guess which boot still held a blade; not to mention having to do it all without Ryian noticing.

And that was only the beginning.

Inch by inch, Amarie began to slide her brother farther across her lap. He wasn't especially heavy, but the angle was awkward, and the strain of moving him while not moving him *too much*, was immense.

There could be no mistakes; no jostling or movement that Ryian would catch out of the corner of her eye. It was Amarie's only chance at success, though for all she knew, Ryian might already be watching, anyway. Their captor could even be creeping over at that very moment, waiting to attack until the last second. Amarie would never know she was there until the blow landed…

But no, that wouldn't do.

She blinked once, hard, and made herself calm back down. Focus. Continue.

Finally, through nerves and forced-calm alone, Amarie felt as though she'd shifted Prinidan far enough to access his boot. So, with her teeth clamped together tightly, she began twitching her hand down his body at a hundredth of its regular speed.

She first encountered the rough fabric and hard thread of his winter tunic, and from there, her fingers brushed against the soft leather that lined the garment's base to keep out snow. The leggings he wore were thick and fur-lined, and she found that a few of the seams were beginning to fray near the edges. Great crusty patches of what could only be dried blood scraped against her touch as she moved along, and then her fingers landed against the cold, hard leather of his boot.

Bracing her arm against his knee so she wouldn't lose track of where her hand was, Amarie then began the arduous process of discreetly searching across the top of the boot—inside the leather, as well as around his actual leg. In time, she was sure that she'd felt all around the top of it, yet nothing had greeted her grasping fingers.

No luck.

Cursing and screaming internally, and barely holding back tears, Amarie started gradually moving her hand over to locate his other leg.

Another great boom of thunder shook the stone of the mountain, making Amarie jump, but she used the moment to cut her hand across Prinidan's body and save herself a great deal of time.

"Gods!" Ryian cursed, and though Amarie's heart lurched to her throat as she heard Ryian leap to her feet, the guard rushed to the large window, and not towards her. With wide eyes, barely conscious of what she was doing, Amarie began rifling across the top of Prinidan's second boot while Ryian's footsteps slowly grew farther away.

The dagger had to be there.

She dug and dug, more frantically by the second, twisting her fingers painfully inside the stiff leather, until finally, at long last, she hit the cold metal of a hilt. It was wedged against his leg tightly, but Amarie didn't have time to spare worrying about whether or not it was going to cut him.

With only the slightest wince, The Earth Queen secured her hold on the dagger and ripped it free of her brother's boot. She slammed it underneath his tunic to hide it, throwing caution to the winds, and feverishly covered it up within the folds of fabric.

"What of the storm?" She croaked, once she was sure that the dagger was hidden from view.

"Illa is hovering in front of the cloud cover, some way off from the rock. Her storm is hammering the mountainside below us like it has a mind of its own." Ryian's voice was shrewd, though not entirely awed.

Amarie's mind began to buzz. Ellion and Zeraphall would be fighting against the very air they were breathing—unless Illa had already drowned them where they stood, of course. But surely, Illa wouldn't steal the oxygen from the entirety of the battle… she couldn't. It would doom the Vague's own soldiers as well as the true royals, and Amarie doubted she would have already worked out enough finesse to pinpoint who she attacked in that way. Even Prinidan rarely used that aspect of his gift, for it was far too risky. It was an extremely dangerous practice to use on a mixed battleground; unless the wielder didn't care who got in the way, that is.

Amarie shivered.

"The eel and the demon are making good time through the mountain," Ryian added, resorting to Lakon's names for the royals. "They might be having quite a time at the holding pens after all," She added quietly, referencing Amarie's earlier question about where they kept the hostages.

"Holding pens?" She echoed all the same.

"You were right enough. Keeping the strongest and most unique powers nearby makes it easier to pass the magic along, when needed."

Amarie blinked in mute disgust. Of course, that's what she and her siblings had assumed the Vague did with many of the Attinian prisoners, but it was quite another thing to have their assumptions confirmed.

"You keep them in *pens*?" She repeated in shock, that key piece of information an unwelcome surprise.

"That's what their quarters are called," Ryian amended slowly. "We keep them all as healthy as necessary to ensure a continual source of power for ourselves. It wouldn't do if they died and stole our magic."

Amarie fairly snarled at the idea. How could the original owners of the powers steal them? It was their right! Their spirit-given birthright!

"You keep my people hostage and trade their soul song between yourselves like it's nothing more than a goblet to get drunk off of!" She could feel herself losing control by the second. Her body began shaking. "You're all gluttonous fools!"

"It is what we have been *forced* to do, to keep hold on our power," Ryian replied in a hard, even voice. "It's not *our* fault that the spirits of Attina chose your people to bless and my people to scorn. Why else do you think we serve and worship our own gods? Even the animals of the mountains received magical gifts from your saints. *The animals!* What, are we no better than common beasts? They do not deserve our praise." Her voice turned deep and dangerous, but Amarie did not balk. "For too long have the powered found favour in Attina." Now she'd stood up, and her footsteps were approaching quickly. Amarie had only a half-second to ensure the fabric was still covering Prinidan's dagger before she was upon them. "The Vague have had enough, and our monarchs have risen to balance the scales. *Our* Four against *Attina's*." Her last words came out as a sneer. "And look how it's going so far."

The thunder clapped at a painful volume, as if to highlight her words.

"What scales? There's nothing to balance!" Amarie barked somewhat frantically over the gale, barely resisting the urge to stand up. She knew that picking a fight with Ryian served no ultimate purpose, but the tension of the morning was finally breaking, and she dared not stop. "We didn't take *anything* from you. What me and my people have is our birthright; our magic is something we've always had! We stole from *no one*! If you're angry over what you and the rest of the Vague lack, take it up with the spirits or your useless gods, and leave the realm out of it." Amarie was breathing hard, reveling in the feeling of her anger as it flowed hot and fast through her veins. "Maybe there's *a reason* your horrible people were overlooked."

"You're saying you're better than me?" A whisper.

"No need to," Amarie snapped. "You've already made it perfectly clear."

Ryian roared in indignation, slapping Amarie's face with a burning hand. Amarie reeled back in surprise and banged her head on the wall, not having known Ryian had gotten so close. She covered the spot while pain itched its way through her skin and the burn settled.

"Don't fool yourself," Ryian hissed. "You're not special, Amarie, and you never have been—you were nothing but a baby who was born at the right time and given a pretty rock to play with. If I'd been given the same rock, it would be me in your place, and you'd be nothing more than a low-level Earth wielding *cripple*."

"That's not true," Amarie said in dangerous tones, but Ryian jeered at her and closed the distance back to her original place in the center of the room. The Earth Queen took a few breaths to slow her anger as her captor finally strode off, mastering herself as best she could, before gripping the dagger tightly against Prinidan's unconscious form.

She would not miss.

—

"Zera!" Ellion shouted, hurling a great sliver of ice over his sister's head a mere second after she ducked.

The shard imbedded into the chest of the woman who had been sneaking up directly behind the Fire Queen. It pierced her body and sent her crashing to the floor. She had been armed with a wicked-looking knife, and had clearly had some measure of fire-proof magic which allowed her to get so close to Zeraphall's armour of magma and fire in the first place. When the icicle sank into her chest, however, the pain was evidently too great for her to keep hold of her gifts. Her skin started blistering in Zeraphall's heat as soon as Ellion's attack hit and her fire-proofing vanished. Her death was quick and brutal.

Zeraphall straightened and gave a nod of thanks to her brother for the assistance, though she shouldn't have needed it. She *should* have been paying proper attention, but she was feeling a little bit out of sorts. They'd just fought off a woman who had shown up and tried to steal her magic. She had undoubtedly been one of the powerful Vague members intended to cut the royal's gifts away; though fortunately, her attack on Zeraphall had failed. The tide of the battle would have turned, and quickly, if it had succeeded.

All the same, it had left Zeraphall feeling shaken.

It had felt like hanging above a canyon on a rope and almost having it tugged out of her hands, only to clamp on at the last second and hold with all her might. The lurching sensation in her stomach had been enough to greatly disturb her, but the fire in her soul, thankfully, had remained.

"Again, Rana!" One of the members blocking the woman from view had screamed, and Zeraphall had felt another tug, but that time she was prepared and had held on more firmly. She hadn't even been sure what she was holding onto—it felt like the essence of her soul—but whatever it was, she didn't let go.

Anger had all but blurred her vision, but before either she or Ellion had been able to do anything in retaliation, a further swarm of Vague had poured into the bottleneck chamber and the woman, Rana, had disappeared with a host of others.

To make matters worse, sometime between Rana distracting Zeraphall, and Ellion trying to fight for all three of them, Prinidan had disappeared. He'd been behind them one moment, hacking away at anybody who came too close with his daggers, and the next, he'd been gone. In a panic, his siblings had fought over to where they'd last seen him, but there was no sign, other than a puddle of blood that was frozen to the icy floor, and a dead Vague man.

The horror of truly realizing that the Vague had him only increased the vigour with which the remaining pair fought, spurring them on into a near frenzy. And just in time, it would seem, for the full force of the Vague was quickly rising up against them.

Not every member that came at them was gifted, but there was more than enough magic being thrown around to make up for any who lacked; and even those without stolen elements were still dangerous, armed to the teeth as they were, with spears, knives, and other weapons. Worse still, an out-of-season storm had broken outside, bringing with it hurricane-level winds and lightning.

It was surely Prinidan's power at work.

It also became clear that the design and location of the chambers within mountain lair had been precise, planned to leave intruders open to elemental attacks from all sides. The wind fairly howled through the open-walls of the bottleneck chamber as the siblings tried to move forward, throwing them off balance and ripping at their clothes. The duo started catching glimpses of a person hovering in and out of view as they fought past the windows as well, and they could only assume that it was Prinidan's thief at last. Whoever they were, they were certainly starting to get the feel for his magic.

The building pressure system finally brought the rains as well, which Prinidan's thief could do nothing about, so Ellion took full advantage of it while he still could. He funneled all of the mountain-cooled water inside before it froze to snow, forming it into powerful whips and jets that lashed out at any oncoming attackers. Some of it, he allowed to harden to ice, and used it as physical weapons meant to slice, puncture, and disembowel. He kept the rest malleable, which was all the better for twisting around and neutralizing his prey.

Once or twice, Ellion even brought the molecules of the air's moisture together to form huge columns of water and clear swaths through the lines of approaching enemies, but such largescale attacks were quite tiring, so he used them sparingly. When he did use them, though, he would direct them side to side like great battering rams, catching the members unaware and sending them over the edges of the mountain; however, he could not keep up that level of power forever. Fortunately, Zeraphall was always there to pick up the pieces.

Side by side, few could stand against them.

Fighting through the growing wind, the Fire Queen decimated all who stood in her way; and any that escaped her brother's wrath. She did have to be mindful of Ellion's proximity to her, though, for if she truly unleashed herself on their enemies all at once, he would surely feel the brunt of the attack, too. He could do similar damage to her, if he tried, but Zeraphall's fire was more deadly than his water, at least in the short term—so she had to be aware. It didn't slow her down, though, for there were more than enough enemies to pick from.

Many of the Fire wielders had some measure of resistance to heat, depending on the level of their strength, and Zeraphall was frustrated to be finding them cropping up more and more. She would be attempting to burn down an oncoming group, only to find that not all of them would fall, and those remaining would come at her with attacks of their own. Her magma-coated body did wonders in keeping them away from her physically, because even those resistant to her would be foolish to come in so close, but it did nothing to hinder them from trying to attack her in other ways—with physical weapons especially, like knives and throwing spears.

They started getting smart, as well. No doubt seeing that the siblings were a force to be reckoned with when working together, Fire and Water-inclined members began heading off the groups that rose against either royal, all the while shielding others behind them.

The ones in the front would block (or absorb and sacrifice themselves) the initial attack, then break off to free up the firing lane for those who came behind them.

And they just kept coming. It seemed that the bottleneck chamber was where the thieves had decided to hit them with full-force, and the tide of them felt endless.

A veritable army hidden within the mountains.

The Earth thieves were out for blood as well, for everywhere the royal siblings looked, they could see boulders and rocks coming at them from the floors and walls. Some rocks melted before they reached Zeraphall, or froze and shattered before reaching Ellion, but many others broke through with bone-rattling contact.

The Air thieves, too, were taking all the help they could get from Illa. The wind was already so strong that it seemed all-too easy for even the weaker Vague members to simply redirect it into more hazardous angles to distract and delay. Some of them were stronger, and could actually buffet the royals or hit them with pockets of pressure, but many and more simply used what was already there to their advantage.

Zeraphall had just turned to Ellion to shout that they needed a new and better tactic, when the stone lurched violently under their feet and everyone in the cave was thrown off balance. Vague and royal alike exclaimed in surprise and fear as they hit the floor. Millions of pounds of stone groaned and creaked around them on all sides as the rock came alive, and suddenly, they felt ever so small.

"Amarie's gifts!?" Ellion yelled to his sister, struggling to stand as the mountain shuddered again. Zeraphall shrugged mutely as she attempted to stagger upright as well.

Their questions were answered seconds later, when a massive horse-like animal smashed up through the floor from the chamber beneath, just a short distance away from where the siblings stood. The rocks splintered away from the beast as it ascended, as though the stone was as breakable as glass, and in seconds, it had found its footing.

The royals were vaguely aware of their enemies still in the archway of the room, but they had little attention to spare as the monster turned and fixed them with a large, black eye.

The animal's body looked to be made of obsidian rock; black, unforgiving, and lethally edged. Instead of a mane, the horse had spikes of rock travelling down its neck, all of which ended in needle points, and its hooves were so sharp that they left gouges in the stone where it stepped. The creature's angled face was long and otherworldly, with a snout that tapered off into a jagged spike, and a mouth full of rocky, paper-thin teeth. It looked at Ellion and Zeraphall for all of a second before it let loose a bellow and bent into a charge.

It was all either of the royals could do to throw up weak barriers of flame and ice and dance out of the way as the creature galloped across the floor. As it raced past, its sharp flank clipped Ellion, despite his best efforts to dodge it, and whipped him around with a great heave. The blow was powerful enough to cut through and shatter the ice armour on his shoulder, and his vision blurred in pain; however, Zeraphall seized him and yanked him back around before he could truly stumble.

"It's wearing an empty saddle," She hissed, shaking out the cold in her hand that Ellion's ice-covered skin had left when she'd grabbed him. In seconds, the flames had pooled back on her hand.

"They *ride* them!?" Ellion said somewhat hoarsely, eyes now trained on the beast as it finished its charge and began a wide, taunting circle. The remaining Vague fell back in dismay as the horse neared them, but it seemed that the royals were its target. Ellion flexed his arm and called the moisture in the air to his shoulder, which quickly thickened and repaired the damage that had been done to his armour; unfortunately, however, it did nothing for the pain.

He could feel the blood trickling down his arm from the point of contact, as well, but he didn't have time to inspect it. Instead, he directed the inner layer of his armour straight towards and into the wound. The ice formed and grew where he commanded it to, and though it was quite uncomfortable, he pressed it against the injury and thickened it still more. Extreme cold applied directly to the wound would force his blood vessels to constrict and hopefully let his body form a clot more quickly, which would, in turn, slow or stop the bleed until he could look at it more closely.

It certainly wasn't as effective as Zeraphall's cauterization, but in the moment, it would have to do.

Ellion completed his quick-fix solution, but the creature was already roaring again. It thrashed its head at them from across the room, and as it did so, the mane-like spikes of rock on its neck dislodged and were hurled towards the royals. The animal was a good distance from them, but even so, the shards of obsidian flew at the pair with troubling speed. Both siblings reacted, slicing their hands through the air to neutralize the threat, but Zeraphall screeched in pain only a short moment after.

A thick spear, coated in ice, had become impaled in her back, right in the meat of her torso. It was already melting due to the heat of her armour—ice, wood, stone, and all—but it had done its damage. She took a breath through her teeth, turning around to zero in on the Vague members still alive in the chamber, who were now clustered around the arch to the hallway.

They were cowards, all.

With a snarl, the heat pouring off of Zeraphall's body became even more intense, and the wood of the spear sagged. The heat was so strong, and so sudden, that Ellion had to jump back from her.

The Earth horse reared up to charge again, but Zeraphall had turned her back on it. She had already lifted her hands and began igniting the bodies of the Vague that still stood in the cavern. It was a reckless use of power and energy—surely, she could have found a more conservative way to dispatch them—but she didn't care. The screaming only lasted a few seconds, but by then, the monster was almost upon them.

Fortunately, Ellion was prepared. With a swivel that momentarily put his own back to the beast, he did a few things simultaneously.

While he spun around, Ellion changed position rapidly and ripped the remains of the spear out of his sister's back. He secured the weapon in his hand, and at the same time, brought his other arm through the air and towards the archway where Zeraphall was burning the bodies. With merely a wave of his free hand, he commanded a great barrier of ice to form there, floor to ceiling, intended to keep any new attackers at bay while they dealt with the beast. Then, before he even completed his spin on Zeraphall's other side, he hurled the half-melted javelin with all the fury and might of a hardened spear fisherman.

And, as the weapon twisted through the air towards the incoming animal, Ellion's eyes sparked, causing deadly-sharp ice to reform and lengthen the spear's point, on and on, until it could have pierced a whale.

It hit with deadly precision.

Even as the horse screamed and fell to the ground, the ice continued to grow, through its body and saddle and down into the rock, making escape impossible. The sharpened edges of the animal's hide left gouges in the stone underneath it, but struggle though it might, it could not get away.

It had all happened so quickly that Zeraphall hadn't even reacted to the spear being ripped out of her by the time it was over. As the beast's initial bellow of agony ceased, she doubled over in pain while the heat of her body closed the wound. After a second or two, she managed to straighten, but her teeth were set. The wound might be closed, but not even fire could heal the damage that had been done internally. Fortunately, Ellion's quick thinking with the ice barrier had afforded them a few extra minutes to collect themselves, as best they could, before moving on.

"How are you doing in there?" She croaked when she figured she could speak, tapping a finger against her brother's ice-encased chest as they turned towards the archway. His armour hissed and sputtered at her touch, but reformed almost instantly when she removed her hand.

"Well enough, I suppose," Ellion said, his breath coming in shallower than he would like. "I don't know if I'll last much longer if Amarie's thief makes an actual showing, though."

"Nor I," Zeraphall agreed grimly, the veritable hole in her torso pulsing with her heartbeat. "Prinidan's, either."

The figure that had been swooping in and out of the far clouds during the initial battle in the bottle-necked room had finally become still. Ellion and Zeraphall could just make them out, hovering in front of the growing storm network outside. The thief's hair was in disarray, and their arms were spread wide, as if to embrace the tempest.

"It makes me uneasy," Ellion admitted, stalking up to the ice barrier he'd created and melting it to water with a touch, once he was sure there was no one on the other side. "Why haven't they come and just blown us off the mountain?"

"They might be scared of us." Zeraphall tossed out her curly hair, which released a few puffs of smoke. "After all, it just takes one hit that's bad enough to be a distraction for them to lose their power."

"Maybe," Ellion reminded her.

"Probably," She countered, refusing to let go of the one belief that might provide them with a chance to see victory.

They'd seen a few Vague members lose their gifts during the recent skirmishes, but there was no definitive way to be sure it was because of distraction or pain that the magic had disappeared. Rog had claimed as much back in the palace dungeons when they questioned him—anything strong enough to hold the mind's main focus would do it, he'd said—but he was still Vague, and therefore, his word was not entirely trustworthy. But Zeraphall had to hope.

The siblings eventually left the chamber and the body of the beast behind, still turning everything over in their minds, and crossed into another windowless hall. For a moment, they merely stood there, leaning against the close-set walls, reveling in the reprieve from the ceaseless winds in the open chambers.

"I'm tired, Ell," Zeraphall admitted, massaging her temples with a burning hand. Rarely had they had cause to push their magic to such extremes. Ellion hummed in pained understanding.

"How many have we fought, now?" He frowned and tried to recall. The different encounters had started blurring together.

"Three or four main bodies of attackers?" Zeraphall guessed after a beat. "A thousand?"

"They can't have many more soldiers to throw at us… can they?" Ellion asked quietly, meaning it more as a rhetorical question than anything. He knew they *could*… but he also knew that if they *did*, it might mean terrible things for the realm.

"We haven't even met the strongest ones yet, Ell," Zeraphall reminded him. "They tried and failed to take my magic, but you haven't been attacked yet, and Amarie's thief hasn't even shown up."

"Maybe they won't show up," Ellion tried hopefully. "Maybe they'll just take my magic and leave you alone."

Zeraphall allowed a tired smile, but shook her head.

"It's going to get worse before it gets better, Ellion."

Once they'd rested for as long as they could reasonably risk, the exhausted royals moved on. The followed the thin windowless hall into another series of empty rooms and curving lobbies, until finally, they entered a circular amphitheatre. There were still windows on either end that revealed twin balconies outside, but everywhere else, the stone walls rose up on lazy angles until they met the ceiling high above. The room had a disturbingly arena-like feel to it, but it was at least still empty.

They also had a much cleaner view of Prinidan's thief by then, after having traversed the curving halls of the mountain below. The storm outside had reached its peak, it seemed, though had not yet boiled over, but whether the thief was waiting for something, or if they simply didn't know how to finish the job, Zeraphall and Ellion had no idea.

The duo closed the distance to the nearest balcony and gazed out.

At first, to their great surprise, the woman looked to be of the Air bloodline after all; upon closer inspection, however, they found that her hair was not white, but rather the yellowish colour that many of the Vague members had so far sported. Her hair was whipping all around her, and though she was facing the storm with her back to them, she painted quite the frightening picture. Torrents of wind were visibly rolling off of her in a show of power that not even Prinidan had ever displayed.

"Look at that supercell," Ellion murmured, his eyes reflecting the churning clouds above them. They'd purpled, and the lightning had now become focused deep within it, highlighted every so often by deafening thunder. The winds, as well, seemed even stronger than they had moments before.

"Is she forming a tornado?" Zeraphall asked as she massaged the still-prickling injury from the spear. She had spent less time learning the in-depth workings of Prinidan's pressure systems than Ellion had.

"Not yet," Ellion muttered. "But she might figure that out soon."

The cloud system outside was easily larger than the mountain itself was, in both width and height. It had come together into a massive circular formation, with the outermost walls of cloud turning lazily, but picking up speed by the second. Looking out from the balcony, Ellion and Zeraphall could see up and into the storm system, as though it were a gigantic, hollow cylinder. They couldn't look at it for long, though, for the sheet lightning within it was so aggressive that it hurt their eyes.

"Can she actually control that thing?" Zeraphall asked skeptically, blinking as she turned to her brother.

"No idea," Ellion replied. "I could pull the ice particles and moisture away to stop the lightning, but I'm not sure what good that would really do. The wind and pressure would still be there."

Then, as if the storm had entered the cavern and suddenly surrounded them, a loud gurgling noise bubbled up from across the room.

The pair spun to face the far balcony where the sound had originated, putting their backs to Prinidan's thief, just in time to see some kind of mass land on the sculpted rock with a surprisingly loud *splat*.

At first, the siblings were too stunned to react. Whatever the writhing ball was, it had barely held its shape through the fall to the balcony, and was just sitting there, pulsing and dripping. It was poison purple, from what they could see, with sickly green and white speckles coating it—not unlike some of the mushrooms that Amarie had created back in the palace forests.

But then, before they'd fully registered what it could even be, an arc of twisting water shot from within the jiggling form and barreled into Zeraphall with alarming force. She heaved as the wind was knocked out of her and the injury at her side all but screamed—even though Ellion evaporated the water to mist as soon as contact was made—but had no words, for the creature had taken the split-second of distraction to unfold and reveal itself.

Thick, dripping tentacles oozed out from the main bulk of the body, where there had been no tentacles before. On and on they stretched, as painfully purple as the main body itself, and blindly searched the room for something to hold to. Too far, too long, they just kept coming across the chamber. More arms, and more, far more than any octopus or spider that the siblings had ever seen or heard tell of. Over the floor, up the walls, across the ceiling, the tentacles continued to roam.

As the beast unfurled, its body finally straightened out, which allowed it to fix the duo with countless sets of rolling red eyes. Its pupils were dilated and moved around ceaselessly inside of the wet, red orbs, catching on the royals for a second or two, before twisting up behind the lids and back again. The entirety of the animal shivered and moved as its eyes rolled, solid but not solid, as if it was made of pure water and pulsed with the heart of a haunted sea.

Another gurgling moan attacked the royals' ears.

"What *is* it—" Zeraphall gasped, finally catching her breath, but Ellion sliced a hand towards the creature before he'd registered her words. He made a quick but powerful attempt to control the water within the monster, call it to him—conquer it. It seemed as though the animal was *made* from water, so then logically, Ellion should have been able to master it.

But somehow, someway, the beast resisted; not only resisted, but *fought back*. Even as Ellion twisted his arms to find a hold, the creature alighted onto a swift wave of its own making and flew into the chamber towards them.

Seeing no other option, Ellion rushed on to meet it.

Zeraphall lifted her own hands to attack alongside her brother, but then she felt a telling prickle in the back of her conscious mind. It was the familiar itch of flame—burning hot despite the rain outside—but it was not one of hers, and it was old… so old… as if it had been burning since the beginning of time.

The Fire Queen spun.

On the balcony now stood another monster, this one so great, that Zeraphall had to fight not to trip over herself in an effort to put space between it and herself. For a moment, the only thought in her mind was to *get away*. She would take the octopus over what now stood before her in a heartbeat.

A gargantuan red and black lizard, all scales and teeth, stood crouched in the rain like a snake ready to strike, its eyes fixed directly on her. Its neck was impossibly long, and curved red spikes grew from its head, down its back, all the way to the lethal barbs of its mace-like tail. A tongue with long forks swept out of its mouth to taste the air, and horror-size wings unfurled from its back, hooked and clawed.

An empty saddle was strapped to the upper spikes between its wings.

Zeraphall couldn't even express her surprise at seeing something like that on such a beast, before it unleashed a roar so aggressive and so powerful that, that her mind was almost wiped blank in shock. And, as the behemoth's cry thundered, a mountain of blue-violet fire erupted from within the depths of its black throat and cascaded towards them.

"Dragon," Zeraphall breathed in awed and horrified disbelief, leaping to press her back into Ellion so that she could protect him from the flames rushing forward. The magical fire didn't want to listen to her, but with a great effort, she tamed it before it reached them; however, it took so much strength and focus that the glow of her magma-armour lessened slightly.

Dragons were of legend in Attina, and were the only living things rumored to have been elemental *before* the great spirits had arrived. There were few—if any, Zeraphall had thought—dragons left in existence, and though the Four had been taught of them in children's stories and songs, they'd never expected to meet one.

Perilously smart and evil to the core, dragons were not creatures one met and walked away from. But all the same, when the thing sent out another blast of fire that Zeraphall barely managed to control once more, there was no mistaking it.

The Vague had tamed a dragon.

Or, more likely, they had somehow convinced it to work with them. But how they had gotten a saddle on it was a question that Zeraphall couldn't even begin to fathom the answer to. She pushed her confusion and wonder to the back of her mind as both creatures began a slow approach.

It was time for a final, great fight.

Ellion had managed to stop the water beast on its wave before it got too close, but he had only barely kept it at bay. Thankfully, he didn't have to split his focus, for Zeraphall was dealing with the monster behind them; if he'd been alone, he would have surely been overcome.

With grim focus, Ellion tuned into the main body of the octopus, which he could only assume was also the head, but even as he did so, tentacles rained down from above. They would grow and fill with water in a steady rhythm, as if in time with the monster's heartbeat, and would eventually become so full and heavy that their suction on the ceiling would fail. As a result, the stinking, elongated tubers would crash down to the floor, creating waves powerful enough to shake the royals on their feet. Once expended, the limbs would shrink back into the main body to refill, before leeching out again, creeping back to attack anew.

And though he was putting up a magnificent fight, Ellion couldn't seem to find a hold on it. Every blast of moisture he sent its way was somehow absorbed, as if the beast was taking his strength and sending it back at him, magnified. Just as he thought he might have found a strong enough grasp, a crack of lightning hit the corner of the balcony in front of him, and Ellion was momentarily blinded. He cursed himself for not dispersing the storm earlier, but it was too late. The creature, who had not been facing the lightning strike with any of its many eyes, recalled some of its legs and bunched them under itself to come at him with speed.

Zeraphall was faring no better. She was managing to tame all of the fire being belched towards them, but the dragon was so strong that she could get no hits in of her own. The only redeeming factor about the situation was that the beast seemed too large to be able to fit into the chamber from the balcony door.

Even still, Zeraphall was fighting a losing battle.

At one point, she tried to attack rather than defend, sending a blast of flame-laced power towards the creature, but it did little and less. It made contact, to be sure, and though the beast faltered for a moment, it barely batted an eye in the end. She then tried to leech the fire from it, calling whatever she could claim, and though she felt a welcome surge of heat bolster her own magic, the beast simply bellowed at her and reignited of its own accord.

It was like she could find no tether of magic to snip free. She could pull and pull as much fire from it as she wanted, but it seemed endless. Every time she thought she'd gained ground, the dragon would only ignite even hotter than before. Was this how Zeraphall's own wells of power had felt to the Vague woman who had tried to rob her earlier? Hopelessly deep, and impossibly secure?

Zeraphall even attempted to lean into the inrush of power from the creature as it attacked again, but without a set defensive plan in mind, a stray blast of fire that she hadn't absorbed washed over them. Zeraphall felt no pain, of course, but Ellion, who stood nearby as he fought the octopus, felt the armour melt off of his back.

The attack he'd been instigating plateaued, pulsing with enough power to possibly send the Water monster backward a few paces, but then ceased entirely.

"No," Zeraphall snarled as her brother gave a rare howl of pain and fell to one knee. She tripped backward and withdrew the heat from his burns with one hand, while doing her best to shield him from the dragon with the other.

What she did wasn't comfortable, but it allowed Ellion to focus past the worst of the pain and reform his armour. He didn't even have the strength to thank her; all his focus went into thickening the ice over his burns before the octopus refilled and attacked again.

To give him as much time as she could, Zeraphall heated and detonated two soaking wet boulders simultaneously with a clench of her fist; one bomb went off beside the Water beast, and the other exploded beside the dragon. She felt the sap on her dwindling strength immediately, but she gritted her teeth and stood strong.

For a hopeful moment, it looked like the bombs would actually do the trick and subdue their enemies; the dragon grunted in pain, and the octopus was thrown onto its back, revealing an underside pockmarked with massive suction cups and a huge, clicking beak. Unfortunately, any rock shrapnel that would have done real damage to the animals was caught mid-detonation by an invisible force, and thrown harmlessly to the ground.

There was an Earth wielder somewhere nearby.

"*Conflagration!* I can't overtake this thing," Zeraphall snarled, focusing on the more prominent problem as the dragon reared to attack again. "Fire can't touch it; it's *too* hot—and there's an Earth thief in here somewhere."

Neither of them had the breath or energy to worry if it was Amarie's thief come at last.

"I can switch," Ellion spat through his teeth, sending a rocket of frozen rain towards the octopus while it righted itself. Finally, his attack made contact. The animal yelped as its seemingly-delicate skin was pierced hundreds of times over, but the siblings had already switched positions.

Before the octopus had managed to shake free of the tiny spikes, Zeraphall let loose a roar of her own and encased it in a cage of floor-to-ceiling flame. The fire burned hot, matching the queen's rage, and grew hotter every second.

Most of the tentacles still covering the walls writhed as the monster withdrew them, streaking them through the fire to fold them underneath itself, but a few of its arms burned off before it could pull them to safety. The severed appendages fell and smashed to floor, twisting and squirming while the nerves slowly died.

She locked her teeth together as fatigue began settling in her soul, fighting to hold the wall of flame in place as the animal unleashed all of its strength against her. It formed a waterspout around itself, which spun and built until Zeraphall could feel the pressure buzzing within her own blood. Every time even one *spark* of that flame was stifled, she pumped her heart's song into it and rekindled it once more. She refused to surrender an inch.

Behind her, Ellion had gone to task against the dragon.

It continued sending forth fire while Zeraphall severed the octopus' tentacles behind them, but Ellion was prepared. Each time the flames rolled towards him, he called up a great wave of rain and ice to stifle it. It was close, sometimes, but he was not burned again. At one point, his water began to boil due to the close proximity of the dragon, but he didn't let it slow him down, and he didn't let it evaporate. As long as he stayed vigilant, it remained in its liquid state, and continued to bend to his will.

The pouring rain outside was already so cold from the mountain air, that freezing it to snow and ice took but an afterthought from the King of Water. What had started as rain pelting against the dragon soon became snow and tiny blades of ice. It bellowed, more annoyed than hurt, but Ellion swept forward into its distraction like the tide.

In a heartbeat, he froze the deepening puddles on the balcony and sent them upward with as much force and speed as he could manage, honing their icy points until they resembled the wickedest of knives.

The dragon was hit so hard by Ellion's magic that it was almost thrust into the air. It screamed as its underbelly was pierced and flayed wide, and it threw out its massive wings in apparent panic. It caught him in its gaze and hissed at him, but then it leapt into the oncoming rain. It rose into the air, rushing to latch onto the rocks, as if it planned to climb up the outside of the mountain simply to get away from him. The beast was howling in agony, and Ellion could now see copious blood mingling with the rain on the stone terrace; unfortunately, his attention was snagged by something else.

When the massive animal had moved, a man was revealed.

With a twitch of the stranger's fingers, two pillars of stone came hurtling towards Ellion. The rocks slammed together, missing their target by a bare few inches. The columns clattered to the ground on contact, a testament to the man's use of unfamiliar (and stolen) magic, but then even the gravel began shuddering at his command.

While all of this was happening outside, Zeraphall had finally managed to shrink the ring of fire enclosing the Water monster. Little by little, the creature was weakening. It was proving to be surprisingly hard to kill, but the end was near.

Each sibling was so focused on their own respective battles that neither of them noticed the woman who was now standing near the edge of the chamber where Zeraphall was fighting. She was meek, with drab brown hair and dark olive skin. Her small hands were folded behind her back, and her teeth were bared in deadly aggression.

Back on the balcony, Ellion swung a whip of ice towards the man who could only be Amarie's thief, twirling still more moisture to him in a fantastic cyclone of rain and wind-fueled power, but then he fumbled. His hand was extended before him, but suddenly, he grasped at nothing.

As he watched, the ice coating his hand melted off, and powerful nausea built up within his soul. With a deafening boom, the water he'd been controlling sloshed to the ground.

—

Amarie palmed the dagger in hand, still hidden by Prinidan's cloak, and set her jaw. Time was of the essence. She was keenly aware of it trickling away by the second, almost as if she could *feel* the lengths her siblings were pushing their bodies to.

It had to be her.

And it had to be now.

She tried to clear her dry throat to speak—distract Ryian, call her back over, something—but then a shudder came up through the stone floor, followed by a loud and echoing roar.

"What was that?" Amarie asked, her focus shattered by her curiosity and nerves.

When Ryian replied, her voice was strained.

"The sound of a steed. It is a legendary beast, sworn into servitude of the Vague. Kanen has entered the fray at last."

"I thought your Four didn't want to fight," Amarie said slowly, forcing the panic that was blossoming in her gut out of her voice. "Isn't that why Illa has opted to attack from so far off, with the storm? Why has Kanen entered, now?"

Ryian scoffed.

"If he could have avoided it, he would have," She spoke harshly and without caution, as if Amarie had offended her.

"Why don't your monarchs want to fight?" Amarie asked a moment later. "Isn't that the mark of a true leader? To go to war to protect the people?"

"Kanen is too important to jeopardize. If he were to fall, everything would turn to chaos. The members should have been able to deal with your siblings without him having to risk himself," Ryian cursed, sounding stressed to the point of breaking. "He should not have had to resort to it."

"And the others?" Amarie prompted when she didn't continue.

"What?" Ryian snapped, voice angling back towards her.

"I asked why your *monarchs* didn't want to fight," Amarie said. "You only mentioned Kanen."

"No, I didn't."

"Yes, you did. You said *he* was too important." Amarie frowned. "Why is he the only one you fear for?"

"He isn't. I fear for all of our leaders; it would cripple the Vague for any one of them to fall. Kanen is just—I mean, he and *I* just—" Her mumbling stopped dead with a little intake of breath, as if she'd revealed her hand on the last play of the game.

Amarie seized it, the hesitation telling her everything that she needed to know.

"You're lovers," She gasped, the pieces clicking together, but then Ryian was upon her.

Before Amarie could even consider pulling the dagger out to meet her, a fire-ringed hand had closed around her neck. She choked as the smell of her own burning flesh coated her tongue and throat.

"*Never*," Ryian snarled, spit flying into Amarie's face. "*Repeat those words.*"

"Does Illa know?" Amarie forced a wheezing laugh around her burning skin.

Ryian snarled and threw her back against the stone wall with surprising strength. Amarie almost lost hold of the hidden dagger as her head knocked painfully against the rock. She winced and took a gasping breath, but at least Ryian had let go of her neck. She reached her free hand to cup the now-blistering flesh of her throat.

Some assassin she turned out to be.

Prinidan would never have missed such an opportunity.

"Illa seems to think," She choked out, digging even further into the nerve she'd uncovered. "That she and Kanen are mates."

"And she will *never* have reason to think otherwise," Ryian whispered.

Amarie's brain started turning around the possibilities. It had been Kanen who had suggested Ryian should be the one to guard her, initially. Illa had agreed—so she knew nothing about the two of them, obviously.

What other treachery was at play, there? What was Kanen planning? And how could Amarie swing it to her and her siblings' advantage?

She did her best to recall Ellion's interrogation of Rog back at the neutral palace, though it came in a hazy blur. It seemed like an age ago. To the best of her memory, the royals had surmised that pain might constitute a strong enough distraction to cause a Vague member to lose hold of their stolen magic. A great surge of pain—physically, Ellion had assumed.

But could pain of the heart do the same thing?

Another bellow came up from whatever kind of animal Kanen's steed was. It was painfully loud, and impossibly close.

"It sounds like they're right outside," Amarie gasped.

"We should be so lucky," Ryian growled, retreating to the far wall. When she spoke again, she was some distance off. "Your siblings made it quite far. They're out on the last balcony before the throne room, some hundred feet below us. I—" She cursed, and a yelping-roar sounded from outside at the same time. "Gods!"

"What!?" Amarie sat up and jostled Prinidan.

"Your bastard brother just hit the dragon," Ryian's voice was a hiss. "He *dares*—"

"Dragon?" Amarie interrupted with a splutter, trying and failing to wrap her head around Ryian's outrageous words.

She'd heard of those beasts in the fairy tales that the palace attendants used to tell the Four before bed, but that's exactly what they were; children's stories.

"Dragons don't exist anymore—" Amarie gave a quick shake of her head, even as another pained roar filtered through the open wall.

"Not so, little queen. There are monsters in these hills that would make even *you* stop and look twice." She swore again seconds later. "It's crawling up the stone!"

"What is?" Amarie squealed, terrified of the answer she already knew.

"The dragon, idiot girl! It's trying to get away from your accursed brother!"

Amarie inhaled sharply. If there was one thing the stories had taught her as a little girl, it was that dragons were, and had always been, ruthless and as evil as anything could be.

"Will it recognize you as an ally when it gets up here?" Amarie hissed, hands tight against both Prinidan and the dagger.

"Well—I'm not... That is to say… it's sworn into the Vague's service—Kanen's service." Amarie waited. Ryian eventually snarled. "No, it will not recognize me."

"Will it even fit in here?"

"How should I know?!"

"You'd better clear off from the window, then." If the dragon *was* coming in, she would be in far more danger than Ryian; but she needed her captor to sit still for a moment. It was now or never.

Finally seeing reason, Ryian's footsteps skittered a little way back, away from the window. Her breath was coming in hard, but blessed saints, she slowly sat back down. Amarie didn't have to see it to know that their guard would be facing the window, and not her and Prinidan.

The sound of the dragon—crackling energy, crunching stone, and a deep thrumming moan—grew ever closer.

Amarie drew the dagger out from the folds of cloth.

—

Ellion gave a strangled gasp, his eyes swiveling back into the chamber and locking onto the hateful woman as she stripped away his magic. She crowed in victory even as the gravel pieces continued shifting and began to lift him up, commanded by Amarie's thief.

Up Ellion went, higher, and then it was spilling ever downward, as if in a land slide, bringing him closer and closer to the center of the terrace, towards the sneering man. He struggled against the tide of rocks furiously, even though he knew it was useless.

Before Zeraphall realized what had happened, the wall of fire she was keeping against the octopus faltered in earnest. Suddenly, not only was the octopus pressing against the fire from the inside, but something *else* was pushing at it from the outside.

Something *other*.

Zeraphall turned towards the sound of female laughter, and was shocked to see Ellion being borne away on a river of gravel. Confusion bubbled to the surface of her mind, until she realized that her brother wasn't fighting back.

A woman who had not been there before stood by, and Zeraphall was too slow to make the connection. She watched, dumbfounded, as the woman's hands flexed, and a huge mass of water rose up and swallowed her flames, bolstered by the octopus on the inside. Anger surged through Zeraphall's veins as the creature escaped and began slithering its poisonous, dripping limbs across the floor once more, like an unstoppable disease. She turned with a hiss and attempted to melt a great swath of rock out of the ceiling, directly above Ellion's thief, instead, but somehow—perhaps through Zeraphall's exhaustion, or even the woman's own strength—her enemy reacted faster. With two wicked slices of her hands, the rain and molecules of the air shifted and thickened, and before Zeraphall knew it, water was coming at her.

It came on so suddenly that she barely managed to throw up a protective sphere of flame around herself before the water was on all sides. Up it surged, and around, eventually connecting together with a great roar, encircling Zeraphall's sphere of fire and covering it.

Drowning it.

Realizing she was about to be trapped, Zeraphall heightened her body temperature to great levels, and even though she burned hot enough that the water around her began to boil and evaporate, the thief took back control of it before it turned to true vapor, just as Ellion had done against the dragon. Zeraphall tried again, screaming in fury within her quickly-sealing prison, but the Water octopus then added its own jets to the woman's tide, and together, they locked the royal in place.

She couldn't fight it.

She was so tired…

The octopus melted closer, red eyes ever-rolling until they pinpointed her and finally stuck fast. It was far larger up close, and its shadow easily swallowed her up. Purple and green tentacles dripped from their suctioned-positions on the ceiling overhead, and even through the roaring of the water, Zeraphall could hear the *click, click, clicking* of the beast's great beak as it moved closer to her. For all of a few seconds, Zeraphall managed to hold them off—but then she was tumbling head over feet as the water surged in around her and the currents took hold.

Pockets of air remained around Zeraphall's head so she could breathe, but the rest of her body became saturated in a few short moments. She took great rattling breaths at first, but she soon realized that whatever air still flowed within the bubbles wasn't enough to properly fill up her lungs. If she breathed too hard, the pockets would fully deplete, and she would surely drown.

Ellion scrabbled against the gravel as it lifted him and carried him along, but it was no use. He fell to his knees in exhaustion and tumbled into the wave of rock. As he toppled in a somersault through the chaos, he caught a bare glimpse of his sister being engulfed by waves back in the chamber. The gravel and loose rocks quickly blocked his view. On and on he tumbled, in perpetual motion, getting battered and thrown by the gravel all around him.

By the time he finally stopped falling, he had been deposited fully outside the chamber and onto the terrace, directly below the still-moaning dragon as it made its slow ascent up the rocks. Hot blood mingled with the rain hitting his shoulders and soaked him in a cascade of red.

Nothing could be done as Amarie's thief flicked his hands and caused the stone to rise up and clamp around Ellion's own wrists. He pulled against it with all of his remaining strength, searching for the tidal waves that he knew should live inside of him—but he came up dry.

His soul had become a desert, devoid of water.

"Meena!" The man called over the wind and thunder. "Do you have the Fire witch under control?"

"For now," Ellion's thief shouted back in a deceptively sweet voice, giving Zeraphall a simpering grin as she did so. "I've never felt such power." Zeraphall could barely summon the strength to glare at her attacker as she felt herself double over, her lungs heaving and screaming for more air.

Ellion's mind whirled, back out on the balcony.

So, his thief was named Meena, and somehow, she had been smart enough to render Zeraphall useless—something not even he had ever done with great success. Ellion fought to turn his head towards the chamber and glimpse his sister once more, but the rock now locking his wrists in place did not allow it.

"Send for Rana," The man continued, gazing down at Ellion coldly. "Get her to try for the Fire again. If she fails once more, drown the hellion and let us be done with it."

Ellion yanked against his bonds with renewed vigour, reeling at the idea of Zeraphall's life teetering in the balance. This Rana woman had already failed to take his sister's power once—she would not succeed a second time, either.

Did that mean Zeraphall's fate was sealed?

"Let her go," Ellion rasped, the words crackling from out of his dry throat. The Vague leader ignored him.

"What are you going to do with him, Kanen?" Meena called out from the chamber, referring to Ellion, even as she continued to twist the water around Zeraphall.

"We'll get him locked up and secured while you chaperone the demon," Kanen replied, sending Ellion a nasty smile. "We can stick him with the other two—keep him nice and safe for you."

"Don't you harm him, Kanen," Meena cautioned.

"Of course not!" Kanen barked over the storm, but the glint in his eyes, which Meena would not be able to see from within the cave, told Ellion a different story. "In the meantime, send someone out to my mate. We don't need this accursed storm any longer! It turns out the Promised Four were nothing to be feared, after all."

As if in reply to his words, a great burst of lightning crackled out from the spinning clouds and struck the uppermost rocks of the mountain. Ellion was at first blinded, and then deafened entirely as the resulting thunder fairly rent the air around them. The dragon high above let out another echoing holler of unhappiness, and Ellion felt rather than heard a great lurching of air as the creature leapt off the rocks and steadied itself into a descent. Clearly, it had decided to brave the terrace as opposed to facing the angry storm.

Kanen cursed and threw out a hand towards Ellion.

The stormy sky and descending dragon were blocked from sight as a great roof of rock stretched out above Ellion's body. He cowered, but it appeared that Kanen had saved him; in the moment, at least. As the thick stone grew into place overhead, great chunks of what could only be falling rock from the lightning strike hammered down on top of it.

—

A great burst of lightning broke through Amarie's concentration. She'd never heard it from so close by before, but the stinging *crack* of electricity could have been nothing else. All semblance of calm she had been building was shattered, for it sounded as though the storm had all but entered the chamber and struck within the room itself. Ryian screamed, and though the resulting thunder was nearly deafening, Amarie made out the distinct sounds of rocks crashing and tumbling down from their roosts on the mountain.

The dragon, closer than Amarie had even anticipated, gave a howl of dismay. The floor of the chamber shuddered, and she heard the great beast launch away from the window, probably trying to escape whatever rocks were now cascading downwards.

"Damned lightning—I can't see a *thing*," Ryian snarled.

Amarie tried not to get distracted by the blessed irony of her guard being momentarily blinded, and refocused into the chaos.

—

Zeraphall saw a great flash of lightning outside, and she heard a muffled version of thunder through the water and ice holding her in place. She squinted through the wall of her cage towards the balcony, but could only manage to see highly distorted images of the scene outside. She thought she could make out a sliver of Ellion's back through the open wall, but nothing more. To her horror, she then saw the forms of blurry rocks falling and smashing to pieces against where she'd sworn her brother had been moments before.

In seconds, the open wall had been blocked by rubble.

"Ellion," Zeraphall gasped, her voice barely louder than a whisper, though she'd tried to shout. She pounded her fists against the walls with lackluster fury, but only resulted in soaking herself further and destroying the delicate air pockets. "Ellion!" This last shout was meaningless, bubbling sound as the water rushed against her face.

The thief named Meena did not allow her to draw breath again until black spots were forming behind her eyes.

—

The makeshift roof over Ellion's head crumbled and fell to the sides, as did the boulders that had broken free from the mountainside; however, his stone shackles remained frustratingly solid. He gave them a rattle for good measure, but it didn't help.

Kanen, who had clearly steered the falling rocks away from himself as well as Ellion, flicked his wrist and caused a few more of the bigger pieces still above the Water King to shift and tumble further out of the way. Ellion glanced up once it was all clear, and noted that the supercell storm had grown even in the last few moments; the purple-grey clouds were now circling at a dizzying speed.

He also caught sight of an Air thief who was heading into the storm. It was slow going, for the wind was significant, but it seemed as though they were heading towards Prinidan's thief—hopefully to tell her to stop battering the mountain before things got out of hand, as Kanen had demanded.

Ellion didn't spare his attention for long, though, for his eyes were magnetically drawn to the still-bleeding underside of the massive dragon as it descended through the sky. In seconds, his field of vision was entirely monopolized by the huge creature, and a mere moment later, it landed on the back end of the balcony with a great quaking of rock. If Ellion's hands and forearms hadn't been secured by the stone shackles, he might have even lost his balance. Kanen turned and spoke to the dragon in a hard voice.

"I expected you to take off after the boy injured you. You aren't much good wounded, Ynfernu. Crawl back to your nest until you are of use to me."

Despite himself, Ellion was blindsided by Kanen's blunt words. In all the stories he'd ever heard, dragons were the proudest beings in existence. To speak to one in such a way, and to use its *name* while doing so, no less, had to be the epitome of foolishness.

To his further surprise, however, the dragon merely rustled its leathery wings at Kanen's harsh tone.

You know of our ways, Kanen… There is a debt that must be paid…

Ellion shook his head in apprehension as a voice whispered through his thoughts, unbidden and unwelcome. The dragon hadn't opened its mouth, but the voice couldn't have belonged to any other being. It was ancient and wicked, serpentine and wholly disturbing.

It was like *hearing* a chill as it crawled into one's blood—like listening as crackling decay slowly crept over one's bones.

The monster turned a great orange eye on Ellion, as if it could sense his attention. Its eye was catlike, or snakelike, perhaps, but distinct in its own way. The pupil was thin and curved, with white slashes that seemed to ripple as the beast held him in its gaze. Ellion felt more aware than ever that he was incapable of moving or protecting himself in anyway.

"Ah yes," Kanen continued speaking as though he were addressing an underling, rather than a beast of myth and death. The dragon's words had clearly whispered into his mind, as well. "There is the little matter of your retribution, isn't there?" He looked back to Ellion, his voice turning sickly casual. "You see, *Your Highness*, the only way a dragon and its war-minded ilk can regain social standing after a serious wound is to kill the one who inflicted it. Interesting; that had slipped my mind." He clicked his tongue, smiling. "Dear dear, Meena won't be happy."

A sour taste grew in Ellion's mouth.

Kanen had planned everything.

He *wanted* Ellion dead, and Meena rendered powerless as a result. He'd waited so long to appear in battle, not because he'd been cowardly or otherwise engaged, but because he had been biding his time. An Earth thief with Amarie's level of magic had no competition; not while in an area such as the mountain, in any case. The whole battle could have been over before it had even started.

But that had never been the plan.

Kanen had wanted Ellion to face off with Ynfernu and injure it—or die trying, what was he to care? Only then could he ensure that Ellion would be killed, and not by his own hand. In a single move, Kanen would guarantee that at least one of his main competitors for power would be rendered insignificant before the battle was even over, all seemingly without meaning to. And, if Rana again failed to take Zeraphall's power, she wouldn't even be a worry. Kanen and Prinidan's thief—who he had called his mate—could rule the country side by side, for they would be the only two remaining individuals with royal-level magic.

Sharing power two ways was easier than three or four, after all.

"Despicable," Ellion snarled once he'd wrapped his brain around the idea of such treachery, shaking out the rain running down his long hair and into his mouth and eyes.

"Beyond retribution, I suppose it is also your duty, as my sworn Steed, to protect me at all costs," Kanen continued as though Ellion hadn't spoken, looking at the legendary red and black dragon like it was nothing more than a simple horse. "The story we will tell is that he broke free of his confines and threatened my life and the prosperity of the Vague. You had no choice in the matter." Kanen's eyes flashed. "We will not mention your revenge."

Without so much as a hesitation, the great beast lurched forward.

—

"Getting tired yet?" Meena prompted, closing the water around Zeraphall's body and robbing her of what little oxygen she did have. Zeraphall's eyes rolled back and she felt her soul's flame flickering within her—weakening by the second. Just when she thought it was the end, Meena allowed the water to siphon in a few more pockets of air.

Zeraphall pulled at them greedily, like a drunkard to wine.

"No more," She wheezed when she was able, her voice reedy and weaker than she'd ever known. Somewhere deep inside of herself, she knew she was begging… but it didn't matter anymore. "Please. No more."

She had almost given up.

"What good are you alive, when Rana cannot use you?" Meena mused in her would-be charming voice, stepping forward and placing a hand on her hips. Zeraphall could only make out her general shape through the lines of ice and water surrounding her. "You are a liability. One in need of disposal."

Zeraphall watched blearily as she began pacing and a few more Vague members filtered in behind her. The octopus remained as well, a massive, colourful nightmare hovering right beyond the line of water holding her.

"I can't be expected to sit here and contain you forever, after all. Surely there are better things to do in this sorry realm." Meena walked back up to the shivering orb, close enough that Zeraphall could make out her face clearly once more. "There are, aren't there? Plenty of untapped resources—powerful people waiting to be enslaved for the greater good…?" She scoffed. "Honestly, you Four wasted the gifts you were given. You had the opportunity to control a great host of people; you could have *made* them do as you wished.

What other empires could stand against an elemental force such as the one Attina could build?" She shook her head in disgust. "No more wasting time singing to the trees and fawning over the winds. It is time to branch out—seize more, and never stop. The Vague is owed. We will use what was given, and what has now been taken."

The small, gathering crowd cheered Meena's blasphemous words, and Zeraphall's resolve shuddered within her. Everything she and her siblings had worked to build, everything they stood for—a land that valued order and worked towards peace and fellowship—would be ruined under the hands of the Vague.

Families would be torn apart by the great war that Meena was mongering, and it would be the end of all good things.

Sometime later—perhaps it was seconds, perhaps it was hours—another face bubbled into view, close enough to the orb of water that Zeraphall could make it out, as well. She knew instantly that it was the woman who had tried to steal her powers during the battle.

Tried and failed.

"This is the time, Rana my love," Meena hissed, her brown eyes flashing as another current swooped into the sphere and disoriented Zeraphall further. "Do it now, or we will close off this well of power for good."

Zeraphall knew that Meena was talking about killing her if Rana failed once again, but for some reason, she couldn't manage to care. She was already all but dead within the watery prison, anyway; her mind didn't even possess the strength to conjure the idea of fighting back.

"You've certainly broken her spirit," Rana mumbled in an accented-voice, staring at Zeraphall as though she were a sideshow at the fair. "It should be easier now." Meena smirked, and closed off the small pocket of air that Zeraphall's head was in as if to prove it further. Water rushed gleefully into her lungs, and the pain was immediate.

It was the end.

Zeraphall felt the water sizzling as it hit the dying remains of heat within her, and with a final breaking of her resolve, she inhaled. Try as she might to fight it, her lungs pulled at the water, searching in vain for oxygen. It was pain beyond pain, a burning she had never known. The pressure in the sphere seemed to intensify, and suddenly her lungs were folding in on themselves, crushing her soul in their attempt to draw breath.

But then, with the feeling of being dragged back to life, the water was pulled from within her and another small channel was opened to the air outside the sphere. Zeraphall hacked and spluttered, moaning in agony, as her lungs expelled the liquid and refilled with what little oxygen she had been allowed.

"Enough," Rana barked to her mate, and Meena backed up a few paces. "Let us be done with this."

Rana's eyes—a curiously striking green—shuttered and she reached a hand forward towards the ball of water. Zeraphall's head had lolled on her shoulders, but she finally found the mental strength to refocus in on Rana's face.

Let her look the thief in the eye, at least, if this was truly the end. She had courage enough for that.

For a few seconds, there was nothing but the raw feeling in Zeraphall's lungs as they reoriented themselves—and then she felt the fated tug. Deep within her, in the very pit of her being, she suddenly felt Rana's intrusive presence. The pull was stronger than before, or perhaps she was just weaker, and the faint heat remaining in her core began to draw away.

"No," Zeraphall whispered in a ruined, utterly haunted way. With a frail snarl, she clamped on to the flickering inner light with her teeth, her fingernails, with anything she could use.

Rana's forehead creased as she met the resistance, and the tug came again, harder that time. Zeraphall felt her magic slip a little bit further out of her exhausted grasp, and her eyes flickered closed. The true understanding of what was about to happen unfolded in her mind like slow-moving lava, but once she realized it, there was no forgetting it.

It would be *so* easy to let go—to let Rana win.

She was holding on by the skin of her teeth as it was, so close to death anyway, so close to a powerless, flameless existence. Would it be easier? Easier to let go? Surely it would be less painful than such a brutal fight; besides, she was the last one.

None of her siblings had the power to fight back any longer—and she was alone.

If she simply gave up, her power would go to Rana, and at last, Meena would release her from the water-laced hell. Never again would she know the feeling of dancing through flames, but nor would she ever need to fight this hard for anything ever again, either. By then they would have her, and it would all be over.

They would hold and control the essence of what made her who she was.

There it was; she could see her magic through her closed eyelids, lifting from the dark spot within her that used to burn so brightly. Rana had it and was holding on with a strength far greater than anything Zeraphall had left.

Her gift.

Her magic.

Her soul.

It appeared to her, in her mind's eye, as the red Stone of Promise she'd heard so much about but of course, could not remember. Just a seemingly inconsequential rock; that is, until it began glowing with her heartbeat, and burning with all the power of the sun.

The stone was slowly being lifted out of her, *pulled* out of her, and she was being left in the cold. She still held on, but her grip was beginning to slacken, for she was so tired; tired of fighting, tired of fear, tired of pushing away the inevitable tide that had her so incapacitated.

From far away, through impossibly deep water, Zeraphall heard Rana begin to shout in near-victory. The thief could no doubt feel how close she was to succeeding—could probably even feel the heat beginning to enter her veins.

Zeraphall's body shuddered in pain, and suddenly her eyes were full of the light of her magic being drawn out of her. It was the last time she would ever feel that precious, blessed heat. What had been black moments ago, behind her closed eyelids, had now ignited. Every colour she had ever known fire to burn—all of the reds, yellows, whites, blues, purples—combined into a beacon behind her eyes.

For a moment, for a mere heartbeat, she was plunged into the sensation of a final, great burst of heat. It surrounded her and encircled her heart, warming up the parts of her that had gone cold. The memory of what it was to be warm, and to be strong, slammed into the corners of her sluggish brain, shaking her to the core.

And that was all it took.

"NO!"

—

As Ynfernu's eyes fell on him and its great mouth opened, Ellion knew it would all be over soon.

A rumbling grew from the pit of the dragon's injured belly, the place Ellion had attacked in exactly the way Kanen had wanted him to, and a snarl rattled out of its gaping jaws. The behemoth took another rocking step forward, hissing evil words into Ellion's mind that he refused to hear or to heed, but it made no difference. The creature's powerful eyes were trained on its target, and though its long neck swayed side to side as it approached, the piercing orange gaze never faltered.

Ellion was nothing more than prey for the apex predator.

Caged. Helpless. Doomed.

Until he wasn't.

Chapter 12

Zeraphall seized her power at, perhaps, the final moment she could, and pulled for all she was worth. Her fury suddenly burned hotter than her pain did, and though she was frozen within her watery cage, the battle raging within her was a wildfire.

A sure spike of adrenaline aided Rana in giving a last, desperate pull on the magic, but Zeraphall was past weakness and well beyond fear. She responded with a ferocious wrench of her own, and finally felt the seed of magic sink back down where it belonged and begin to smoulder once again. Rana's eyes popped in fear and anger, and the tugging sensation within Zeraphall ceased entirely.

Meena's face crumpled in rage as her partner failed yet again. She turned to scream at Rana and tightened her fist as if she was ready to drown Zeraphall and be done with it but she was too late.

Zeraphall had found the strength to fight, and she didn't let it go again.

Instead, she threw her arms out to the side, into the now-shrinking walls of water, and unleashed herself. Trusting that the boulders still blocking the balcony would be enough to keep her brother safe from her wrath, she quickly inhaled every last molecule of dwindling oxygen and used it to ignite.

The water that had so hampered her ability to protect herself and to fight back was no longer an issue, for Zeraphall burned so hot, so suddenly, that Meena had no time to properly react and build the reinforcements back up. Water and ice hissed as it rocketed to boiling in a single blink, then screamed as it evaporated to mist. The moment the walls of water fell away and a greater amount of oxygen surged in, the fight was over.

Zeraphall detonated, and the chamber became an oven.

Waves of bone-melting heat pulsed out with her heartbeat, wider and wider, as if she were the core of the deadliest of bombs.

The Water octopus and all of its accursed legs shriveled at the first touch of that unyielding flame, and the bodies of all the people gathered there fell to ashes in seconds. Zeraphall barely registered the faces of the two Vague leaders in front of her before they, too, were blown away, and the floor became sticky underfoot as the rocks began to melt in earnest.

Flames ignited in the air itself and licked out the still-open balcony on the other side of the room, turning the rain to mist, and finally, finally, Zeraphall was free.

She collapsed in exhaustion.

—

A deafening surge of sound erupted in Ellion's ears, loud enough that it felt as though he'd plunged his head under a great waterfall. The dragon was close enough by then that he could have almost counted its scales, if it weren't for the waves suddenly crashing around inside his head. He took a huge, heaving gasp, like a fish that had been returned to the ocean, and threw his head back to the stormy skies above.

The dragon hesitated as Ellion's neck was bared, no doubt trying to decipher if the display was in either deception or submission, but Ellion barely noticed. He was shuddering as the thrum of power took over the flow of his veins once more, and he could feel the rain again—really *feel* it.

He *was* the rain.

It sang to him, all around and a million times over, like a lover long denied.

Ellion called out to each crystal of snow upon the mountains, and grinned ferociously as the storm itself shifted towards him, unable to resist the magnitude of his power. With razor-sharp focus, he took hold of the rain in the sky, the moisture in the air, and the waves within his heart.

He found the imperfections and cracks in the rain-soaked shackles Kanen had created for him, and filtered water into them and hardened it to ice. They shattered off of him in a blink, and even as Ynfernu recovered and dove to crush him in unforgiving jaws, he leapt up. His eyes burned an untamable blue, and when the dragon opened its cavernous mouth to reveal a glowing, sweltering throat, Ellion met the burning tide with all the power of his soul.

"No!" Kanen screamed at the same moment, as if he had sensed what was about to happen a bare second before. He threw a protective sphere of rock around himself, but had no time to do much of anything else as Ellion settled into his magic.

Bolstered by the rain, the fog, and the melted snow of the peaks—a tidal wave the likes of which Ellion had never formed rose up to hit Ynfernu from every imaginable angle. On either side, atop the beast's head, up into its throat, and against its hulking body, the wave did not relent. It did not fall from the balcony as it spread, either, but instead shot upwards as if it had collided with an invisible wall, only to then double back and hammer the dragon anew.

Whatever Zeraphall had done to Ellion's thief, it had stuck.

In a mere-heartbeat, the tsunami had arced and plummeted down on the dragon from above, catching and holding the beast within it twisting fingers. The water sloshed to the ground and back up again, slamming against the barriers Ellion had created on all sides before raging back towards the center once more. In the span of a few seconds, the balcony became encased in a pool of swirling, rampant water—and though Ellion did not know it, he entrapped the dragon in a large-scale version of what his sister had only just barely escaped.

Kanen's lump of rock was inside the roiling ball of water as well. He may hold Amarie's magic… but he was merely a powerful fool. He was more concerned with self-preservation than he was with anything else. Instead of trying to fight back when the tides had turned, all he had succeeded in doing was securing himself well within the Water King's grasp.

Ellion spun and twisted the water around the Vague leader's quickly-made structure to prove the point, sending it into a deadly whirlpool and locking it there. Kanen would not emerge until Ellion willed it to be so.

The dragon had flared its huge wings in an attempt to keep itself on its feet as the wave surged and roiled around the balcony, but its movement was slow, for the water pressure was immense. Ellion watched on, steadfast and immoveable as currents surged around him, tracking the dragon while it struggled and snarled to no avail.

His hair flowed behind him in a violent blue-green tangle, and his eyes churned in the ecstasy of once more being in tune with his magic. Ynfernu found his gaze and held it defiantly; unending fire against unfathomable water.

"Your dignity's quarrel with me is over." Ellion's words echoed and pulsed through the water, both muffled and magnified. "Or drown here and now."

Ynfernu let out a furious roar. The bubbles that rose from its throat boiled the water around them when they popped, but then the beast paused. Its eyes held great anger, that much was certain, but there was something else there as well. Ellion could not place what it was.

After a few seconds, the reptilian whisper breezed into his mind once more, yet another exhibition of the dragon's old and uncanny magic.

Drowning would be my deepest shame…

A cold, satisfied smile spread across Ellion's face. A legendary beast of fire would never choose death by water—if given the option. Fortunately, Ellion was in the exact position to offer such a choice.

"Then go from this place," He snarled, but did not free the dragon from the water; not yet. He'd managed to neutralize it only due to surprise and pure adrenaline. If he let it go too soon, he was not sure he would get the upper hand again.

All was silent for another stretch of time while the dragon held its substantial breath, no doubt considering its words. It lifted a lip, silently snarling at Ellion despite the position it was in. Its fury was almost palpable through the currents of water.

Release me from my bond to the Vague, and our paths shall not cross again.

The beast's request caught Ellion off-guard, and his eyes were pulled towards the rock where Kanen still lay encased. With the slip of his focus, the tide of the water faltered, and Ynfernu instantly began thrashing to free itself. Ellion managed to take hold again right before the water sloughed off the edge of the balcony. The dragon was smart, and as clever as it was, it was also treacherous.

Somehow though, through measures he couldn't begin to imagine, the Vague, or Kanen at least, had control over the beast of legend before him. Powerful control, of such measure that the creature would not, or *could* not, break it on its own.

"What is the nature of this bond?"

Ynfernu considered him darkly, tilting its head back in a movement so humanlike that Ellion nearly lost his focus all over again.

Of blood.

Ellion's mind reeled, and he tried and failed to bring up everything he'd heard of dragons throughout his childhood. What was the meaning of such an oath? How had it been done, and why? Was it magic keeping Ynfernu from breaking it, or merely a powerful sense of honour? How had Kanen, or whoever had secured this bond, even found Ynfernu in the first place?

The seconds ticked on, however, and as Ellion's initial surge of adrenaline slowly faded, his exhaustion began creeping back. He needed to make a decision, and soon, before the dragon realized that he could not fight forever.

"Then, as one of the true kings in these lands, as decided by the prophecy and The Stones of Promise," He finally said, forcibly silencing his curiosity. "I free you of your service to the Vague. Whatever blood vows, threats, or agreements have been made, consider them broken." His eyes hardened. "My life debt to you is hereby recompensed. You can find a way to repay the realm for freeing you and letting you live, in whatever way you choose. Now go from this place."

Ynfernu dipped its huge head in slow agreement, shuddering in what might have been shame. Ellion did not miss the way its huge orange eyes hitched on Kanen's location, either, but then it flicked its neck backwards in a clear acceptance of dismissal. So, with slight misgivings, Ellion waved a hand and allowed the bulk of the wave to shift.

The black and red lizard gave him one last, mutinous glance, then launched itself backwards and into the sky. However, to Ellion's surprise, Ynfernu did not turn north, to the rest of the mountains and the spirits only knew what else, but towards Kanen's mate. As Ellion watched it fight through the wind, a sudden realization washed over him. Perhaps Ynfernu's bond to Kanen extended to his mate. Maybe Ellion releasing it from service hadn't been enough; after all, he didn't truly know how to break a blood bond.

The Vague member who had been dispatched to speak to Kanen's mate was hovering beside her, as well, and yet the storm grew on. She clearly hadn't heeded Kanen's request to stop, and now the dragon was heading straight for her. Ellion's thoughts strayed to Zeraphall in the chamber, beyond the line of fallen rocks, and to Prinidan and Amarie locked somewhere within the mountain itself. If Ynfernu and the woman were about to join forces, it was highly likely that things would slip back into the Vague's favour.

Ellion squinted, and was horrified to make out Kanen's mate turning and welcoming the coming dragon with open arms. The Vague member beside her flew farther to the side, but Ellion supposed that made sense, especially if the dragon was bonded only to the mated pair, as he suddenly feared it was.

What had he done in releasing the creature from his hold?

Ynfernu was rising rapidly through the raging winds, faster than Ellion would have thought possible, and Kanen's mate still had her arms spread towards it; and yet, Ynfernu didn't seem to be checking its speed as it neared them.

As Ellion watched, Ynfernu opened its cavernous jaws.

He caught a glimpse of the woman slamming her hands together and the dragon's wings getting plastered to the sides of its body as if by air pressure alone, but by then it was too late. With another distant roar that still had Ellion covering his ears, the legendary monster angled its body into a freefall dive, using the woman's own attack against her, and engulfed her and her underling in purple flames. The dragonfire was so intense that not even the Vague members' corpses remained to fall to the mountains below.

Once the flames had disappeared from the air, Ynfernu's wings snapped back out and it pulled up from its dive. Without looking back, the dragon turned and began banking slowly towards the north. Ellion stood frozen to the spot as the lizard shrank into the distance, utterly shocked by the turn of events.

Clearly, Ynfernu had not fancied being indebted to the realm for any amount of time. Whatever Ellion had done had worked, and thankfully, *thankfully*, the beast hadn't had any warmth to spare within its black heart. It had done for the royals what they probably would not have managed on their own; not easily, anyway.

With Prinidan's thief dead, however, the storm did not dissipate as Ellion had expected it to; rather, it seemed to continue building upon itself. The churning air still gained speed, as if what had been set in motion could not be stopped.

But Prinidan would put an end to it.

Ellion turned on his heel to face where Kanen remained imprisoned, feeling slightly bolstered, but also still somewhat distracted by the expectation of seeing Prinidan soar in to tame the tempest. Kanen would be easier to deal with as a pair, anyway, and Ellion was ever so tired…

But Prinidan did not come.

And where was Zeraphall?

Surely the return of Ellion's power meant that she had contained his thief… but at what cost? Was she stuck in there on the other side of the rocks, containing his thief much as he was containing Kanen?

Or had something else happened?

And why wasn't Prinidan reveling in the renewed wonder of his magic?

Ellion's strength and conviction wavered as time dragged on, and though he tried to hold it, his grip on the spinning wave faltered. Kanen must have sensed it, for as soon as Ellion felt it slip, vibrations shuddered across the balcony floor. And still, none of his siblings appeared.

So it was, with a sinking feeling, that Ellion turned to confront Kanen, tired and alone, even as the man shot up into the air on a great pillar of stone.

—

Amarie had no magic left. Of course she didn't.

But with a bit of effort, and a great deal of concentration, she focused her mind in much the same way that she used to—sensing the planes of the rocky floor beneath her feet, as well as listening to the roar of the storm outside, all the while imagining trees and grasses brushing against her mind instead.

It wasn't the same as it had been before, not even close; but as the dragon bellowed below them and the sound of a great rush of water rose up to meet the storm, Amarie began to pretend that it *was* the same. She bent her legs underneath her and crouched, seemingly stretching, but in reality, getting her bearings.

The floor beneath her feet was made of stone, of course, but even so, was mostly smooth. Far different from the soil and grasses of the forests—but still of the earth, in its own way. Amarie twisted her foot back and forth on that stone, memorizing the feel and slope of it, and tilted her head to catalogue the way the winds were whistling from one end of the chamber to the other.

"Is the dragon gone?" She breathed, her shortness of breath almost giving her away.

"It's encased in water…" Rage shook Ryian's voice. "Your brother—" She snarled, and her voice rang louder as she turned back towards Amarie. "—has it incapacitated. I can't even *see* Kanen anymore." She swore, her voice catching in emotion. "But you're obviously still here, so I guess he lives on."

By the lack of her footsteps, Amarie could more or less assume that Ryian had no plans of moving from her spot by the window, as she searched desperately for a glimpse of her lover.

All for the better.

Amarie bounced in her crouch a few times, trying to get the blood flowing properly in her legs after spending so much time sitting, before tightening her hold on the dagger. She took another steadying breath, and began to imagine that she truly *was* elsewhere.

Somewhere far away.

She forced the hardness of the rock, in her imagination, to shift to the softness of a forest floor. What did the ground *feel* like when she had not activated her awareness? Or better yet, what did her distant surroundings *appear* like when she had? She had never been seeing, due to the old beliefs that her ancestors had held, so she didn't know if the images she'd learned over time held true to actual nature, but they were precious to her, and she would never forget them.

There, she remembered the feeling of a great oak standing nearby—a burst of light within her mind—that spread both high to catch the sun, and deep into the earth in search of water. She recalled seeds, millions of them, hiding in the dirt and barely germinated, beginning to pulse with the brightness of life; and there, there was the land itself, splayed out in the vastness of her memory, rolling and stacking and marching off into the distance. Amarie then focused in on a created image of a young tree, standing alone in a lush meadow and rustling in the wind. She crouched at the border of the clearing in her mind, surrounded by the forest and facing that one lone tree.

How did it *sound* when she approached the tree and stood some distance off from it? What did the ground *feel* like underfoot as the dirt approached the tree's roots? The sound of Ryian's breathing and muttered curses, the rustling of her clothes, became another breeze through the leaves of that little tree, and the storm outside became but a murmur in the distant background.

How far off would Amarie be, from the single tree, if things in the meadow *sounded* exactly the way they did at that moment? How would she have to angle her body, just so, in order to hit the trunk with a boulder or a spear of wood?

A distant shout and crumbling of rock sounded below and Ryian shifted, but she did not walk away. She said something, too, perhaps Ellion's name, but Amarie couldn't be sure. She was beyond distraction. Each movement, each breath, each creak of Ryian's bones locked the tree's position in that meadow more solidly within Amarie's mind.

She held fiercely to the image she'd created, and was barely aware of her own body as she stood up and raised an arm. It was a wooden spear in her hand, not a metal dagger, and she stood deep within a forest, opposite a lone tree. There, a few silent steps towards it, careful not to disturb the slumbering seedlings at her feet.

Gentle, gentle… creeping ever closer to that little tree.

Amarie pictured exactly how it would look and feel as her weapon, a burst of natural life in her hand, would pierce the darkness and embed in the bark of the tree before her. She slid a few steps further into the depths of the meadow, her head tilting back and forth with the sounds of her imagined forest. With barely a breath, she adjusted her strength and lined up her body before the tree's rustling leaves, careful not to disturb the slumber of the forest around her. She wasn't far off from it now—perhaps a mere few paces.

Amarie bent her elbow silently as her chin tilted towards the heart of the little tree, so close at hand.

"Ryian," Her breath was a whisper.

"What—!?"

Amarie released her spear at the first hint of sound.

The meager handful of air between them whined as the perfectly balanced dagger sliced through it, one end followed by the other, and then came a wet *thump*.

Amarie heard Ryian attempt to draw a shocked breath, and she felt a weak flare of heat, and then the woman collapsed.

Chapter 13

"Ellion!" Kanen roared, staring down at him from atop the stone pillar with all the fury of a usurper settled into his throne. He had not yet shed an ounce of emotion for the loss of his mate, though he had certainly seen the empty patch of sky where she had recently hovered. "You cannot hope to rise against me!"

Ellion sent whatever he still had the strength to command at Kanen, but it was not powerful enough to be a danger. He funneled the rain and commanded it to batter against him, but Kanen was either too far away, or Ellion had simply become too weak to make any kind of difference. Not giving up, he tried to send water seeping into the cracks of Kanen's rock pillar, as he had done before, and hardened them to ice. Pieces of the stone shattered and broke apart, but Kanen simply called more rock to him before it truly threatened him.

And before he could even do so much as consider attacking again, Ellion caught the sound of rock cracking above him. He threw a wall of ice above himself, as thick as he could manage, to deflect the falling mountain debris that Kanen had dropped on him; but unfortunately, Amarie's thief took hold of the rocks and slammed them down with far more power than gravity alone.

Ellion cried out as the rocks broke through his meager roof of protection, and only barely managed to save himself by shifting the molecules of his body to water at the last moment. His form melted around the falling rocks, but his exhaustion was too deep to maintain the shift for long, and the moment he was out of immediate danger, his form solidified once more.

"A fancy trick," Kanen sneered from on high. "But costly. And I know some tricks, too."

Ellion didn't even hear or register the words before shackles had risen around him once again. These were stronger than before, and larger. This time, the stone melted around his entire body, rather than just his wrists, and rose up past his waist. He kicked his legs feverishly and willed his water to find cracks in these rocks, too, but

Kanen was one step ahead of him. This time, Amarie's thief hadn't simply called new rocks together; instead, he had literally dragged Ellion down into the solid stone of the balcony itself. If there were any cracks to be found, they were too thin to make a difference. Ellion snarled, sending knives of ice at Kanen from all sides instead, but the thief merely encased himself in thick, stony armour. Try as he might, Ellion could not hinder him.

Kanen's pillar began descending down, crumbling and folding in on itself, and soon enough, he was standing on the balcony once more. He smiled wolfishly as the stone beneath Ellion continued pulling him in, and his arms were quickly locked in place. Down Ellion sunk, feeling the chill seep into him as his body petrified inch by inch. He sunk in past his neck, never slowing, until even his chin was beginning to harden into the rock.

He took as deep a breath as he could, and forced himself to speak.

"If this is it," Ellion wheezed, his words coming out strangely due to his inability to properly move his chin or chest. "Then I die proud."

"Proud?" Kanen scoffed, taking a step closer to him. "Proud of what? You've lost, and this awful country and all of its spoiled people are doomed."

Ellion was permitted to stop sinking just long enough to form a somewhat understandable sentence.

"Proud, because—we fought you with everything… Together. Never did we falter—or doubt each other!" Even his voice was tired. He spoke the truth, but his voice was weakening as the rock pressed against his chest and he began to sink once more. "Your mate is… dead—and so are the other leaders. You are alone, but I—I never have been. Not even… in death."

"Illa was not my mate, you stupid child," Kanen scoffed, stepping close and leering down close. "My mate is safely locked away with your blind, useless sister. Soon enough, she and I will rise up, to—"

Ellion never found out what he was going to say, for just then, another sound joined the cacophony of the storm. Falling… it sounded as though something was falling from above. Ellion could no longer move his head to look, but whatever it was, was twisting through the air overhead, and coming down fast.

And then—

A body entered his limited field of vision, rotating one moment, then slamming onto the far side of the balcony with a wet crunch the next.

Kanen flinched away from the impact behind him, as surprised as Ellion was.

"What in the—" He tripped across the ground to the ruined corpse. It took him a few seconds to reach it, and that was when he screamed. "RYIAN!"

Kanen's howl was a sweet song to Amarie, perched as close as she dared to the window's edge—but it was nothing compared to the heady rush that enveloped her at the same second, stronger than anything she had ever felt before.

With a world-splitting earthquake, Amarie's magic was back.

Ellion felt the mountain lurch as though a bomb had gone off below his feet, and the rocks holding his body shifted painfully. Another quake, and another bone-grinding shift of rock, and Ellion found he could move his legs. He thrashed and clawed, and twisted his neck back and forth until he recovered some measure of mobility there, as well. Wasting no time, he then filled the new cracks in the stone with rushing water. Using the last of his strength, he began to shatter and kick and scrabble his way out of the deepening pit where he'd been destined to die only seconds before.

Before Kanen's scream had finished echoing, Ellion had thrown himself to more solid ground and cast his eyes up the mountain. He could still see the marks of Ynfernu's dark blood up its length, but there, towards the top, was his sister.

Amarie's arms were held wide and her legs were firmly planted on the edge of the floor. Her brown hair was loose and whipping around her with the force of the winds, and even from a distance, Ellion gaped at the feeling of renewed power shuddering out from her through the mountain.

Across the balcony, as if in slow-motion, Kanen raised an accursed hand to reclaim the magic that had vanished with the shock of losing Ryian, and Ellion had the good sense to get as far away from him as he could.

He tripped away until his back was against the hot wall of debris separating him from the chamber where Zeraphall had been, and then he threw a shield of ice around himself. It was even weaker than his last one, but there was an overhang of rock above him that he hoped would provide some measure of protection, too, from whatever battle Kanen and Amarie were about to have.

Amarie had been assaulted by the return of her power when Kanen realized what had happened to Ryian. It had been so powerful, in fact, that it had been all she could do to control it before Kanen regained himself.

But she had.

Instead of getting lost in the intoxicating feeling of the rain hitting the top of the mountain or the depth of the stone beneath her feet, she pinpointed all of her rage towards the man that she could feel standing near the balcony's edge, and sent half the mountain crashing down on top of him. It was already falling by the time Kanen reached his hand out to her.

Amarie opened wide her awareness as it crumbled, finding Ellion's familiar warmth down below and encasing him in a shield of her own. She reinforced the rocks holding him, as well as the rocks that supported the chambers in the mountain as a whole, but everything else, *everything else,* she let fall.

Made fall. Encouraged it and commanded it and whispered to it, until the planet itself would have shattered for her.

The balcony was severed, and everything below it turned to gravel as the upper half of the mountain smashed down with unrelenting power. The thunder from the storm had nothing against the screaming of the rocks as they slid against each other, grinding themselves to dust, while everything, *everything* tumbled to the bottom of the valley, smothering any remaining magma in a never-ending cascade. Down and down the mountain tumbled, the sound deafening, until at long last, the earthquake settled, and the cliffs themselves fell once more to ringing stillness.

Amarie swayed near the window once she was sure it was done. The need to be with her siblings was suddenly choking her. She sensed for Prinidan across the throne room, finding him easily, and brought him to her on a bed filled with powdered stone, softer than silk, meant to cushion the side of his body that would never wield a dagger again.

Within the cocoon of stone Amarie had created for him, Ellion let his shield of ice melt away. He couldn't have held it any longer even if he'd wanted to; he was entirely and utterly spent. Safe in the dark, he actually found it quite difficult to keep his eyes open. But he did, and then only a few minutes later, the roof of his shelter split wide and revealed both the storm, and the grinning, tear-streaked face of his beautiful sister.

"Amarie," He breathed.

Amarie felt him scramble out of the remaining piles of debris a heartbeat before he crushed her into his chest. He smelled of sweat and dust and blood and *Ellion*, and before she knew it, they were both weeping.

"Where's Prin?" Ellion croaked a moment later, his eyes sweeping the sky before landing and sticking on the cot. His mind stuttered to a halt as he dared to consider the impossible.

"He's not dead." Different tears now sprung into Amarie's eyes. "But—" She gestured wordlessly, suddenly terrified, and Ellion finally looked upon the shell that was his brother.

If Amarie hadn't just told him Prinidan was alive, he certainly wouldn't have thought so. He was pale, *so pale*—more grey than white. His lips were corpse-blue, and his hair was tangled and matted with dried blood. His tunic was stained red, so deeply that Ellion couldn't recall what colour it had been before. And there, at his right shoulder where the injury from the Air bird still glistened, was a gaping, empty… nothing.

Nausea rose in Ellion's stomach at the *hack job* that had been done to his brother. The wound had clearly been cauterized, but not well, for drips of blood were still leaking out from the corners of the mangled stump and beading against the ruined skin. Even if it somehow healed before it got infected, it wouldn't be a happy recovery. Ellion had no words to say, and only the warm grip of Amarie's hand in his, and her continual reassurance that Prinidan was alive, kept him from shattering.

Prinidan was dehydrated—lethally so. So, through exhaustion so deep it was painful, Ellion began to coax a bit of moisture back into his blood. It was an involved process, but without such help, Prinidan surely wouldn't survive. When it was finished, some of the colour had, thankfully, come back into Prinidan's face, but Ellion's eyes kept snagging on the still-leaking wound.

"Maybe Zeraphall could help—" And only then did his mind catch up to his mouth. "Amarie—in here." He dragged his sister across the wet stones, back to the wall of rocks.

"Those rocks are hot," Amarie warned without touching them, her brow creasing and her scarred eyes flashing back and forth, searching. "I do feel someone inside the chamber, though. Zera, I think," She confirmed, and Ellion felt his heart sag in relief. "She's alone—but it might be too hot for us to get in. The rocks inside have melted."

"Is she alive? Is she trying to get out?"

"It feels like she's prone on the floor."

"We have to get in there," Ellion whispered, squaring his shoulders and tapping into what he felt was the last ounce of strength he possessed in the world. Could he die from magical overexertion? Surely, he would be finding out soon. "I'll cool down anything I have to."

Amarie nodded once, trusting in her brother, and set her awareness against the rocks blocking them from their sister. She could feel that the stones and dirt had formed a closed-off wall, which had most likely saved Ellion and the others from the hell their sister had brought to life inside.

"Alright," Amarie said. "At the top there, left corner."

As she carefully cut out and removed the highest boulder, Ellion prepared to stifle anything threatening that came out; flames, magma, demons… whatever Zeraphall had created. As soon as the rock shifted loose, however, beyond the barest sizzling of rain as it hit the heated stone, nothing happened.

"The other side of the chamber was open, too," Ellion recalled. "Maybe most of—whatever she did—went out to the other balcony."

Amarie focused in, and nodded a half-second later.

"Well, there's no balcony there now. If it was there before, it's melted and gone."

The sibling duo squinted in discomfort as too-hot air filtered towards them once the chamber was properly opened, but were soon rewarded with an open path to Zeraphall, lying unconscious on the floor. Her powerful form was lifted up on semi-solid rock, and with a subtle grinding, was brought out to her siblings.

Ellion lowered an ice-coated hand to Zeraphall's still-burning throat and confirmed that she had a pulse.

"Alright," He whispered, wiping away his tears and holding his sisters. "Everything's okay."

—

Ellion had to fight sleep from almost the moment he sat in the pile of gravel remaining from Amarie's assault on Kanen, even as the storm continued howling above them. The air and clouds had stopped spinning around the valley, but the winds were still vicious. They couldn't guess how long would be until it blew itself out, but it no longer seemed like an issue, in the wake of everything else.

Amarie kept her awareness thrown wide, more out of necessity than actual desire, and did a few sweeps of the Vague headquarters to ensure they were safe. After paying careful attention, she confirmed that there was nobody moving within the mountain.

"Did you kill *everyone*?" She asked quietly, her voice pulling Ellion back from the brink of near-sleep. He shrugged, the movement slow and lazy.

"Most that stood against us. More probably escaped, though," He replied. "But we did kill a lot..."

That number would haunt him later. For now, he needed rest.

"I'll keep my eye on the ground, anyway." Amarie leaned back against the wall and let out a great sigh. For a moment, all was silent, save for the gentle breathing of Prinidan and Zeraphall, and the groaning of the wind above them.

"What happened?" Ellion mumbled into the relative quiet. Amarie knew what he meant without explanation.

"I was taken by Air thieves," She said. Ellion and the others had guessed as much. "It was disturbingly well-executed, and strange… it was a situation I'd never trained for. I could feel the land underneath us, rolling by, but had no concept of where we were in relation to it, so I couldn't hit them with any counter measures."

"Well, you left us a pretty big trail to follow. That was helpful."

Amarie cracked a somewhat rueful smile.

"Well, I was angry."

"Clearly," Ellion agreed.

"And terrified."

"Us, too."

Amarie then explained what had happened once she'd been stripped of her gifts and brought to the throne room, and everything she'd overheard and guessed at since then. When she came to the part about Ryian and the dagger, Ellion actually smiled.

"Then, I figured… if Ryian *was* telling the truth, and she and Kanen really *were* lovers… I figured that dropping her body in front of him would probably be quite the distraction."

"And after you assassinated the *seeing, gifted enemy,* you then cut the mountain in half the second you got your magic back?"

"I knew Kanen wouldn't be downed for long."

"You're magnificent." Ellion shook his head, not only in wonder at such a showing of power, but in complete awe of Amarie's capabilities without magic, as well. It was true that the royals hadn't often trained without their powers, for nobody could have guessed that enemies like the Vague would rise, but he found that he wasn't the least bit surprised that Amarie still managed to be the cleverest person in the room without hers.

"What about you?" Amarie hummed, taking Ellion's rough hand in her own.

He explained about finding the epicenter of the quake and everything that had happened back at the palace as a result, and then skipped over the details of their journey until he reached the Air creature. Next, he explained the sheer number of Vague that he and the others had to fight through, and he also mentioned the strange hold that Kanen seemed to have had over Ynfernu, the blood bond, and how it had been the beast itself who had finally finished Illa off.

"And it killed Illa because you released it from its bonds?" Amarie asked, deep in thought.

"Told it that it could repay the realm another time—turns out, that time was about two minutes later."

And then they started to laugh. It was the sound of release.

Together, they let go of the fear, exhaustion, anger, and every other hysterical thought associated with what they'd gone through over the past few days. On and on they laughed, unsure of what they were even laughing at, until they were bent at the sides and clutching their stomachs.

Once they were spent, they straightened out and lifted their faces to the now-dwindling rain. It was almost nice; being there, together. Perhaps they slept, perhaps they were just finally relaxed, but eventually, Zeraphall's voice crackled into the silence.

"So, we're alive, then?"

Amarie flung herself on her sister, and once they'd gotten through the tears and exaltations, they had Zeraphall recount what had happened to her. She spoke of being trapped and tortured by

Meena until her will to fight had almost run out, and the inner-battle that had been waged between her and Rana.

"Then I realized what it would mean for you three and the country… if I did give up," Zeraphall cast a glance towards Prinidan—she'd noticed his arm almost immediately. "And I just kind of… rejected that reality."

"Well, you couldn't have picked a better moment," Ellion said ruefully, having already filled her in about how he'd gotten his own magic back at the last possible second. She nodded and idly ran a hand over the now-burnt remains of the injury from the spear. It would be some time before it stopped aching. She turned to look at the ruined mountainside, and as she did so, a flicker of movement in the valley below caught her eye.

"There," She hissed, lurching into a crouch as her fists ignited in balls of crackling flame. She felt the sap on her depleted energy, but with will alone, she kept herself burning.

A huge group of people were picking their way across the land far below, heading directly towards the mountain. Some of the strangers were flying above their fellows, and even from their vantage point, the siblings could see flashes of both fire and water twirling in the coming twilight.

Amarie's awareness flashed out, picking apart their numbers and counting how many there were. Her forehead creased in worry, and she turned to her brother and sister. She could feel Earth wielders there, too.

"I'll carry us down. Can you fight with me, if it comes to it?"

Ellion gave a humorless and fatigued snort, dread sluicing through his body, but he said he could; for a while, at least. Zeraphall was more or less the same. She scrubbed a hand across her eyes and gave her head a few shakes to clear it.

"Keep Prin out of sight," She murmured.

"Of course." Amarie twisted her hands. With deft movements befitting the proper royals of the land, solid rock rose underneath them and began transporting them down the side of the mountain.

Behind them, Prinidan's cot was hidden within another column of rock, though left open to the air on the backside, and held steady within to keep from jostling him. What would have been difficult for Kanen, came as easy as breathing to Amarie.

"Steady now," Ellion muttered, drawing the rain to him like a great magnet as they descended. If he could only find the strength to generate a wave, once he let it go, it would do most of the work for him. Gathering it was the hard part.

Zeraphall, too, began melting great pieces of earth that Amarie brought up to her, preparing a magma wave of her own. If they didn't possess the actual energy to put up much of a fight, they could at least look the part.

They were close enough to the valley floor to count the approaching group. It was a disturbingly large number. Even with a rested Amarie on their side, they might not stand a chance.

The royals alighted to the ground running, calling their magic around them like a shield, bending their focus to this last obstacle ahead of them. Zeraphall began arcing her hands, and the lava was quick to follow. It curved high above the trio, while Ellion's wave went below and before them, simply begging to be turned to skin-piercing ice. Amarie ran alongside her siblings, reveling in the ability to do so by herself once more, and began pinpointing where each stranger stood. It was easy enough to calculate how quickly she could bend the earth to swallow them up, if the need arose.

Nobody would threaten her siblings again.

"How many in the air?" She breathed as they ran, deducing that there would be, at least, a few.

"I see nine," Ellion barked, eyes swift even in the growing darkness. Amarie nodded, setting her jaw.

As the distance between the parties closed, each wielding their own gifts and preparing for the final, great battle, Zeraphall screeched for a halt. Amarie stopped instantly, not knowing what Zeraphall had seen, but Ellion was slower to listen.

"What?" He hissed, feeling his water stretch out and begin to lap against the newest group's feet.

"Look at them," Zeraphall muttered in response as she took a few tentative steps forward, eyes bright. She kept her hands out at her sides, magma at the ready, but her face was alight with wonder. Ellion squinted across the shrinking space between them, and once he understood what his sister had seen, he gripped Amarie's shoulder and whispered fiercely to her.

"These don't look like Vague," He breathed.

And indeed, as the two groups slowed, the royals took in the people before them properly. The ones flying were thin, with pale skin and flowing white hair. Those wielding Fire had skin varying from red to deep brown, and were of the largest in the group. Some of the smallest people were manipulating the ground they were walking on, and the ones seeming to wield Water boasted hair and eyes in blues and greens. For a beat, neither party moved, and not even the wind above could break the silence.

Then the strangers fell to their knees as one.

—

It turned out that those in the new group were all reasonably high-powered individuals. They had been captured by the Vague and held at a site nearby, as Ryian had claimed, so that their powers could be traded and shared amongst the thieves.

Some had been locked up for decades.

When Zeraphall and Ellion had started dispatching Vague members in their battle through the mountain, just as Amarie had considered, some of the citizens had started to feel their magic rushing back to them. Sensing a change in the tides, they'd bided their time until enough of them were powered once more, and then they'd waged a battle of their own and fought their way out of the cells.

"We heard the landslide and the earthquake." One individual peered towards the still-crumbling mountain. "We figured it meant that you'd either won… or lost. But either way, we wanted to be here."

"We didn't all get our magic back though," Said another person, stalking to the front of the group. The royals turned to him. He was clearly of the Air bloodline, and his hooded eyes were cold.

No wind circled at his fingertips.

"There was nobody moving around within Vague quarters when we left." Amarie's eyes flashed green as she swept through the mountains once more. "There's nobody in the surrounding valley, either. If there are still Vague out there, they aren't here."

The Air clansman's breathing hitched slightly at the conviction with which she spoke, possibly witnessing such power at work for the first time. After a moment, however, he nodded.

"We go south from here," Zeraphall called to the group at large. "Once we've arrived on safer ground, my siblings and I will take inventory of everybody who still doesn't have their abilities and mark down which could be an issue if left unchecked."

A wave of murmurs swept through the crowd as they accepted Zeraphall's words.

"Those with Earth and Air awareness, to me," Amarie called as the group turned south. She sent a few of the Winged to fly ahead and inform the palace of what had befallen the royals, but she kept many and more Air folks with the group. They needed as many eyes on the land and in the skies as possible.

She didn't feel quite the same desire to use her awareness, as she had before—especially after having had such a powerful experience without it—but she did accept that for the moment, it was necessary. She didn't know how many Vague had truly escaped her siblings' wrath, and there was still the possibility of elemental beasts to contend with.

"It won't be an easy journey over some of these peaks," Ellion remarked to Zeraphall as Amarie cleared her thoughts and began calling out orders. "At least until we can find Amarie's path again."

His sister chuckled.

"I'm sure she could smooth out the road a little bit for us."

"Where is our King Prinidan?" Asked an Earth clansman, after having made his way over to Zeraphall. His eyes were on the storm above, clearly wondering why Prinidan hadn't dealt with it, yet. "Is all well?"

"Well enough." Zeraphall placed a hand on the man's shoulder. "Our brother is resting."

She wouldn't say anything more. It was Prinidan's story to tell.

As the night wore on and eventually bled into dawn, the party hiked on.

Battling through their exhaustion as one, bolstering each other as they went, they fought to the top of every mountain that rose up before them. Amarie's trail provided something of a path, but it was quite some time before the hiking became noticeably easier. By the time night rolled around once more, however, the large group had made it a good distance from the mountain of the Vague.

Amarie had provided assistance to many of the Attinians citizens who were unfit for the strenuous journey as they'd travelled. Much of them were frail after their time with the Vague, and the Earth Queen wanted to make the trip as pain-free a possible. It was not far dissimilar from what she was also doing for Prinidan. The Air King had remained hidden from public eye for the entirety of the journey, and was being regularly checked on by his siblings. His colour had finally returned in earnest with continued help from Ellion to maintain his fluid levels, and his breathing had deepened as the day wore on.

By the time Amarie and the other Earth wielders had finished creating a camp for the group in the early evening, he was stirring.

When he finally opened his eyes, his siblings were right there with him.

Many tears were shed, and in fact, had begun to fall well before he'd actually woken up.

"There you are," Zeraphall growled, testing his body temperature and ensuring he was comfortable. "About time you woke up."

"Beautiful creature," Amarie wept, closing her hand around his own, and holding fast. Prinidan offered them all a quiet smile, but when he reached to grip Ellion's hand, his face fell. Something felt… *off* about the movement.

He felt as though his head was moving through murky fog, and though he knew there was something he had to realize and remember… he couldn't for the life of him figure out what it was. Besides that, the pounding behind his eyes was life-altering, and stole his focus and his ability to think.

He lifted his hands to rub his eyes, and that's when he knew what was wrong.

The realization would have been too much to survive if he'd been alone, without his brother and sisters. He couldn't have accepted it on his own; no way he *would* have accepted it. He didn't understand. Ellion and Zeraphall had all but fought a war together, and he'd done almost nothing—yet still, it was him who would carry such a grievous injury for the rest of his days.

Denial and fear rose up within him like bile as the minutes dragged by, but his siblings never wavered. They didn't try to tell him it was alright, and they didn't try to cheer him up.

They were simply there. Beside him.

They cried with him, withstood his screams, and held him when his energy was spent. Then, when his rage broke through his exhaustion again in the middle of the night, and he began hurling accusations at them, they weathered that, too.

None of the royals slept.

But by the time the morning light once more coloured the distant horizon, Prinidan felt that he could, perhaps, face it.

"One day at a time," Amarie whispered, cupping her beloved brother's face in her hands. "One day at a time. We're here for you." She planted a kiss to his forehead before ducking out of the makeshift tent.

"Prin," Zeraphall spoke just as Amarie left, leaning in close. "If and when you need someone to get mad at, I'm here." She placed her hand on her chest before kissing him, as well. Then, with a turn that left the barest scent of flames in her wake, she left, too.

Silence flowed around the brothers, for a moment.

"Ellion—" Prinidan's voice was low and wary. He caught his brother's hand and heaved himself upright, wincing against the terrible, itching pain in his non-existent arm as he did so. "How do I get past this?"

Ellion fixed him with an assessing stare.

His brother's fair skin was bruised and shadowed, nearly purple with lack of quality rest and comfort. There were demons there, too, circling behind his eyes. He was also holding himself at an awkward angle, injured shoulder up, as though his good side was weighing him down.

Moving gently, Ellion put his hands above each of Prinidan's shoulders, where there was no fear of touching a sore spot, and straightened him out. He held him for a moment, and looked closely into those wise, grey-silver eyes.

"You don't get past it."

Prinidan blinked, caught off guard.

"I—what?"

"You don't," Ellion repeated, removing his hands from his brother's shoulders. "Not right away. You work at it—every day. You wake up; you work at it. You go to bed; you try not to let it keep you awake. You work yourself to the bone, every day, and you *still* won't be past it… until you are."

Ellion's words faded into the silence of the gathering dawn, and Prinidan turned them over in his head. It wasn't encouraging… it wasn't optimistic… but somehow, in some way, it was exactly what he'd needed to hear.

"Okay…" Prinidan said slowly, weighing how he felt about it.

"We'll be there with you, you know," Ellion said, standing up and offering his brother a hand. "Every step of the way."

Manufactured by Amazon.ca
Bolton, ON

21904048R00144